THEY LIVED BY THE SWORD

H. BEDFORD-JONES

THEY LIVED
BY THE SWORD

H. BEDFORD-JONES

ILLUSTRATED BY
HERBERT MORTON STOOPS

ALTUS PRESS • 2018

PUBLISHING HISTORY

They Lived By the Sword originally appeared in the December 1939–March 1940 issues of *Blue Book* magazine.

THANKS TO

Everard P. Digges LaTouche and Gerd Pircher

TABLE OF CONTENTS

THEY LIVED BY THE SWORD

THREE MEN sat at a wineshop table. Above them, the upper Isère valley stretched to the passes of the Little St. Bernard; beyond, the Alps towered icily, but this quiet little village was nestled cozily out of the October winds.

"War and war and war!" said the village mayor gloomily. "Where will it end? Now the whole world is in upheaval, with fire and death and starvation everywhere! Spain is swimming in bloody ruin. All northern Italy to the Alps is in rebellion against the *fasces* of Rome. And now the African hordes move up the Rhone like a countless swarm of locusts—whither? No man knows."

"Perhaps Mancinus, who used to be a Roman, knows," said the second man, a brawny Gaul with long henna-dyed mustaches and hair. "Explain, Mancinus! Why are these Africans here? They're not marching against the Romans, who hold Marseilles and the seacoast towns, but they pour out of Spain against *us!* We pay tribute to Rome; we have a small Roman army here: but that's no reason for sixty thousands Africans to bring us fire and sword!"

Sipping his wine, Mancinus nodded, and eyed the other two. They were simple, untutored men, honest and friendly; yet his was the prestige of being a Roman, even though broken and exiled. Five years he had dwelt here among these Gauls, adopting their dress and customs and speech; he still stood out from among them in looks and manner, a different being.

The uncouth garb of his tall and massive figure, the unkempt light-brown hair and beard, could not hide the difference. He conveyed an impression of vital energy and power. The deep eyes, the careless winning laugh, the strongly carven features, marked him with intelligence far above those who companied him.

"The earth teems with men; there's the secret," he said slowly. "Rome is but a little state with few allies, exhausted by her wars with Carthage; now she's at war with the entire world. This country of Gaul, and the northern forests, pour forth uncounted myriads of warriors. There's not enough land and treasure for all. Last year, in Spain, Hannibal destroyed a hundred thousand men in one battle, and scarce made a gap in the population. Gaul, Spain, Germany, provide soldiers by the million; the earth teems with men!

"These vast masses of wild fighters are helpless against dis-

ciplined legions. Rome and Carthage fight for control of Spain; now Hannibal leads his army into Gaul. Why? He means to march against Rome."

"He can't reach Italy from here." The local mayor jerked a thumb toward the mountains. "The Alps prevent."

Mancinus shrugged. "So you think. So Rome thinks. A great man might think otherwise. Why, you ask, this unwanted war? Because the time appointed by the gods is at hand. There arise insensate waves of struggle, a generation or two apart, when whole nations rush to conquest and slaughter; a mass hysteria seizes them, and they're drunk with dreams of glory and loot. They're led to it by the magnetic character of some great leader. Hannibal is such a man, from all accounts."

The two Gauls eyed one another.

"I don't understand all this," said the village chief helplessly.

"We're content to farm and till and raise our families in peace and comfort. Why should this storm burst on us?"

"You Gauls are proud," Mancinus rejoined. "If the Africans seek to pass your lands, will you permit? No. Like your tribes along the Rhone, you'll fight first—and be destroyed. Why? Because the earth is too full of people. Perhaps the gods seek to thin out the race of men."

I N O N E corner of the wineshop sounded a stir and a rustle. Throwing off a robe of skins, a man rose with a yawn and lifted his astonishing presence before them.

"Spoken like a philosopher, Roman!" he exclaimed briskly. "But you're wrong; there are no gods. I defy the gods, I deny them, I war against them everywhere! And I'm a useful person. If one of you gentlemen will buy me wine, I'll give him first call on my services."

The three stared at him, stupefied. He was extremely tall and thin, with a bald head, a long straight nose, a long neck; immediately one thought of a stork. His keen, twinkling, birdlike eyes heightened the resemblance. He had abnormally long arms, hands hanging nearly to his knees, and was clad in rags and tatters. From his girdle hung a pouch and a lissome sling of leather.

"Who the devil are you?" demanded the local mayor.

The stranger grinned, the weather-wrinkles about his eyes crinkling whimsically; a harsh, croaking laugh escaped him.

"Pelargos, being Greek for *stork*. My father was Greek, my mother Spanish, and I've traveled the whole wide world. Beyond the Pillars of Hercules to Tartessus; in Sicily and the African shores; in the isles of Greece, in Crete and the lands beyond, my name is known. Gentlemen, you behold the best slinger on this earth!" He touched the sling at his girdle. "With this, I can bring down a soaring hawk or drop a running hare at a hundred paces. As for men—*pouf!* No armor is proof against my missiles. I've killed Gauls, Numidians, Greeks, heavy-armed and light-armed; and in Sicily I blinded an elephant with two bullets and slew his driver with the third!"

"Why, here's a lusty braggart!" Mancinus burst out laughing. "Ho, landlord! Wine for the Stork, who brags of the impossible!"

"You may change your mind about that." Pelargos surveyed him appraising. "Ha! A Roman of consular rank, looking and living like a shaggy Gaul!"

Mancinus lost his smile. "How do you know my rank?"

"By your eye, friend; by your tongue, by the set of your head…. Thanks to you!" Pelargos received his wine and gulped at it amiably. "Aye, I know Romans! I got here an hour before dawn and have been sleeping ever since. Do you gentlemen know that Publius C. Scipio and his headquarters staff will be here any minute? His army has gone to Marseilles and thence to Spain. But he himself, being bound for Italy—"

"What? Here?" yelped the mayor in dismay. "The Roman general coming here?"

"Precisely." Pelargos swigged his wine and winked confidentially. "That's why I'm here myself, having no desire for Spain. The whole army knows me. You can't hide from an army, but staff officers are fools; anyone can trick them. In plain words, gentlemen, I'm a deserter. Yes, Scipio is due here early this morning, and will probably stop for food and wine—"

The two Gauls were up and off at a run, shouting to rouse the village; a visit from the Romans was the signal to rush girls and goods to hiding. Pelargos, chuckling, eyed the impassive Mancinus and gulped more wine.

"Mancinus, they called you. That's odd! There was a Marcus Gaius Mancinus in Sicily, during the last Punic war. He commanded the Fourteenth Legion; I was attached to that legion with a company of slingers. Boy as I was, even then I was better than the best."

Mancinus surveyed the man with narrowed eyes.

"That man was my father."

Pelargos nodded, as though not surprised.

"I see. He was sentenced to loss of citizenship and exile. His whole command was caught in a trap; he marched away on parole to save his men's lives. Saved my life, too." Pelargos grinned. "Your blasted Roman Senate said he should have fought to the death. I don't agree! A cousin was given his estates and rank.... Hm! I owe you gratitude because he saved my life, and for this wine. I believe in prudence and safety, and the gods be hanged! That's my motto every time."

"YOU'RE A profane blasphemer," said Mancinus, a twinkle in his eyes.

"What soldier's not? Bah! Every tribe and nation has different gods. What have your Roman gods done for you? Landed you here in exile. And you still love Rome, eh?"

"I hate Rome with my whole soul!" said Mancinus harshly. "Rome broke my father's heart, and he died of it."

"The old Latin virtue of filial piety and so forth, eh? But don't hate all Romans; they have pretty girls there." Pelargos peered at him, head on one side; with his bald pate the fellow did look like a stork. "Your whole life, background and ambi-

"Who the devil are you?"
demanded the mayor. The
stranger grinned. "Pelargos,
being Greek for stork," he said.

tions gone to hell; and you still a young man in your twenties! What are you doing around here?"

"I have a farm."

"A farm!" Pelargos grimaced. "You, a soldier if ever I saw one! A farm! Hiding your face among barbarian Gauls, overcome by an inferiority complex, as we say in Greek, eh? See here!" Sudden animation lit up the seamed and weathered countenance. "I like you. I'll make a bargain with you—give you an ambition, a future, a glorious future! First, money. With wealth, a man can do anything, even repair a shattered life."

"Money? I've enough," said Mancinus. "But not wealth."

"Nor I; but I know where it's to be had for the taking. Enough to buy all Rome! And I'll share the secret with you; that's why I deserted, to get back into Italy. But there's something else." Pelargos spoke with brisk assurance. "Do you, perhaps, know the lady Drusilla, daughter of the former consul Quintus Veturis?"

"No." Mancinus frowned in retrospect. "No. I used to know Veturis; he was a Roman of the old school."

"Which means superstitious, arrogant, headstrong! Well, he's dead. He was serving with Scipio and was badly wounded some months ago; Drusilla came from Rome to be with him. She's the last of the family, and they're all afraid of her. You'd fear her too. She's one of these women who command the world by reason of their virtue and wisdom and beauty; in fact, she knows the gods intimately. You've seen the type. What she needs is to be triced up and given fifty lashes to take the arrogant nonsense out of her. Just the same, she's a raving beauty."

Pelargos paused for breath, gulped the last of his wine, and went on:

"She's with the staff; Scipio is taking her back to Rome. I'm the only person who's not afraid of her; I can handle her. Well, I was with Veturis when he died, and at the last he spilled a few secrets. I'll share those with you also, like a good comrade."

"You're drunk, or a fool," said Mancinus with some contempt.

PELARGOS GRINNED widely. "Think so? Guess again. I offer you wealth uncounted, which means power; and for a bride, the lady Drusilla—properly tamed, she'll be quite all right. In short, the world's at your feet! In return, give me clothes and your friendship, for I see by your eye that we'll be friends. We'll go into Italy together and conquer the world. Yes or no, my friend?"

Mancinus regarded the man steadily, somewhat startled by his winning ugliness, his confident air, his ribald cheerfulness. He took in the knotted muscle of those ungainly arms, the poise of the long, lean frame, half a head taller than other men, and the deep, steady glow of the bright eyes. He was on the point of replying, when a shout lifted outside, and a chorus of voices joined in; a clatter of hoofs resounded on the crisp October air.

"Ha! There's Scipio. I'll take no chances," said Pelargos.

He dived for the corner and seemed literally to vanish. His lanky frame folded up; the skins were pulled over him, and there was only a shapeless something in the corner. Just in time, too; for armor clanked, and a Roman staff-officer strode in.

"Wine!" he curtly addressed the innkeeper. "Let's have a look at your stock. Send some bread and cheese out to the General, while I see if you have any decent drink."

RISING, MANCINUS hooked his rough woolen mantle over a shoulder and stepped outside. Half the village was crowded in the street, staring. A score of horsemen had dismounted. Scipio, a harsh and forceful figure, was standing in talk with a lady and two officers of his staff. Mancinus looked at them, and a bitter hatred welled up within him; no hatred is so deep and terrible as that caused by injustice and injury to one beloved.

Five years ago! Time slipped away. He actually recognized most of these men; some of them he had known well, in his boyhood. Shaven, steely men, hard of jaw and of eye, like no others on this earth, a breed apart; tall men, punctilious, masterful beyond belief, rather machines of iron and granite than fragile human beings, with a pride of race that was coldly indifferent to all around. Once he himself had been like that, not like the brute beast he now was. He was sharply wakened to himself; anger and horror leaped through his brain....

Abruptly, all his thoughts were jarred awry. He saw her standing there with Scipio, so unutterably lovely that he caught his breath and stood agape. She was slim and white, swathed in mourning, so it was only her face he could see, but this was

Scipio and Drusilla

enough. An oval, it was lit with beauty more than earthly; a regal but laughing loveliness, with tenderness beneath its pride.

"That hulking barbarian should be in the army," said one of the staff officers. "By Jupiter, would you look at the build of him! And the intelligence! Why, he has the manner of a very Hercules!"

Mancinus' was aware of quick, sharp glances, but he looked only at Drusilla. For a moment he met her eyes, blue, lively, filled with glinting lights; and in those blue depths something quickened and kindled. Color came into her cheeks as she met his gaze. Then an officer gestured at him and spoke in faulty Gallic.

"Who are you, barbarian? Why aren't you serving the eagles of Rome?"

Mancinus turned to him, and knew him, and disdained to hide his name.

"Because, Cnais Lentulus, your father and other Romans preferred that the son of Marcus Mancinus serve the enemies of Rome."

The defiant, laconic words were like a slap in the face. Astonished, recognizing whom he must be, they stared and muttered. The case of Mancinus had been a famous one. The lady Drusilla, however, took two steps toward him, looked into his eyes, and spoke in a clear quiet voice, with a perfect composure as though unaware how her words must shame these others. Romans were given to uttering their exact thoughts, without regard to the feelings of their hearers.

"You are that man's son!" she said. "Then accept my sympathy and friendship—for the sentence given Mancinus was unjust. It was only one of many things which have angered the gods. My father Veturis was among those whom your father saved. May the gods reward him and you!"

"They have. He is dead."

The harshly sardonic words rebuffed her. It cost her little enough, thought Mancinus, to fling an alms of sympathy to an

uncouth man by the roadside whom she would never see again! Yet in her face he could see how unjust was this thought of his; and as she turned away, he regretted his own lack of courtesy.

She turned to her horse, drank the wine given her, and mounted. The others hastily gulped down their drink, and without further word for Mancinus, Scipio and his staff drove in spurs and were on their way again for the coast.

The Gaulish chieftain came up to Mancinus, and pointed to the road at the edge of the village, in the direction whence the Romans had come. Three crows had alighted there and were pecking away in the road.

"An evil omen," said the Gaul gloomily. "Crows follow the eagles, eh?"

"Suppose we change the omen," struck in another voice. Mancinus turned to see the tall ungainly figure of Pelargos, who had emerged from the wineshop.

Reaching to a pouch at his hip, Pelargos took something out, slipped it into the broad end of his sling, and whirled the sling about his head. The birds were two hundred yards away—an impossible shot for any sling and stone.

"The crow on the right," said Pelargos. "He has two white feathers in his tail."

He loosed the sling. Mancinus found himself unable to sight

the missile or to follow its flight; but the crow to the right spilled over in a mass of rumpled feathers, and the others took wing. Pelargos broke into a run, retrieved the dead bird, picked something up and pouched it, and came back grinning widely. He held up the bird, then tossed it aside.

"I told you he had two white feathers in his tail."

This was true. Mancinus looked hard at him.

"How did you know a thing impossible to see? And with all your skill, what sort of missile did you use, that it carried so far and true?"

The merry eyes of Pelargos twinkled, at the open amazement of the whole circle.

"That's my secret," he rejoined. "If we're comrades, I shall have no secrets from you. Do you accept my offer? Are we comrades or not?"

MANCINUS WAS conscious of a thrill and surge within him. Destiny, destiny! This man appealed to him. Cast off the shackles of circumstance! Away with the farm, with the hopeless attempt to bury ambition; out, and fight! No matter for what, no matter where. Those merry but keen eyes wakened things dormant within his brain—suppressed desires and hopes, crushed aspirations.

After all, the world was ruled by force, by the strong hand. Life was cheap; slaves were everywhere. As he himself had said, the earth teemed with men…. Here was a person, grotesque and therefore unlike others, who offered him release from himself—seize the chance!

"Done with you!" said he. "Come along home with me."

But, as they walked together up the road to the mountain farm, he knew in his heart that it was not the company and the offer of Pelargos that had wakened him to life; nor had hatred for Rome touched his ambition and roused sudden horror of himself and what he was. No. All this, and far more than this, had come from the clear and steady eyes of a woman; eyes that burned and lingered in his memory, and called him to a future.

CHAPTER II

PELARGOS SEEMED cheerfully and utterly irresponsible in his personal ambitions, habits and desires. By the time they settled down before the fire in the rude farm cottage, that evening, for definite discussion of the future, Mancinus had his new comrade ticketed. Pelargos had wandered and warred all over the world, and his contempt for human life or suffering was absolute; he was possessed of a humor that could be gay but was usually of a grisly cast, an abnormal capacity for liquor, and certain fundamental qualities quite out of the ordinary.

Grex, the wolfhound, took instant liking to the lanky rascal. He was a fierce and half-wild beast, with little affection for Mancinus or anyone else, but Pelargos tousled his head and roughed him about, and he responded with obvious enjoyment.

"Never feel fear, and you've got any beast in your hand, from dog to elephant," said the slinger. "Feel fear, and they know it; they sense it somehow; sweat fear, and they fly at you. Actually, it's a smell of some kind, I'm convinced."

"Never feel fear? Easier said than done," commented Mancinus.

"Precisely. I'm really a valuable acquisition for you," said Pelargos, grinning. "I do actually see farther than other men, as you noticed in the case of that crow with his two white feathers; that, also, is a gift. You may comprehend more easily that my peculiar build enables me to use a sling with peculiar force and accuracy; but here, too, my intelligence prevails. Most slingers are content to use stones or leaden balls. I'm not. Being a competent smith, I make my own missiles. Look here."

Half ironic, half serious, he fumbled in his pouch and extended what was, apparently, a mere jagged lump of iron. Upon fingering it, Mancinus perceived its odd balance, and the sharpness of its pointed faces.

"I see you get the point," punned the other, chortling. "Instead of merely hitting, it tears; at close quarters it even bites through armor. I keep a small stock of these bullets for emergencies; as I must forge them myself, it requires time and occasion."

He replaced the sharply jagged lump in his pouch. The flickering oil lamp lent his weathered, long-beaked features a sinister air, but his eyes were twinkling.

"I'll keep my promise and unfold the whole secret of the treasure," he went on, leaning forward. "You may know that the Veturis estates are in Samnium, north and east of Rome."

Mancinus frowned. "There's no such province. The name's loosely given to some of the old Latin tribes—"

"Call it Umbria, if that suits you," struck in Pelargos. "In common speech, Samnium is usually used; you're too damned literal-minded, like all Romans. The Villa Veturis is not so far from the town of Reate. Close to the estates is the grotto or cave of Lamnia the Sybil; you must have heard of her?"

"Of course. A famous witch or prophetess in ancient times; her cave became an oracle. A hundred years or so ago, the place was closed by order of the Senate. I don't know the details."

"I do. Your Roman Senate is the most superstitious body of men extant," Pelargos said dryly. "Because of some public calamity—I think it was about the time the Gauls sacked Rome—a halfwitted priest declared the evil could only be remedied by closing the grotto of Lamnia. So the cave was walled up, and a curse laid on anyone who broke through. Which," he added thoughtfully, "is a bit odd, if you stop to think of it! The Roman Senate had some good practical reason for spreading this yarn and closing the cave. Can you guess it?"

"I'm not fool enough to try."

"Treasure! Some of the treasures of Rome were hidden there, from the Gauls. Then the city was destroyed; those who knew the secret died. When Rome rose from its ashes, the secret was lost. Do you see?"

MANCINUS SHRUGGED. "What the devil has it to do with you or me?"

Pelargos chuckled. "Veturis, when out hunting, discovered a hillside opening and made his way into long caverns; he told of it in delirium, when he was dying. Because of the curse, he never went back or mentioned his discovery to a human soul. He saw the treasure, then learned this was the grotto of Lamnia, and it was finished for him. A more superstition-ridden people than you Romans, it would be hard to find! Well, I know the secret. I know how to find this cave entrance; no one else does. And there, comrade, is wealth and fortune for the taking, with the compliments of Rome!"

Mancinus sipped his wine, frowning. Pelargos was right about Roman superstition; however, most people were superstitious, on account of the nearness of the gods, who might be found anywhere by river or forest or road. He himself somehow lacked this quality of mind.

"I share neither Roman superstition nor your atheism," he observed. "I credit the power of the gods; I also believe in the power of men."

"Ha, I knew it! A man well balanced, a man of common sense!" Pelargos slapped his lean thigh in delight. "A fit comrade for the Stork! So, then, the treasure is all explained and we've only to reach Umbria."

"If you're talking about the town of Reate, it's in the Sabine country, which is in the province of Umbria."

"A plague on your petty divisions!" Pelargos grimaced. "My friend, I'm not strong on geography. To any man who's seen the wide world, your Italy is a crowded confusion of backyards. To make all safe, say we're bound for the Villa Veturis and be done with it. So that's settled. Now, how about the woman? Is she to your taste?"

"Don't be absurd."

"What d'you mean by *absurd?* The secret of getting somewhere in life doesn't lie in looking at the ground, but at the stars; look far ahead, fasten mind and will upon some distant objective! Nothing can stop you from forging ahead to it."

"What's yours?" demanded Mancinus.

The other shrugged.

"Whatever comes into my head. I've commanded armies, won women, ruled provinces; now I prefer less distinguished roles. The man who stands out above the rest, is easiest hit. At present, I want wealth and what it'll bring. Bah! Between us, we could make you consul of Rome, if so sorry a position were worth while. This African, Hannibal, will soon destroy Rome. Wealth and a woman—there's the objective for you!"

"And for you?" persisted Mancinus, smiling. "Don't evade; what's your goal?"

Pelargos tapped the leather sling at his belt. "This makes me the equal of senator or knight, captain or consul! Any girl will do for me. Achievement I like for itself. My goal? Damned if I know." He laughed and rubbed his bald head. "Whatever interests me. Just now, you interest me."

"The crow on the right," said Pelargos. "He has two white feathers in his tail."

THE WOLFHOUND lifted his head, cocked his ears, and growled.

"Wolves outside, Grex?" Mancinus stroked the dog's head, but Grex heeded him little. "I've enough money, Pelargos, to take us into Italy. Go to the coast and take ship, eh? I'm supposed to be in exile, but no one will pay any attention to me."

"Why not go across the mountains?"

"No road. The passes are held by wild tribes. On the other side of the Alps, the Gauls around Turin are all in revolt against Rome. Not even Scipio could go across those mountains. By the way, you said a moment ago that Hannibal would destroy Rome. For the past few months he's been pushing up the Rhone with sixty thousand men. Why think you he's aiming at Rome?"

Pelargos stared. "Why? You said so yourself, in the wineshop this morning. Marching against Rome, said you."

Mancinus laughed. "I was only talking for effect, to impress those Gauls." The dog growled again. "Silence, Grex! Let the wolves prowl and be hanged."

"Well, perhaps your heart spoke better than your head," said Pelargos. "Those Africans may cross the mountains, join the Gauls revolting there, and burst on Rome like a storm."

"Bosh! Use your wits! Any such march would be impossible for an army with supplies, baggage and even elephants, as I hear this army has. If Hannibal tried to fight his way through those wild tribes, he'd lose half his force."

"What of it? Human life is the cheapest thing going." Pelargos shrugged. "As you said this morning, the earth teems with men! If he reached Italy with a mere twenty thousand, those

Gauls and the other Italian peoples who hate Rome would all join him."

"And Rome would wipe them out of existence," said Mancinus. "An ugly little city, but somehow a mighty force. Let's be practical and stop dreaming. When do we start for Italy?"

"As soon as you can sell this farm."

"I'm no tradesman. Devil take the farm! Shall we leave with morning?"

"Agreed. How about some decent clothes for me? I borrowed these from a scarecrow, in exchange for my uniform."

AGAIN GREX growled sullenly. Mancinus, who had no great love for the dog and distrusted his savagely wolfish disposition, ignored him and went to a chest in one corner of the room.

From the chest, he tossed garments to the bed, and followed them with weapons. Then came a leather coat to wear beneath armor, and the armor itself, a shirt of flexible steel plates. He held this up.

"My father's; good Spanish steel. I'd better try it on."

"Aye, and shave that beard," cackled Pelargos, beginning to strip. "Any veteran can tell you beards breed lice. Especially in Italy."

"We've no razor here."

"I'll trim hair and beard with my knife. You look like a wild beast!"

"Why not? It's all I am."

"Get out of that accursed mood." Pelargos, though far too lanky for the garments, arrayed himself swiftly and helped Mancinus get into the coat and buckle his armor. "You're out of the old life, into the new! Before I've finished with you, my friend, you'll be a god. Get rid of your Roman name, first off! Pelargos, who wars against all gods, now helps to create one—ha! I have it. Ramnes! A good name."

"Ramnes? Not bad," said the other. "Ramnes! Etruscan, isn't it?"

"I suppose so. Might be anything." The lanky Pelargos inspected him with a glitter. "Ramnes! Or do you cling to your Roman name?"

"Plague take it! I cling to nothing from the past, which holds only sorrow. Mancinus is dead, and Ramnes lives. A good omen! Shake on it."

Pelargos shook hands, and grinned. "There's your Roman superstition again. Get rid of all talk about omens!"

Ramnes, as he now was, laughed and made the armor fast. To his astonishment, it was small for him, yet his father had been a large man. A hulking barbarian, the staff officer had said truly. It came to him that he had lived these latter years like a wild animal, sunk in morose and hopeless despondency, bewildered and blinded to the chance of any future.

Ramnes! A good name. He threw out his arms; he had not thought much about himself, lately, but this armor made a difference. Beside this Pelargos he bulked huge, immense. Barbarian! There was a change in him tonight, and it astonished him, though he realized it only vaguely. All his Roman heritage had been swept away with boyhood and exile. In sullen flaring hatred and resentment he had tried to forget Rome and everything connected with it. He still was a man, however, and tonight a new man. How and why?

It came to him suddenly. Across the years, pride and hope and youth had all been crushed down. Today, these had leaped and burgeoned, surging up full force; this day, all he had lacked was come to him in flooding force.

"That sentence was unjust. May the gods reward him and you!"

The only words of sympathy ever given, and too late arrived to reach the broken-souled captain of Rome who was gone. A few words, a look, something kindling in the blue eyes of Drusilla. And how had he answered? Like a boor. Ah, but now he was awake! And he must find her again. He had read this message in her eyes, and it sang in his heart. He must find her again!

"And, by the gods, I will!" he muttered aloud.

Pelargos flung him a glance, surprised the expression in his face, and slapped him on the shoulder.

"Ha! Whatever it is, you'll do it, and I with you. Comrade, you've come to life; you and I together could tear Olympian Jupiter from his throne! Now let's have a whack at that long hair and beard. If you have any grease around, trot it out so we can knead it into the leather coat. The garment's stiff as a board."

"There's grease outside. I'll get it."

RAMNES! HE liked that name; it had a dark Etruscan sound in the mouth. He had a suspicion that Pelargos had not chosen it at random, but it suited him. He could never use the old name in Italy, anyway.

Outside, he found the pot of grease on the shelf, and as he came back left the door ajar, carelessly. He settled down on a stool, armor and all. Pelargos, knife in hand, hacked at the long hair and attacked the beard, jesting gayly the while.

WHILE THEY were thus engaged, Grex made a sudden dash for the door and forced his way out. His barking was furious and sustained.

"Let him go; he can take care of himself," said Ramnes, rubbing his cheeks. "Not bad, not bad at all! One could almost shave with that knife of yours."

"I used to, until the Gauls captured me two years ago and pulled out my beard, hair by hair, to make face match head." Pelargos, whimsically grinning, stood off to survey his work. "Well, what emerges from the shrubbery might definitely be called good, my honest Ramnes! I'll wager you've lost two pounds' weight of hair—look at it on the floor! By the way, something occurs to me."

"What?"

"This: If you're to help me down the old gods, comrade, you

must flow with the stream of destiny. It came for me when I met you; it hasn't come for you yet." Pelargos broke off and cocked his head. "Strange! The dog's fallen silent."

"What are you driving at?"

"Oh, I'm not sure myself!" Pelargos relaxed, and laughed shortly. "Some men are marked out by destiny, above the common herd of mankind; men different, men fated to do strange things, different thinks! I'm one, you're another. We all roll down the same torrent of death in the end, it's true, but some of us have more intelligence than others. What do I mean? Hard to explain, hard to find words; it's something I feel."

Ramnes smiled, a bit uneasily. Then Pelargos, looking up, gulped suddenly—gulped, and froze, slack-jawed, staring. Ramnes turned his head. That talk went unfinished for a long while....

The door had opened silently. A man stood there, looking at them.

A rather short man, swarthy, with dark curly beard; the rest was gold and gems. Golden helmet, a furred golden cloak much worn, and beneath it golden armor, somewhat battered; jewels flashed everywhere about him. A gaudy, jaunty, spendthrift figure, but every inch of him a soldier. In his hand was a javelin, short, steel-tipped. Close behind him crouched two dark figures, bows bent and shafts notched; the arrow-points glittered in the light.

"The gods! The gods have come to life!" gasped Pelargos.

"Steady; you're covered. Keep your heads and you'll not be harmed," said the amazing figure in mixed Gaulish and Latin. "Are you Romans?"

"Romans? No, by Hercules!" exclaimed Ramnes.

"You look it. No harm's intended; we had to kill your dog, for he attacked us. I'll pay you for him."

"Pay for him? Pay?" With a choked oath, Ramnes came half erect. The hand of Pelargos thrust him down suddenly.

"Steady!" said the slinger. "Steady, comrade! Here are Africans."

Africans! The word, commonly applied to the troops of Carthage, brought cool sanity and comprehension. Ramnes relaxed. Something more here, something greater, than a dead dog.... Caution smoothed his first rush of anger. From the outside night came a murmur of voices, a confused sound—horses, men. The cavalry of Carthage. War!

"You appear intelligent. You can't be Gauls?" asked the intruder.

"Nor you a god," rejoined Pelargos, his assurance fully recovered.

THE DARK man laughed gayly.

"I am Maharbal, commander of the Numidian horse in the army of Hannibal," he said, pleasantly enough but with slow speech.

"Ah!" Pelargos broke into a swift guttural chatter. The Numidian's face cleared, an exclamation of relief and joy escaped him; he became animated, talking rapidly in his own tongue. Pelargos talked as fast or faster. Both of them laughed together. Question leaped upon answer, back and forth, until Maharbal half turned, made a gesture to his two bowmen, and they disappeared. He closed the door, and stepped forward.

"Comrade, forget the damned dog," said Pelargos, hand on shoulder of Ramnes, with warning grip of fingers. "Rather, consider that in his death he's led us into the very stream of destiny I was talking about! This man wants to take us to his general. I've told him a bit about us—enough, that is. He wants guides; he has them, if you say the word."

"Guides!" Ramnes frowned, bewildered. "Guides? Whither?"

"To Italy," said Maharbal, quick eyes flitting from one to the other.

"Italy, comrade!" rang the voice of Pelargos. "Here's our chance; they're here, they're here, do you understand? Africa is here! They're heading over the mountains. They're not sure of their guides, and are getting more—they want us! Hannibal and his army, do you understand? No time to argue, no time to hesitate. It's yes or no. Can you guide them?"

Ramnes came to his feet. Italy! The mere word shook him, lifted him erect, blazed in him with a wild savage comprehension.

"By the gods—against Rome!" blared out his voice. "Yes, a thousand times yes! Rome, the cruel and pitiless, the killer of good men, the ravening wolf—yes! A jest, what a jest, that I of all men should guide them!"

Harsh mirthless laughter burst from him. Grex was forgotten, everything else was forgotten in this tumultuous and ecstatic moment. The son of Marcus Mancinus guiding the deadliest foes of Rome to death-grips! Why, the whole world had turned over for him this day—his day, the flood-tide of destiny!

Maharbal stood eying him, appraising him, listening to him, then quickly smiled and put out his hand. Ramnes gripped it, and was oblivious to the swift anguish his grip caused the smaller Numidian. His face was alight.

"Rome, the enemy and destroyer! Not you, not Hannibal himself, is the enemy of Rome that I am!"

"What has Rome done to you?" demanded Maharbal, freeing his hand with a grimace.

"Nothing. But to the father I loved, everything! Where do we go? When?"

"Now," said Maharbal. "To Hannibal. We have spare horses. Take what you desire to take, and go."

So it was done, and as though in dream, Ramnes found himself riding away into the night.

Pelargos was beside him, bestriding a horse; dark men all around, Numidian cavalry, with Maharbal close beside, and tongues clacking. Hour after hour they rode, until the cold stars and the chill wind brought sanity of a kind.

Ramnes cooled to it at last. It was real. In a few short hours he had leaped entirely out of his old life, shedding it as a cicada sheds its skin. Since his meeting with Scipio's staff, the old dull hatred for everything Roman had grown into a searing flame; everything Roman, except the blue eyes of a woman.

WAR? LAUGHING, jesting men of Africa all around, a pair of Gauls from the Rhone, everyone talking freely—was this war? No plundering, no killing, but an iron discipline; it was not war as he had heard of it. Maharbal, he discovered, was one of their chief captains, second only to Hannibal. The army was marching for the upper Isère valley, but was uncertain of the spies and guides at work.

Italy! The word was on every tongue. Those who stopped the way would be massacred without mercy. Italy, and the loot of Rome! Once over the Alps, the Gaulish tribes of northern Italy would welcome and join them—those same tribes that had utterly destroyed Rome a few generations ago. Nothing could stop this army, nothing!

Sixty thousand men had left Spain with Hannibal, and a third of them had perished in Gaul. When Ramnes thought of those high passes, already deep with snow and habited by savage barbarians, he recoiled mentally. Madness, madness! This one word wormed at his brain. He knew those passes, those barbarians. He knew the iron legions beyond. These gay Africans with their high talk and brave spirits marched to ruin.

What of it? He would march with them, and damnation to Rome! The city once destroyed could be destroyed again. Boyhood memories of the mean, crowded buildings on the hills inside the Servian wall, rose in him; narrow, twisting streets, houses hastily run up after the Gaulish ruin, temples built anywhere. Ramnes, Ramnes! The name sang to the clatter of the dark hoofs. It had a fine solid ring, this old Etruscan name.

DAWN WAS at hand when they rode in upon an enormous camp whose fires glimmered for miles. The fitful flames revealed figures strange and wild and fantastic to the eyes of Ramnes; black Nubians, tattooed Berbers, Spanish slingers from the

Balearic isles, heavy-armed troops of Carthage; an army that slept without tents or cover. Every man, Maharbal said, a chosen athlete inured to Spartan ways, but not a man of them the equal of their general.

Vaguely weird shapes upheaved through the gloom; elephants, nearly fifty of them, picked for size and strength. And at last the embers of an open fire surrounded by guards, two men asleep with their feet almost in the ashes; two men, wrapped in mantles against the heavy dew and the Rhone mist.

The party dismounted. Maharbal went forward to waken the sleepers; wood was slung on the fire and a blaze went up. The two wakened, yawned, sprang up—man and boy. The elder was a towering, massive figure, close-bearded, wearing a stained army blouse and an old cloak; yet he was young, no older than Ramnes. The boy was cast in the same mold.

"There we are." Pelargos was at Ramnes' elbow. He looked at the two, with whom Maharbal talked rapidly. "There's destiny, comrade. Hannibal and his brother Mago, they tell me. Find tongue, now! There's a god in the flesh if ever such a miracle happened."

HANNIBAL TURNED and beckoned, and spoke in Gallic.

"Come, you two! Let's have a look at you. I don't understand this at all. You're not Gauls?"

Ramnes stepped forward to the blaze, aware of the keenly probing scrutiny from man and boy. A handsome fellow, this boy, open and frank and eager.

"No Gaul," Ramnes said. "I was born a Roman."

Hannibal regarded him attentively for a moment, then turned to Maharbal.

"Get us some food. Order the light column to be ready to march in twenty minutes; your scouts in advance. The main column follows with elephants and baggage—sure there's no trouble ahead, eh? Very well."

"Now," and he swung around to Ramnes again, "let's have

it. Roman by birth, eh? Talk fast, my good fellow. Either you're a spy, some scoundrel sent to trick me, or else you're a gift from the gods! Your name?"

Ramnes talked freely, as trumpets began to sing through the camp across the dawn.

Here was Hannibal, already a noted figure of romance and legend: the African leader, owner of fabulous gold mines in Spain upon which he maintained this entire army, the soldier whose one aim was to drive a sword into the throat of Rome! It was hard to credit; yet no harder than for the African to credit that this stalwart man in Roman armor could hate Rome also. He said so frankly, and Ramnes blazed out at him in harsh words. Then they both laughed, and the spell of unreality was gone. They were man to man.

If the grim vigor of Ramnes impressed the other, Ramnes himself was astounded by the quick spell that Hannibal cast over him—the fiery energy, the almost hypnotic wave of personal charm, power, capability.

"Enough. We'll find a place for you. Welcome!" Slaves were bringing food and wine. Hannibal caught the hand of Ramnes, pressed it warmly, and shot a glance at Pelargos. "Who's this staring baldhead?"

"My friend," said Ramnes. "I answer for him."

"Good; sit down, be comfortable, eat while you can. Now tell me what lies ahead. Can the army cross those mountains? Can you lead us through the passes?"

Amid swift questions, Hannibal slipped into a coat of mail, buckled on a sword-belt, and attacked the food. Ramnes shrugged.

"The very idea seemed fantastic madness; now, since meeting you, I'm not so sure. Yes, a crossing is possible, and I can show the road, or a good part of it, but you'll lose heavily. The mountain tribes are fierce, treacherous, savage. You'll have to fight."

"Understood. I have forty-odd thousand men. Get me into

Italy with half that number, you who hate Rome as I do, and I'll promise you the sack of that proud city."

Ramnes emptied his winecup and grunted.

"Perhaps, perhaps. The walls of Rome aren't stones or mountains, but men."

HANNIBAL LAUGHED at this. "No flattering tongue, eh? We'll get on, my friend; you're the only Roman I ever saw who went to my heart. Now, who's this fellow?" he added, with another curious glance at Pelargos.

"The best slinger in the world, my general!" spoke up the latter, who had been silent long enough. "Give me the proper slings for various distances, and I'll make a joke of your best marksmen. Further, you'll find in me an answer to every problem of army, march or battle; in short, the brains that most men lack."

"Indeed? You'll need them," Hannibal said dryly, and beckoned an officer. "Five hundred mounted Balearic slings to accompany us. Give this man whatever equipment he desires. Mago, take command of the heavy column. Ready, friends?"

The boy Mago mounted and was off at a gallop. As by fresh magic, Ramnes found himself riding amid half a hundred aides, staff officers and guides, all swept forward by the furious energy of the one leader. Somewhere amid the throng, he heard the raucous laugh of Pelargos.

Well ahead, Maharbal was gone with a few squadrons of Numidians. Behind, the light column drove along, slingers and arches and horse. Far in the rear came the heavy troops and elephants and baggage, under Mago. All up, moving, on the way, in a matter of minutes.

AS HE rode, Hannibal was covering all headquarters details: aides were continually dashing off or spurring back again.

To Ramnes, surprise piled upon surprise. He had supposed this African host a wild, barbaric horde ravening on the pillage of the country. He found it the contrary; aside from the strict discipline, the supply service was organized to minute detail, and it was the army's boast that not a man had ever missed a meal.

Then, when a dozen riders closed around and began to ply him with searching questions on the nature of the defiles and passes ahead, he discovered they were engineers. They talked of heat and cold, of blasting rocks and building roads, of crossing rivers and scaling precipices, of chemicals and stress and weights. Madness? Rather, the slow planning and preparation of years. He began to see the venture, the whole venture, everything around and behind it, in a new light. The weapons, the men, the elephants, the money behind all this supplied from Hannibal's private funds—yes, there had been years in the doing. Scipio had not turned aside from a skirmish or a battle, but from an imponderable weight of fate. And this momentum was carrying Hannibal forward.

After talking steadily with other guides from Gaulish tribes, some thousands of these men accompanying the army as auxiliaries, Hannibal beckoned Ramnes forward and shot at him swift, incisive questions regarding the passes. Ramnes described these as far as the summits, which he knew personally, and Hannibal squinted at the snowy peaks.

"If you report aright, we'll find battle ahead. Tonight?"

"Tomorrow morning. As I said, you'll have nothing to worry about after nightfall. The mountain tribes come out to fight only by day, knowing that no advance is possible by night. Snow and darkness and rocky passes will halt even you."

"You have yet to know me, my friend!" said Hannibal, and laughed a little.

Long before noon, Ramnes recognized the country he knew so well, his own village, his own farm; all was deserted, for the Gauls had fled. The column rode on without halt, and he looked back at the little farm.

Pelargos brought his horse alongside.

"Someone you know, back there, comrade?"

Ramnes turned to him with a nod.

"Aye. A rascally farmer named Mancinus. He died yesterday, thanks be to the gods!"

Pelargos grinned. "You forget, comrade. There are no longer any gods; they're all dead except one."

"What one?" Ramnes laughed. "Blasphemer, you actually admit that one god exists?"

"Aye. He who conquered the Pyrenees, and who has the Alps yet to conquer, and after those the Apennines—if he'd reach Rome," said Pelargos, and nodded at the figure of Hannibal. "And if you think he's no god, Hercules come to earth again, ask the army!"

As though he had caught the words, Hannibal turned his horse and rode over to them. A trumpet blew, others made silvery echo in the distance. The long column drew rein.

"You, baldhead!" said Hannibal, his eyes twinkling. "While we breathe the horses, make good your boasts. Our Balearic slingers are the finest in existence; prove your words and you shall have a place among them."

"You mistake, African." Sliding to the ground, Pelargos rubbed himself gingerly and peered up. "Blisters on the backside don't hurt the throwing-arm; but you mistake. I want no place among your slingers."

"Then what the devil do you want?"

"Command of them."

"Very well." Hannibal lost his smile, and his eyes hardened. "Win it, or be crucified."

CHAPTER III

THEY CAMPED that night far up the Isère valley. The Gallic auxiliaries had made contact with the tribesmen hereabouts, and reported there would be fighting on the morrow, where the valley narrowed and was commanded by

the heights on either side. Yet despite the towering Alps, the
snow ahead, the certainty of death and suffering, the column
could talk of nothing but the new commander of the slingers.
For Hannibal had been true to his word.

Ramnes eyed his comrade curiously that night, while about
the campfire the captains drank his health, and Hannibal, who
drank not, praised his skill. Ramnes would have expected Pelargos to be wildly braggart, but he was not.

"You did feats today that I'd have sworn were impossible,"
Hannibal declared. "Take care of yourself; I need men like you.
Though others perish like ants, you must live; you're worth
thousands. Remember."

"I'll remember, General." Pelargos seemed sober and almost
gloomy, and of a sudden Ramnes realized that it must be the
effect of the wine, for the man had drunk deeply. "Ants? Aye,
to a god like you, men are no more than ants; a good com-
parison. You're not like the Romans, who never forget they're
mere men; they can't cross the street or move camp without
seeking omens from the gods."

"I make my own omens," Hannibal said curtly, eyeing Pelargos as though finding new worth in him.

"Precisely." The Stork spilled a little wine from his cup. "Oblation to a living god! Your health, general!"

A burst of laughter and acclaim rose on all sides, but Ramnes
caught the irony under those words.

SILENTLY HE wandered about the camp that evening,
listened as Hannibal and Maharbal and Mago questioned the
guides—and turned away, in frowning silence. Finding Pelargos
again, he stretched out beside the tall man.

"Best watch your words, comrade," he said. "You may be a
great man and commander of the slingers; but I think Hannibal suspected the mockery in your oblation."

Pelargos chuckled. "Why not? He's a god, sure enough;
beloved by the soldiers, sharing all they do and suffer, led by a
divine genius. He can see half the world die under his heels

"I make my own omens," said Hannibal curtly.

and think nothing of it. Can you?"

"I hope I may never have to pass such a test," Ramnes said moodily.

"That makes my point; you're not a god, comrade, merely made in the likeness of a god. Some day you'll be hailed as a god—"

"Stop your damned nonsense," Ramnes growled. "Those guides are betraying us."

"Eh? Impossible. Tell the general about it, not me. I distrust and defy and war against all gods— even the general! But upon occasion I can treat 'em well. Tomorrow you'll see me win the heart of this African god of ours."

"You're drunk. I tell you—"

"Tell me not, but go to sleep. Let 'em betray us; that'll mean fighting. We'll have work tomorrow; I intend to get into Italy with a sound skin and a click of silver in my pouch. Then we're off on the trail of destiny, you and I."

"But you've taken oath to serve Hannibal!" Ramnes protested.

"Bosh! I'll give him his money's worth. See that you swear no oaths, because you'd keep them. Now go to sleep; tomorrow we earn passage into Italy."

With morning, too, Ramnes found Hannibal beside him, as they broke fast; and here was sudden choice dinning at him. Choice between the vagrant witless fantasy of Pelargos, and the solid assurance of rank and command and golden future.

"What will you have of me, Ramnes?" demanded Hannibal abruptly. "I've appraised you, and you're worth while. Army rank? Name what branch of the service pleases you. Wealth? What I lack, Italy will give; but I don't lack. Power? It lies ahead for the taking. Only swear true service, and ask what you will; I think you respect an oath."

"Too much to give one lightly."

Hannibal eyed the savage rocky defiles and heights ahead, nodding thoughtfully.

"Once in Italy, I can put you to use," said he. "You're no ordinary Roman; you can be of great service. Yes or no?"

Ramnes could not miss the voice of opportunity, which made swift appeal to all the solid Roman depths of him; in the same instant, he recoiled. His brain sang with flittering glints of thought: The sardonic, ominous warning of Pelargos. Oaths that would bind him down. The blue eyes of a girl, somewhere afar over the horizon.

The stern Roman instinct in him died, before a rush of boyish, reckless impulse. He laughed gayly, lightly, eagerly, so that Hannibal gave him a frowning scrutiny.

"My hatred of Rome serves you—not I," he said, and smiled. "You're generous, and I thank you. At present, I'm guiding you over the mountains—"

"Others are also doing that," broke in Hannibal.

"Yes. I heard you talking with the guides last night. They're leading you into a trap where the savage tribes will crush you. Take the valley to the left, said they; take the defile to the right, I warn you."

Instantly all else was forgotten. Hannibal looked him in the eyes, and caught his breath, and leaped up.

"Good! I trust you. To arms!"

TRUMPETS PEALED. The column broke camp and moved; Hannibal delayed, and Ramnes saw him talking with a little group of half a dozen Gauls. Something familiar about them struck his attention. With a shout of recognition he headed his horse for them, only to be swept aside by Maharbal and the column of Numidian horse. Laughing, Maharbal caught his reins and drew him into the swirling vortex. Only the vision of those Gauls, friends from his old village, remained, and he saw them no more.

"Aye," Hannibal admitted, later. "I had them brought in for questioning—about you. I trust you on the evidence of my own senses, but I prefer to get confirmation. I got it."

All this later. For the moment, riding with the gay Maharbal, the world was tossed into chaos; the whole army was rushing impetuously forward, hurling itself up the valleys as though to conquer the shining peaks at a single charge.

At first, in this mad confusion, Ramnes thought his warning had gone unheeded, for the valley of the upper Rhone was tempting to the eye. He knew, only too well, the narrow, gorges beyond, the impassable defiles, the precipices skirted by mere tracks a foot wide. Just when he gave up hope, aides came on the gallop. Maharbal was shifted to the right and the Numidians went tearing off toward the Little St. Bernard peaks.

PELARGOS PROVED his boasts this day, and earned his passage well. When the heights to left and right suddenly sprang to life, with blast of horn and wild yell, when huge rocks began to crash down and rend the column apart, carrying men and horses away with screaming death, it was Pelargos who led

the light-armed slingers up the heights and cleared them. They
fought all day along those hillflanks and the descending shades
found the army still entangled in narrow defiles and faced by
seemingly hopeless precipices. Late in the afternoon, Ramnes
was summoned, and Maharbal with him.

Hannibal awaited them, with several other leaders of the
advance and a number of the guides. Pelargos came, grimly
exultant; the whole army was already chattering tales of his
deeds this day, as it made camp for the night.

Along the heights ran suddenly a blare of
war-horns. On the slopes, on the peaks, Gauls
appeared by the thousand. The slingers and
light troops went desperately at the enemy.

"The guides say we're headed wrong," said Hannibal abruptly. "To the left would have been better going, they say. Now,
Ramnes, speak out."

"The guides lie," said Ramnes quietly, scratching lines in the
snow. "You were headed for better going, yes; that road would
have taken you on to Geneva. You would have been lost among
the mountains, utterly lost! This way, the defiles open out. Tomorrow we'll come to Chambery and clear valleys along the
Isère; then on to the Little St. Bernard and the summits. I've
been that far. I know the way."

Clamorously the guides insisted that it was utterly impossible to gain Chambery, where lay the chief fortress and village
of the local tribes. Ramnes laughed shortly.

"True enough," he said. "But if there's no opposition, your
army can get through. And the trick is to gain those heights
tonight, when they're undefended, and seize them."

"As I foresaw," said Hannibal, with a nod. "The council's
ended, my friends; sleep until midnight. Then, Ramnes, to
work!"

There was little joy that night in the camp, lost in the winding
defiles. Despite the roaring fires, the advance guard was appalled
by the situation; the bitter cold, the snow, the narrow ways,
terrified African hearts. In the rear, the engineers were at work
making the trails passable for the heavy column that followed.

Midnight. Ramnes was wakened. He joined Hannibal, Pelargos, and a number of picked captains. A hasty meal, and they
set forth upon the starlight, while the army fires twinkled below.

This climb along the unlit ways was a frightful memory.
There was no enemy, except the bitter darkness. Here and there,
wild mournful cries resounded, and a clash of arms from somewhere below, as men slipped to their death; these noises followed persistently. Ramnes kept close to Hannibal, and this
was something to boast about. Hannibal seemed imbued with
superhuman and untiring energy; the supreme athlete in his

own army, he was impervious to any human feeling, and his body seemed of pliant steel.

They went on and on, until the defiles began to open into the valley ahead, leaving parties of men to occupy every height. With dawn, masses of the enemy appeared, war-horns blared, and disconcerted though they were, the Gauls attacked fiercely, only to be held off by the slingers and archers, until the first parties of shivering cavalry struggled through into the open. Then the enemy broke and, with a few thousand men, Hannibal swept on up the ever-rising slopes.

NIGHT SAW the fortress and town occupied, open country beyond, and messengers speeding back to bring up the heavy column of the army. Three days they lay here, the men resting and gaining strength, while scouts probed the way ahead. Here Ramnes was at work, riding as far as the chief village of Conflans, where the elders of the Gauls decided on peace and sent back guides and gifts to Hannibal. He at once brought up the entire army in column, the elephants and cavalry in the lead. This was a two-day march, and that night, after talking with the Gauls, Hannibal showed up suddenly beside Pelargos and Ramnes.

"You know these local people better than our guides do," he said shortly. "We've scouted the gorges ahead; but I'm worried more about the people than the ground. If these Gauls intend treachery—well, what do you think?"

"What you do, evidently," said Ramnes. "The gorges up ahead are narrow defiles, bad ones. If these hillfolk mean to trap us there, they can do it; and I rather think they'll try it. The safest plan would be to camp here for a week or two and send detachments on to secure the trails and the heights."

"A week or two!" Hannibal laughed harshly. "In that time, the elephants will all be dead; the cold will kill them. We've lost three already. No! We march at dawn, and if these Gauls mean treachery, we'll fight through at all costs."

Pelargos made half-sardonic comment.

"We've lost four thousand men already; a few thousand more or less are of no moment, General. Sacrifice ten thousand lives to the gods of victory! It'll be cheap at the price. It'll cost you that many if you push through at all costs."

"At all costs," snapped Hannibal, oblivious of any deeper meaning behind the words, and issued his orders on the spot. Elephants and light cavalry in the van, this time, with the heavy infantry—baggage and heavy cavalry in the rear.

THE MARCH pressed forward during two days, in peace; the second night, however, saw the worst stretch of gorges ahead.

That second evening brought Ramnes curious gifts from the fates. Marching order was lost; anyone joined any group that had firewood. Pelargos and Ramnes were warming themselves at their own blaze and awaiting mess-call, when others drifted in upon them. One, a lean graying man wrapped in furs, sat at one side by himself and wept; no one knew why or cared. Two others came; a Spanish archer, and the prisoner he guarded, a Roman named Lucius Alimentus.

This Roman had been brought from the lower Rhone; Ramnes had seen him more than once, but avoided him, for he was a bragging and insolent fellow, full of talk. Now he eyed Alimentus without love and kept a closed mouth in his presence.

Mess was served. The fur-clad man ate, dripping tears into his bowl. Pelargos was windy with big words. The Roman prisoner prated of what would happen when this haphazard army of Africans encountered the Roman legions.

"Ha!" said Pelargos, who had been talking long with Hannibal that day, giving him full details on the latest Roman army affairs. "Ha! I can tell you one thing that'll happen. This is the best cavalry in the world, and with the elephants opening the way, it will trample your legions flat."

"You forget that Rome has cavalry," said Alimentus with a sneer.

"Not I! Mounted legions, my good fellow; and once in the

saddle, your legions aren't worth a curse. The Roman cavalry is like the elephants of Greece—there's no such thing. It's a standing joke in all armies."

Alimentus turned pale with venom. "You'll learn otherwise," he spat out. "Mancinus is building up a cavalry force in Italy now, has been doing it for the past year; and you'll see your Numidians scatter like autumn leaves before it!"

RAMNES JERKED up his head at that name. "Who did you say?" he demanded in astonishment.

Alimentus turned to him.

"Ha! You speak Latin of the purest, do you? I said Lucius Hostilius Mancinus, head of that family. A man of great ability and honor."

"So?" muttered Ramnes. "I've heard otherwise."

"What have you heard, barbarian with Latin tongue?" jeered Alimentus. "Are you not the man Ramnes they've been talking about? An Etruscan name, that. Who are you?"

Ramnes ignored him. Lucius Hostilius Mancinus, eh? This distant cousin had taken over his father's rank and estates; a man of ill omen, a name of sly cruelty and unscrupulous ambition.

Alimentus, rebuffed, grumbled threats.

"You ragged barbarians will soon find how little you know of Rome," he went on. "I've met Mancinus; he's the most promising man in Rome today, of the younger generation. He's raising and training cavalry among the Samnites and other Latin peoples—"

Not trusting himself to talk with the man, Ramnes rose and strode away. He halted curiously beside the fur-clad man, who had dried his tears for the moment.

"Who are you?" he asked. "What are you doing here?"

"Waiting for speech with you, lord."

"With me?"

"Yes. He sent me." And the man pointed at the figure of

Pelargos, beside the fire. "He said to come and find you, for only the gods could help me and you had influence with the gods. Help me, lord, and I vow a tenth of my salary all this year to you!"

Scenting some ironic joke of Pelargos, Ramnes suppressed an oath.

"What's all this about, you fool? Who are you?"

"Lars Masena, chief elephant-trainer."

"Lars Masena! Ho, that's no Punic name! Sounds Etruscan."

"Yes, lord. I came years ago from Asculum, from across the Sabine hills. I was slave to a Roman, who took me to Sicily and was killed in the war; I was captured and sent to Carthage. There the elephants liked me. Now I'm chief trainer, I have money, I rank as captain—and I'd give all, all, if I only had Pinktoes back again!"

"Pinktoes!" echoed Ramnes, staring at the figure. "By the gods, what kind of a jest is this?"

"Lord, for me it is tragic." The other stood up, a lean man, old in the face but of great vigor despite his graying hair and beard. He spoke with a simple dignity. "He was the largest of the Getulian bulls, lord, and the noblest elephant I ever trained. Two days ago he died, and I've grieved for him. Now I fear lest his brother Lotus Ear go the same way, for he's been ordered into the lead tomorrow. You see, they don't know that these Getulian bulls cannot stand the unbroken defiles; they must always have a trail or a road, else they become nervous and wild. They can follow others, but not lead. And the worst is that poor Lotus Ear is delicate in the feet—"

Ramnes with difficulty restrained a laugh. Pinktoes! Lotus Ear! It was ridiculous; but it was fact, and to Lars Masena it was tragic fact.

AFTER SOME talk, Ramnes had the man lead him through the camp to where the elephants were bedded. Here, speaking with the officers in command and not hesitating to use the general's name, he soon had everything arranged to the delight and satisfaction of the elephant-trainer.

Then, ridding himself of Lars Masena and his gratitude, Ramnes came back to his own fire at last and found Pelargos alone.

"What's the idea, putting that elephant-trainer on my trail?" he demanded.

Pelargos grinned and gave him a cup of wine.

"Drink that and listen. The man's interesting; he has secret desires."

"Who hasn't?"

"Ah, but you don't understand! This Lars is a fellow of infinite value, looks older than he is, has brains. He knows the Umbrian country like a book. He's longed for nearly thirty years to go back there, has lived for that moment, yet loves his damned elephants too. We got drunk together the other night in that mountain town, and he opened his heart to me. I told him you'd bring all his lifelong dreams to pass."

Ramnes stared. "Eh? Are you crazy?"

"Of course. You're inhuman like all Romans, trampling on the hearts of men, self-sufficient. But it's in the hearts of men, common men, one finds miracles." In the dirt, Pelargos drew half a dozen converging lines, coming into one, and pointed to it. "There's strength, as in a rope of twisted strands. Destiny's like that, too, made up of little things coming together."

"Oh! You mean our plans?"

PELARGOS NODDED. "Don't we go to Umbria? We'll take Lars; he'll be worth while."

"Why? You have reasons that you're keeping secret."

"Right. Now look how destiny works for us! First, this man; we'll be glad of him, later. Then this Roman prisoner, what's-his-name, who knows your precious cousin. I milked him of more information, after you left. Your cousin is not only in

Umbria also, but he's in the very spot we're going, the town of
Reate! What's that but fate at work?"

"Fate be hanged, and my cousin to boot!" growled Ramnes.
"I don't want to see him."

"No matter; I tell you, here's destiny! If we get through the
Alps alive, we'll see some fun down in those Sabine hills. Where
did you go with Lars?"

"To arrange about his blasted elephant in the line of march."

"I thought you would; now he's a friend for life. You're not
so inhuman after all."

"Shut up—go to sleep. I'm worn out."

Ramnes rolled up and fell asleep with a cackle of sardonic
mirth in his ears....

Mid-morning of next day found the column deep in the
rocky gorges, painfully climbing; the cavalry were far out-strung
along the line of march; the elephants were uneasily picking a
way along the narrow trails. Ahead, the defiles began to widen
out. Then along the heights on either side, suddenly ran a blare
of war-horns. On the slopes, on the peaks, in the wider stretch-
es ahead, Gauls appeared by the thousand. Rocks began to
thunder down, huge boulders that brought with them trees and
small avalanches.

Amid this wild uproar and confusion, the Gauls attacked.
Battle was added to destruction. Arrows and javelins rained
down. In the rear, the column was broken in two; here the Gauls
attacked openly, and also at the van, endeavoring to destroy the
whole force.

The elephants, luckily, terrified the foes ahead and drove
them back, giving the cavalry a chance to emerge from the
gorge. Men and horses were struck down by the missiles from
above; multitudes of the light infantry were trampled to death
by the maddened horses. An elephant was down. The stream
ran crimson.

The slingers and light troops went desperately at the enemy
and slowly won a way upward. Every crag, every hillside path,

ran blood. Pelargos was in the thick of it, and Ramnes repeatedly saw the lanky slinger bring down enemy chiefs at seemingly impossible distances. He himself, however, had scant
leisure to watch others. More accustomed to such mountain
trails than most, he was in the thick of the onset, slowly toiling
upward, wielding javelin and sword with grim insistence.

It was a mad scramble, but gradually Hannibal made good
his words and fought through. His column suffered horribly;
as the afternoon waned, he got them out of the defile and in
makeshift camp at the wider valley ahead. The fighting died
away with sunset. The wounded died, or came crawling on in
the darkness. The rear of the army was cut off somewhere
behind; and darkness drew down as exhausted men dropped
where they stood.

Then, with roaring firelight limning the bloody scene,
Ramnes saw why this army held its chief to be a god. He accompanied Hannibal everywhere, aiding the wounded, lending
the surgeons a hand, bringing order out of chaos. By midnight,
discipline and organization had prevailed, the troops were in
some semblance of formation; and Ramnes, at his last gasp,
flung himself down near Hannibal and was asleep instantly....

He wakened to movement all around, and to stifled sobs
close by. Sitting up, he stared slack-jawed at Lars Masena, who
crouched at his elbow in the dawn-light.

"Help me, Lord Ramnes!" exclaimed the elephant-trainer,
chattering with cold.

"You again! What the devil is it now?"

"No one will listen to me. The trappings for the elephants
are with the baggage in the rear. I must have a blanket to pad
the back of Lotus Ear, for it's rubbed and sore, and they
command to load the worst of the wounded on the elephants,
and no one will give me a blanket—"

"Here, take mine." Ramnes scrambled to his feet, laughed,
and flung his own blanket at the man. "We may all be dead
tonight—off with you!"

Lars departed joyously, a blanket being just now a treasure above price to the Africans. Ramnes turned as Pelargos approached with some food. The commissariat still functioned.

"Gulp it, comrade, gulp it!" ordered Pelargos. "We're attacking in five minutes—attacking, mind you! There's a general who knows his business."

And for once the ungainly slinger was not sardonic.

CHAPTER IV

T HE GAULS ventured no further battle; none the less, the advance became a nightmare, swirling with horror. The enemy attacked invisibly, rolling down boulders that swept away men and horses, but this was by no means the worst.

Snow fell. The army, reunited once more, struggled on without fires for cooking or for heat, since there was no more wood. More elephants died, there being no way to cook the flour-cakes on which they were fed. Men died from wounds or sheer cold; many went over precipices with the baggage-animals and wagons, since of these the thundering boulders took fearful toll.

YET, WOUNDED and stricken, the army dragged itself along, There were no guides; Ramnes knew the summit, but he had not come by this passage, and the snow made the whole country look different. Consequently there were many false starts before the best way was scouted. And with each day more men were gone, more of the baggage was missing.

Eight days of hell; on the ninth day the passes lay behind, the enemy was gone, and they staggered to the open summits at the crest of the final pass, bleeding feet turning the snow to crimson behind them. And here, during two gasping bitter days, the exhausted army rested, looked forth upon the vista of Italian plains far below, and gathered strength for the final work while scouts pricked out a possible descent. Debilitated by cold and

wounds and labor, the men were like skeletons, the elephants were starved and weakened, half the baggage was lost.

"Did you hear the reports today?" asked Pelargos, as he and Ramnes huddled for warmth on the night before the march wag resumed. "Now see how a god thrives on fhe blood of men! This general of ours came into Gaul with sixty thousand in his train, He had forty-six thousand nine days ago, when he attacked the Alps. Today the reports show fourteen thousand African infantry, eight thousand Spanish and Gallic infantry, and seven thousand Numidian cavalry; forty elephants left. The Africans and the horses are dying like flies. If we reach Italy with twenty-five thousand men, we'll be lucky. One bite for the Roman legions!"

"Perhaps," muttered Ramnes gloomily. "But the Gauls of Italy will join us."

"Granted, So much the more to perish. A god doesn't see men die; but their comrades do, their friends do! Whether your god be one person, like Hannibal, or many like your Roman Senate—do the tears of women reach their hearts? Never."

"You're bitter against Hannibal."

"I'm not. I admire him enormously, as a general; not as a god. I distrust all gods! Their chief business is to kill off mankind; I desire to live. Even your own private god of hatred is a silly thing; it breeds destruction. Comrade, I'd give my good right arm, my slinger's arm, if I could make you see the folly of the gods!"

"Aye? What would replace them?"

"Reason. Contentment and peace in life; happiness that comes with construction." Pelargos spoke with deep and surprising earnest. "I've been talking with Lars Masena; if you could look into that man's heart, you could see the reality. Now he has one elephant whom he cherishes more than life. Let's hope he loses his damned Lotus Ear soon."

"Eh? Why such a hope?" queried Ramnes.

"Because then Lars will be ready to follow his heart's desire. That elephant is, at the moment, his god. When this beast dies, he'll shed tears and become a man again—with a horizon. While a man clings to his little god, he has no horizon. He needs one. We all need one."

"I thought you an aimless drifter?"

"HERE IN this damned snow, comrade, I'll tell the truth. I'm no such thing, though I pretend; aye, and jeer at fate to hold my courage up! I've a wife and two sons, taken from me during the wars. They're in Italy now, in a certain city—never mind the details., I'm on my way. You'll help me, I'll help you; Lars Masena will help us both, and we him. What was the first thing I gave you? A horizon. A woman and wealth."

"Damned nonsense," growled Ramnes, but thought again of blue eyes in warmth.

"Maybe; nonsense is a wise thing at times. You're in process, like an elephant half tamed. I need you. I'll use you, or Hannibal, or your cursed Roman Senate, anything and everything, to reach my horizon."

"Then your wife and children are, in your own words, your gods."

"No; they're human. And human desires, like that which burns in the heart of Lars, aren't gods. I'll tell you the difference. Once, in Sicily, I met a fellow from some far eastern land near Egypt. I don't know the name of it. He was a merchant from Tyre, and his country lay somewhere about there. We liked each other and talked often. He used to tell me about the god of his people, and the odd thing about it was that it was a different kind of deity. He used to tell me over and over that his god was a spirit—just that."

Ramnes laughed. "Queer kind of a god, sure enough!"

"Well, there's something to it, and that expresses what I mean; a god is a spirit. The only real god there is. Poor Lars is a humble fellow, has craved with all his soul for thirty years, and when he gets to his goal, will be disappointed; no matter. I tell you he can make or mar all we do! So much for him. For me—why did I desert from Scipio's army? Because he was sending his army to Spain. He himself was going to Italy. I couldn't go with him, which was his misfortune, so I started by myself and found you. Together, we'll be a team to drag down the gods! With Lars, we're invincible."

"Why?" demanded Ramnes. "Why Lars—a weeping, broken man?"

Pelargos snorted. "Broken, my eye! Weeping, over his dead god, yes. What chance have any of us in this man's army? None. We can't be ourselves. We're all overshadowed by a god, by the grind of events. Get free of it and serve our own ambitions! One battle, and either Hannibal will be destroyed, or he'll smash the legions. In either case, be ready to go our own ways. Agreed?"

"Agreed," said Ramnes, and wondered what Pelargos could see in the elephant-trainer that was worth while. Upon the puzzle, he fell asleep.

Two more elephants were found dead in the morning, when the army marched out. An evil omen, said someone on the staff, at which Hannibal cursed all omens. But new snow had fallen in the night.

The descent was far steeper than the ascent from Gaul; it wound down the face of precipitous cliffs, the new snow had hid the old surface, and ghastly tragedies occurred every hour. With afternoon came heartbreak. The advance guard were in a gorge so deep and abrupt that the sun never reached the bottom, which was a sheet of solid ice—and went on over the edge of a precipice. Here was death for many, ere the situation was realized.

BACK ALONG the column, trumpets shrilled, the army halted; and with sunset the engineers arrived at the head of the line. It was bitter cold. To go on, meant that a road must be built around the lip of the precipice for a good three hundred yards; the living rock had to be blasted out.

Luckily, there was no lack of firewood here, and the engineers went to work by torchlight. Roaring fires were built along the seams of rock. These were filled with water and allowed to freeze, bursting the rock asunder; with tools, with vinegar from the baggage train to soften the rock and help drill more holes, the work went on.

By daylight, the light-armed troops could pass, but for another three days the engineers labored, patiently working farther and farther until by aid of frost and water and handiwork the way was passable for baggage and for the elephants. And as the days passed, men and animals perished from cold or from sheer exhaustion.

Six days in all before they came down into the valley of the Po, leaving a full twenty thousand behind them in the Alpine passes; human wreckage, emaciated and worn, thirty-seven gaunt elephants staggering with weakness, one of them Lotus Ear, the Getulian beast on whose neck sat Lars Masena. A single legion then would have wiped them out. Instead, they were met by the Gauls of Italy, friends and allies against Rome—met with wild rejoicings, with eager hospitality, with news of all northern Italy in revolt and cities waiting to be looted.

The nightmare horror was past. In its place was jubilation, a frenzied exultation of conquest, loot, women, plunder; small wonder that under this triumphantly rolling flood, one man was forgotten.

RAMNES REMEMBERED vaguely that last day or two of the descent, with fever tugging at his brain and his body loosened and failing; then came a blank. He wakened in a little village of Gauls, on the Orcus River; he was alone here, weak and wasted with fever, but an honored guest among kindly folk.

It was days later before he could comprehend just what had occurred.

"Lord, you were left with us; we were well paid," said his host. "One man, very tall, who carried three slings at his belt; he had a bald head. With him another man and a vast monstrous beast with two tails, who obeyed him like a dog. They said you were to wait here for news from them."

"I can do nothing else," said Ramnes, who could scarcely lift his hand.

A terrible despondency enveloped him. Mere skin and bone, all energy sapped away, his companions gone and all the vista of the future destroyed, he lived mechanically but hopelessly. The Gauls tended him with assiduous care. The days drew into weeks, he was able to sit in the wintry sun, and his strength gradually returned; but inertia gripped him.

For this emptiness and loneliness he had bartered his mountain independence far away in Gaul; a glamorous dream that was turned to ashes. Now his future was as blank as his past. After all, the whole vision had been silly, baseless. The story of Pelargos might have been a lie, about the hidden treasure. Drusilla? He smiled bitterly at the thought of her. She had gone her way, all his fancies about her blue eyes were utter nonsense, he would never see her again.

Harsh reality here, and reality hurt. It had been so easy to dream afar! Queerly, though, one thing lingered with him; that confidence in the snow on the Alpine summits, and the words of Pelargos. "God is a spirit." As he lay, Ramnes came to realize what the bald rascal had meant by his talk of warring against the gods, the material gods, and by the deity that was a spirit.

True, perhaps, but he himself had nothing, nothing. Ambition was reft from him. He was a shadow in the world of men, and he had not even a name. As health returned across the weeks, mental health evaded him; he grew more and more hopeless of the future.

The Gauls were simple, kindly folk. News? They had little. The Africans, they said, had captured Turin and were occupying the whole country north of the Po; it was rumored that the Consul Scipio had been defeated in a cavalry battle on the Ticinus. This left Ramnes cold. Hatred had died with the rest; he cared little, he told himself, whether Rome or Carthage won. If hatred were his god, in the words of Pelargos, it had been dwarfed to petty stature. He needed a cause, his own cause, a cause that would fire his heart and soul; and he had none. The dream that had thus far carried him, was gone before the blasts of reality. Fool, to idealize a pair of blue eyes and a moment's passing meeting!

NOVEMBER WENT, and December was in. Ramnes was himself again in body, strength returning full flood; he was an enormous hulk of a man, listless and tormented in mind. The Gauls chivvied him, for his own good, into matching himself against them at running and throwing the javelin and wrestling; the best of them were helpless against him, yet he had no pleasure in his own powers. He had no incentive, no ambition. He took no care to his appearance, let hair and beard grow wild. And so, of a morning in late December, came Croton.

Ramnes heard the hubbub in the village, and then they brought in the man—a small, wizened, blear-eyed fellow with perpetually hoarse voice, and the metal collar of a slave about his neck. He blinked at Ramnes, saluted him, announced himself.

"My name is Croton," he said in Greek. "One Pelargos sent me to you."

"Speak Latin," said Ramnes irritably. "I've forgotten my Greek."

"Very well, lord. I've brought you a horse, garments, money, armor, and a message."

"I want none of them," retorted Ramnes. "Your Latin has a damned queer accent!"

"Perhaps, lord; I come from Reate. I was a freedman of the noble Quintus Veturis, and the manager of his estates there."

Ramnes straightened up on his stool.

"What's that?" he exclaimed. Croton repeated his words.

"A freedman? But you wear the collar of a slave!"

A snarling oath came from Croton, a vicious, hate-hissing oath.

"I keep that collar until I can return home and obtain justice. Lucius Mancinus took me as his slave, by fraud and force; he took other possessions of the Veturis family, also."

"The lady Drusilla?" Ramnes asked quickly, "Where is she?"

Croton blinked at him in astonishment. "You know of her, lord? She is coming to her estates now, poor soul! Mancinus is supreme there in Umbria; he raises men and horses for the army and has much power. There is no love between him and the lady Drusilla, though he intends to force her to his will and marry her, for the sake of her estates—"

"Wait, wait!" broke in Ramnes, putting back his unkempt hair and staring at the man. "By the gods, what trick is this? How the devil did you get here?"

"By gods and devils both," the other said sadly. "Mancinus took me with him when he led his cavalry contingents to the army, because I am skilled in the ailments of horses and he needed me. The Africans defeated us at the Ticinus River. Our cavalry cannot stand up to theirs, for our men are trained, like the legions, to fight on foot. I was captured by the Africans and saved my life by proclaiming my skill, so they attached me to

the army and the bald man, Pelargos, one day heard me talking
about Veturis. He had served Rome under Veturis; so he bought
me and sent me here to you. I gave oath to reach you. My reward
is freedom. I have the letters of manumission here, to be signed
by you as witness, which makes them valid. Also the gifts for
you, outside with the horses; and a letter from Pelargos. He is
unable to write, but I wrote down what he commanded."

This said, Croton wiped his bleary eyes and lapsed into
watchful waiting.

Ramnes caught his breath, and his heart leaped. Drusilla
again! This fellow had known her and served her! And Pelargos
had not forgotten him at all. Ha! The world was not so dark
after all! His spirits mounted. The old sparkle crept into his
eyes and his brain wakened into life.

"WHERE'S PELARGOS now?" he demanded in a new
voice.

"With the army, lord. The consuls, Scipio and Sempronius,
have united their armies in a fortified camp on the Trebia. The
Africans are camped opposite them and are eager for battle,
but the Romans delay. It may come at any time."

"You spoke of a letter. Where is it?"

Croton reached under his tunic, and produced a roll of sheepskin pieces.

"There's the letter of freedom for you to sign." He laid one
aside. "And my passport through the African lines, bearing the
seal of Hannibal; also another for you. Here is the epistle. I
write Greek, Latin or Tuscan."

He handed over a length of the thin leather bearing exquisite
calligraphy in Greek. Ramnes seized it, still lost in wonder at
the apparent coincidence which had led this horse-doctor to
him; but it was no coincidence, as he presently perceived. It was
the quick wit of Pelargos at work. The letter was to the point:

> Greeting, Ramnes. Ask this man Croton about the dagger of
> Mancinus, your cousin. Shave your face clean and avoid Hanni-

bal. Join us. Lars Masena will be ready, for his god is dying. Down with all the gods! Farewell.

—Pelargos.

Ramnes eyed the words, his blood running warmly. He was not forgotten, the dream was reality, the future was not empty! From the depths of despondency, he was abruptly jerked to the heights of vision again.

Shave? Avoid Hannibal? Obvious enough. So the elephant Lotus Ear was dying, and Lars was looking ahead to his mysterious heart's desire—good! Aye, he must up and ride, and lose no time about it; if battle came, Pelargos might well go the way of all flesh, by a Roman sword. Sudden excitement stirred in him, and then he looked up, frowning.

"What does he mean about the dagger of Mancinus?"

"Oh, that!" Croton wiped his wizened features, blinking, with nervous hand. "That is the dagger of Eryx. Your bald-headed friend seemed to think it interesting. What became of Mancinus in the battle, I don't know. He was going back to Umbria to raise more cavalry and to stick the dagger in the Lady Drusilla; possibly he's there now. You see, the Veturis estates are near the city of Reate, where he has his headquarters."

Ramnes felt his brain swimming.

"Am I in fever again? What has all this to do with a dagger? What is Eryx?"

Croton began to laugh amusedly.

"Lord, Eryx is a city founded by Greeks along the coast, east of Umbria; now it pays tribute to Rome but has its own rulers, or did have when I last heard."

"What the devil are you driving at?" cried Ramnes angrily. "Are you trying to say that this damned cousin—that this Lucius Mancinus means to kill Drusilla?"

"Kill her? The gods forbid!" exclaimed Croton, astonished. Then he changed countenance. "Still, she might be better off if he did kill her," he added, wagging his head mournfully. "For I've heard him say that, after sticking the dagger in her, he meant to make her a laughingstock and exhibit her to all his friends in shameless attitudes—"

Ramnes came to his feet, drove his fist at the open door before him, and the stout wood splintered with a rending crash.

"What madness is this?" he roared. "Eryx! Reate! Daggers! Exhibits! By the gods, will you talk sense or must I have you taken out and whipped by these Gauls?"

"Lord, have patience! I'm trying, indeed I am," the little man cried in alarm. "First, Mancinus not only loves the lady Drusilla, but hates her, because she despises him; he wants to marry her, degrade her, break her heart, shame her! Is that clear?"

"Go on," said Ramnes, ignoring the Gauls clustering outside the broken door.

"Second, he means to do this with the dagger. This dagger, lord, is the sovereign emblem of the old Tyrants of Eryx; who owns it, becomes the lord of that city, or so it was in the olden time. It was a gift to one of those rulers from the goddess Athene—"

"Skip all that rot!" exclaimed Ramnes.

"But, my lord, that's the point of everything!" desperately pleaded Croton. "It is a magic dagger, the gift of the divine goddess! No swordsman is secure against its magic power; whoever is pricked by its point, straightway loses all will, all resistance, and becomes the slave of the dagger. This is well known. It's historic fact. If Mancinus only pricks the finger of the lady Drusilla, she obeys him in every respect, like a slave who is made drunk with unmixed wine. This is his intent. He took the dagger by force from the temple of Tinia in Reate. Tinia is the Etruscan god whom we know as Jove or Jupiter—"

RAMNES BROKE into a laugh of ridicule, but his laugh froze midway. He stared at the sunlight, the horses before the door, and the clustered Gauls, and saw them not. Instead, he saw the face of Drusilla, calm and deep of eye, this woman who, in the expressive words of Pelargos, knew the gods intimately. The voice of Croton droned on, telling how the dagger had come to be in that temple and so forth, but Ramnes heard nothing.

His brain was busy; behind these words about magic, he perceived hard sense. He knew now why Pelargos had sent the horse-doctor on to him.

A dagger of magic power, given by the gods—somebody had been clever, back in the ancient days! A dagger, feeding its very point some secret and terrible drug, such as were known to priests and wise men; yes, a simple thing enough, embellished with many a fantastic detail. And a man, powerful, unscrupulous, savage of heart, lusting after beauty and planning to drag it down into the mire.

Ramnes closed his eyes and shivered slightly; he had heard from his father what manner of man was this cousin Mancinus, a young man with the heart of a wild boar. Now, with all Italy in wild uproar and confusion of war, with the allies of Rome, the Latin states such as Umbria and the independent cities like Capua or Eryx wavering in loyalty—now was the time for a man to act. A man like this Mancinus, working for Rome with his right hand, for himself with his left. "Or," muttered Ramnes, looking out suddenly at the sunlight, "a man working with both hands for himself and for a daughter of the gods—a man like Ramnes!"

HE TURNED abruptly to Croton, who had fallen silent and was staring at him.

"Have you a razor?"

"Eh? Yes, yes, my lord," was the hurried response. "Pelargos said you might have need of one. I brought one."

"So? And what sort of armor did you bring me?"

"Excellent armor, lord; Pelargos tested it. Your passport says you are Ramnes, captain of fifty, attached to the elephant division. Pelargos said that upon reaching the army you are to report to someone in that division. Hm! An Etruscan name like your own—"

"Lars Masena, yes." Ramnes! Work to do, a journey to go,

an ambition to seek, a horizon to reach! He remembered that Lars Masena knew all the lower country intimately; a man seeking some mysterious heart's desire across the years. Just as Pelargos sought. Just as he himself—his smile became a laugh, eager and ringing.

"I'll sign your freedom letters, then you may go. Whither?"

Croton blinked at him in a snarl.

"To Umbria, of course. My mistress will be there; she'll see justice done me."

"Hm! The town of Reate, in Umbria. Do you know of a certain grotto somewhere near your estates there? The grotto of a Sybil?"

"Lamnia the Sybil!" Croton gaped at him. "Sealed up and accursed! You know of it?"

"Aye. You have money?"

"Plenty, lord. A full purse is among your things."

"Pelargos has looted well, eh?" Ramnes laughed again, and sobered. "Go and find your mistress; give her a message from me—wait! How do you know she'll not remain in Rome?"

"Lord, the Villa Veturis is her home, and is dear to her. She detests Rome. The villa houses all the family *lares*—relics of the family, gods and shrines of the ancestors—and also the family wealth that I helped Quintus Veturis to hide before he went on this last campaign. My mistress takes after her Sabine mother, rather than after her Roman father."

"Do you know that Pelargos was with Quintus Veturis when he died?"

Croton veiled his sharp eyes and evaded. Ramnes chuckled.

"I see you do. Pelargos warned you to tell no one, eh? Good man! Well, tell your mistress that the person once named Mancinus, whom she met on the other side of the Alps comes to find her once again. That's all."

"Mancinus!" Croton looked up with prying, speculative gaze. "There was a Mancinus years ago, commander of the Fourteenth Legion; but you're young. And Pelargos said she would remember him, too. All this is very singular—that she should know him and you both!"

"Well, let's have your letters for my signature," Ramnes said. "Then off, make haste! Warn your mistress; make her return to Rome, where she'll be safe from this Mancinus."

"From this or that Mancinus?" said Croton, and shook his head. "I know her, my lord. She has the greatest contempt for that man. Her pride would not let her fear him."

Ramnes nodded, and took the strip of leather handed him. "You should write on paper, like the Egyptians do."

"Lord, there was no paper in the camp," said Croton simply.

AGAIN RAMNES laughed. He was still laughing as he affixed his name to the letters of freedom, with a seal borrowed from his Gallic host. He was in a riot of laughter—laughter of upsurging strength and confidence and vision.

For he knew now what Pelargos had meant by all his talk of gods; and those gods were beckoning him forward to a horizon glinting with blood and steel.

CHAPTER V

LARS MASENA the elephant-trainer was weeping again.

Ramnes had timed his arrival in the two-mile-long camp; it was evening when he was passed through the lines, a Numidian guiding him to the elephant division. A bitter cold wind swept down the valley of the Trebia, and men were huddled for warmth about blazing fires. The number of elephants was not what it had been, said the Numidian. The cold was killing them off rapidly.

So they came to Lars Masena, tucked in between two elephants, and weeping.

He greeted Ramnes with a cry of joyful recognition, and spat

a hasty order at a slave who set off, running, into the darkness. Then he pulled Ramnes into the shadow of the giant beasts.

"Do you spend your life shedding tears?" asked Ramnes.

"Lord, I have reason. Lotus Ear died yesterday. All the elephants are dying. I've sent for Pelargos; do you know we're going to fight tomorrow?"

"I heard some talk among the men, yes," said Ramnes. "And I saw the Roman campfires across the river. Pelargos is well?"

"Aye, and a great man now, my lord. Captain of all the slingers."

"Hm! Then he'll not be in any hurry to get away from here."

"Eh?" Lars clapped hand on his arm and lowered voice. "You've not come to fight, then?"

"No. I'm for the south, and no time to lose about it. Umbria."

"I'm going with you, I'm going with you!" murmured the elephant-trainer excitedly. He had abandoned tears now. "I wept, because I thought the gods had forgotten me! But you're

here. Pelargos will go. We'll all go. After thirty years, I'll see Asculum again!"

A HASTY step, a towering figure in gleaming mail and furred cloak, and Ramnes struck hands with Pelargos in the obscurity. The Stork folded up his long legs and sat with them, cursing the smell of elephants.

"I came into camp after dark," said Ramnes, "hoping to avoid Hannibal's eye. I've no mind to figure in any battle. There's work ahead."

"Then the man Croton found you," Pelargos said with his croaking laugh. "Good. This time tomorrow night, all three of us will be on our way. You'll see something tomorrow, comrade! I've just come from Hannibal. By Hercules, what a wonder he is! I'm winning the fight for him tomorrow—you'll see. We have to fight quickly, before all the elephants are dead. No front-line work for me, either; I'm one of your bloody commanders now, with a dozen aides and nothing to do but see that all goes well. Content to wait?"

"No," said Lars Masena. "Lotus Ear is dead. The others are dying. I'm all through here. I want to go!"

"Tomorrow night," said Ramnes. He could not keep the vibrant thrill from his voice. "If this is true, tomorrow spells Rome or Africa! Confound you, Pelargos, I may get into the fight yet and strike a blow against the legions!"

"Cool off, comrade," Pelargos retorted, with cynical calm. "Never mind enthusiasms; they're dangerous. Bunk here with Lars tonight. I'll join you in the morning; my post is close by, anyhow. Twenty-two thousand of your Romans over yonder, and as many more of their allies; you'll see widows in Rome by next sunset!"

"Are you sure," asked Ramnes softly, "that you want to go to Umbria?"

Pelargos was silent for a moment; then:

"I can't blame you for that question. You're young, ambitious, ignorant of the world. You know nothing of the hearts of men. You don't know the one enduring drive that holds a man through thick and thin; the one vision that dies not. Why did I get you here? Lars Masena, there, knows. For thirty years Lars has had a vision, and now he sees the reality approaching. Eh, Lars?"

"Yes, yes!" sniffled the elephant-trainer. "I've lost all that I had; nothing now remains except the dream."

"Dreams are the only realities, comrades," said Pelargos, and his voice sounded mournful. "With your help, mine comes true. With my help, you attain your own. Ramnes, here's your answer: I have three of the best horses in the army ready. Tomorrow pause a little while, to watch something that will echo down the world. Then we mount and ride, we three. Content?"

"Content," said Ramnes gravely. "If Rome's beaten tomorrow, you'll lose a lot by going to Umbria. Fame, position, rank—"

"Be damned to all that!" broke in the other. "What awaits

me, beyond Umbria, is greater than all else. Don't you think it's
hard to be patient? Good night."

He rose abruptly and stalked away, his abnormally tall figure
glinting upon the next firelight. When he was gone, Lars
Masena spoke gently.

"He told me, one night in the Alps. His wife and two sons—
somewhere."

"Yes; he told me also."

"Are you comfortable here? Might as well bed down on this
straw between the beasts. I have some food ready for you, and
wine." As he spoke, Lars produced a bowl and a leather bottle;
apparently he was not critical in the matter of food. Neither
was Ramnes, at the moment. Having cared for his horse,
nothing else mattered. He relaxed, ate, drank, pulled up the
blankets, loosened his garments.

"Any danger of these beasts rolling on us, Lars?"

"No." The trainer chuckled. "They're careful, my lord—"

"Don't 'my lord' me," grunted Ramnes. "My name's Ramnes.
We're comrades. Tell me where you're bound for in Umbria—
the town of Asculum, isn't it?"

"Aye. Just beyond Reate, for which you're bound; between
Reate and the coast. Eryx is on the coast."

"Eryx!" That was the city Croton the horse-doctor had talked
so much about, the Greek city. It was the dagger of Eryx which
Mancinus now had.

"Aye," said Lars Masena. "Eryx. That's where Pelargos hopes
to find his wife and two sons. You for Reate, I for Asculum,
Pelargos for Eryx."

RAMNES WHISTLED softly. Here was news. A shrewd
and canny man, this Pelargos, and could keep a close tongue.
A man not to be doubted, yet endlessly serving his own pur-
poses.

"You haven't told me, Lars, why you seek Asculum. Home-
sick, after these years?"

A pause in the darkness. Then the older man's voice, reflective, evasive:

"Only when we've drunk unmixed wine, when the tongue is loosened—then I'll tell you the truth. Otherwise, a man lies to avoid thought of his own heartburnings."

"Yours have had thirty years or so to burn out," said Ramnes, somewhat irritated. "Do you spend your life between tears and elephants?"

"The elephants are dead or dying; the tears are spent: my life now lies in the future," replied the other, with a touch of restrained dignity. "Don't disdain me, friend Ramnes. In the Latin cities to the southward, in the whole of Italy where the power of Rome reaches, you and Pelargos will walk in hourly peril, but I'll go in security."

Ramnes was puzzled by the man. He knew Pelargos had picked Lars as a companion, not blindly but for some deep reason; what it could be, eluded him.

"Peril for us? How so?" he asked.

"Somebody has talked; perhaps Hannibal, who knows? You no doubt remember that Roman prisoner, Alimentus, who was with us in the Alps. He was exchanged and has gone, but learned too much before he left. He more than suspects that you're a Roman and that Pelargos is a deserter from Rome; and, since we're going into territory that's subject to Rome, look out! The Latin cities hold safety and aid for me, even were I blind and starving, but without me they'd hold scant security for you."

"Why are you so sure of yourself?"

The elephant-trainer chuckled softly. "Wait and see! I'm not sure enough to boast of it, except when I'm drunk; the first Latin city we reach, will tell whether I'm right or wrong. Time enough then to boast. Here, feel this."

Ramnes found a rope-end thrust into his hand.

"Feel it, pull it apart. How many strands are there?"

"Three, of course. All rope has three strands."

"Good rope," corrected the other, and chuckled again. "I

"I'm going with you!
After thirty years, I'll
see Asculum again!"

learned this from Pelargos. A strong man can break one of those strands; but not three. You or he or I, alone, might be helpless; together, the three of us can attain what we will."

RAMNES LAY quiet long after the other had fallen asleep, and his brain flittered with uneasy conjecture. Disturbing news, that about Alimentus; despite war and ruin, Rome would not be too busy to stir a relentless pursuit of deserters or traitors. A pity that Alimentus had been exchanged and let free, to tell what he knew!

The mystery about Lars Masena had deepened, but the little parable of the threefold cord was to the point, significant. Ramnes comprehended that upon these two, as upon the thousands all around, weighed an ever-increasing suspense. He caught the contagion of it, could sense it on every side. The feeling had taken hold upon him, also. Here along this river on the morrow would be settled the destiny of nations; but what was more vitally important to every man there, the fate of personal ambitions and desires and hopes, the life or death of selves and comrades.

With morning, Ramnes slept late; the whole army slept late, snug against the chill searching wind and the driving gusts of rain. Ramnes wakened to movement and confusion on all sides; here was Lars Masena with a huge flask of wine and a huge bowl of hot stew, and fresh-made bread. Crouching, the bowl between them, Lars vented his news.

"*Brr!* Snow today, if I'm any judge. Three more elephants dead, the rest barely able to stagger. Listen!" A blare of trumpets, thin and distant, pierced athwart the rain. "The signal; that means they're coming. Maharbal's Numidians have been riding around the Roman camp to tempt them—the legions are coming! They'll have to ford the river. No hurry. The orders are to eat and drink hearty. Thank the gods I'll not be in the fighting line! Such a day for battle I never saw in my life. The wind's like a knife."

They ate. The elephants were being led out and caparisoned with mighty armor of steel and leather; many of the poor brutes were so far gone with cold that they could scarcely stand and their trumpetings were pitiful.

Time wore on. Presently only the hulks of the dead beasts remained. The rain was coming down harder, mingled with

Ramnes

occasional bursts of sleet. The leaden, sullen skies boded snow. A courier, pelting along in the mud, paused to fling excited words.

"They're crossing the river! Crossing, and forming up!"

"Come along," said Lars, wrapping himself in a long skin robe. "I know where to find Pelargos. What a day, what a day!"

Close by, on a little rising ground, Pelargos was stationed, giving final instructions to a crowd of officers. A new Pelargos, brusque with authority, wasting no words. He nodded greetings and went on with his orders. Ramnes eyed the slingers with surprise; each was wound about the head and about the body with two slings, and carried a third.

"Why the extra slings?" he asked Lars.

"Some notion Pelargos has—to be used at varying distances. Ha! *Look!*"

The line of battle was marked by the elephants, placed in pairs in the van, each pair a hundred yards apart. Behind these, the ranks of heavy infantry; behind these, again, the crowded masses of slingers. Between gusts of rain, cavalry appeared in the distance. And opposite, coming up from the river-line, the legions of Rome, slowly advancing, increasing, swelling in number as more crossed at the ford, spreading out to right and left.

The crowded officers about Pelargos burst into a yell, turned, and scattered at a run. A few aides and couriers alone remained. Pelargos came to Ramnes, his eyes glittering eagerly, and exchanged quick handclasps with the two.

"All's set," said he. "Hannibal's off to the right with the headquarters staff—won't bother us. Look!" He pointed to a line of trees lessening in the distance. "Mago and a division of light Numidians are hidden there, to take the Romans in flank. Ha! Look at our Spanish infantry, and those heavy Numidian regiments! Then look at the Roman legions—comprehend the difference, Ramnes?"

Ramnes nodded. The legions were open and uncrowded, with a man's width between every two men; but the African heavy infantry was like a human wall, with shields locked, the men in close formation. Ramnes felt the blood pound in his temples as the shouts rippled along the line, as the advancing lines of the legions gave birth to some thousands of skirmishers who came forward at a run toward the elephants. Lars squatted on his heels and squinted across the rain.

Pelargos gave his croaking laugh.

"There we go! Watch, now—watch! Lead bullets for distant work; stones for closer business; and for hand-to-hand work with the infantry, big stones as large as eggs. That's the program.... Ha! We're at it—we're at it!"

The slingers went out at a run, past the heavy infantry, past the elephants. They came to an abrupt halt. The Roman skirmishers were leaping forward—only to melt suddenly, to fall in windrows, to break and stagger back. Unseen death smote them from afar, as the leaden bullets of the slingers sang, and the ranks were lost.

MORE MEN rushed from the ranks of legions—light infantry of the Latin allies; a wave of them, thousands of them.

From somewhere on the wings, to right and left, came the din of battle, the flutes and horns, the thin yells of men; but Ramnes could not take his eyes from the scene before him. The Roman infantry survived the lead bullets, but each slinger now took his second sling, and a perfect hail of stones stormed upon the mailed ranks; and as they came still closer, the largest sling of all came into use, hurling great lumps of stone that battered armor and smashed skulls and men together.

Pelargos kept his staff busy—now ordering up fresh supplies of ammunition, now sending messages to division commanders. Yells of exultation rippled up from the African lines as the Romans, unable to endure that frightful rain of missiles, broke and drew away, and hastily reformed their stricken lines, while the legions swung forward to take the brunt of battle. Whistles shrilled. The cloud of slingers melted, fell back; the Spanish and African lines moved forward between the elephants. The elephants moved. The whole line of weight was in motion, hurtling forward at the famed legions of Rome.

THEY MET, with a crash of conflict. Snow swept down in a whirl of flakes, rain and sleet coming in gusts. To see much of anything was impossible. A horseman came up at a gallop and drew rein before Pelargos.

"Orders!" he yelped excitedly. "The Roman cavalry has broken, and Maharbal is killing them like flies! The general says to have the hot stones ready and not fail; and can you spare any slingers for the center?"

"I'm sending him a company at once," said Pelargos, and dispatched one of his own aides. He beckoned another, as the courier went off at a hammering gallop. "Move up the furnaces and the hot stones; let 'em have it at once."

He turned, chuckling, to Ramnes. "Red-hot stones, comrade! Another little trick of mine. Selected men can handle 'em in link-mesh slings. Comrade, you're seeing something! I never saw such a battle as this—do you realize that hardly an arrow has been shot? This rain has ruined the bowstrings. Ha! Listen!

That means Mago has fallen on their flanks!"

A tremendous rolling blast of trumpets broke upon the storm, but to see what was happening at any distance was impossible.

Under the impact of the African wall, the legions reeled; and the elephants rolled in upon them at the same time. For one moment, Ramnes thought the whole Roman line was swept away. But it reformed, the legions drew into ranks again, the elephants were halted.

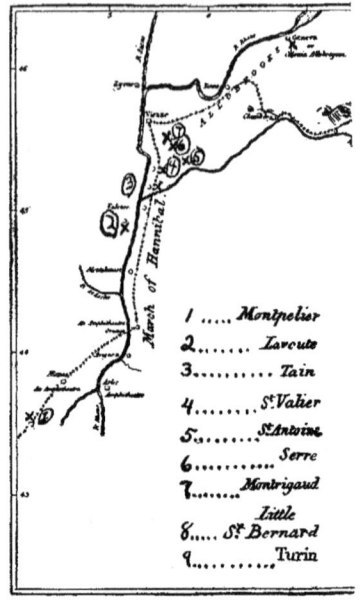

1 ..... Montpelier
2 .... Lavoute
3 .... Tain
4 .... St Valier
5 ...... St Antoine
6 .... Serre
7 .... Montrigaud
8 ..... St Bernard Little
9 .... Turin

Lars Masena shook his head sadly.

"I said they'd be no use!" he croaked. "They can't fight; they can hardly stand! And the snow will kill them all."

Those stubborn Roman ranks were unyielding now. Their array was taken in flank by Mago and his hidden troops. Maharbal's cavalry, sweeping around, came in upon the flanks also; their retreat was cut off by the river—but they did not retreat. Back and forth surged the massed ranks of men. To the eye of Ramnes, it was a wild turmoil, a furious mob conflict, but the trained gaze of Pelargos knew better.

"Well, comrade, it's all over," he said. "You've seen your first battle, eh?"

Ramnes gave him a glance. "What do you mean, over? Those legions aren't yielding!"

"No," said Pelargos calmly. "They're dying. Our Numidian cavalry is in on 'em from the flanks, and that settles it. They can't get back across the river to their camp. The whole scheme

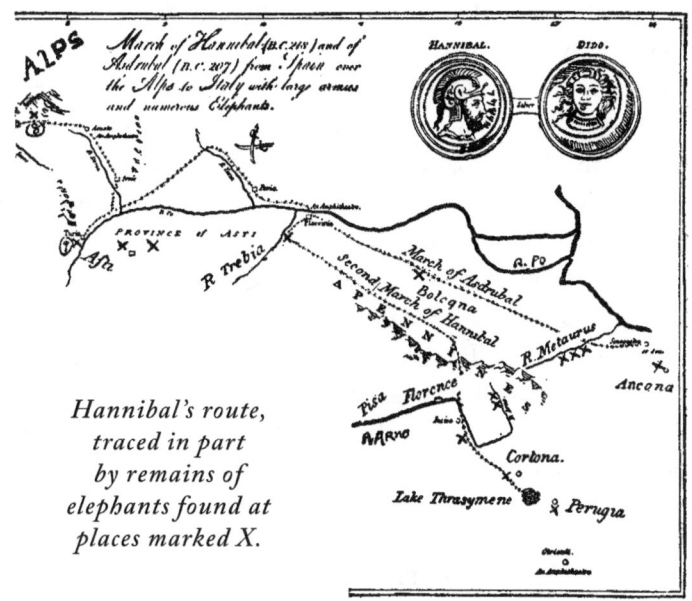

Hannibal's route,
traced in part
by remains of
elephants found at
places marked X.

of battle was absolute perfection. I didn't believe the Romans would be foolish enough to attack, but there they are! And they won't surrender. Romans don't."

"No," said Ramnes in a low voice.

PELARGOS EYED the rain-lashed, snow-whirling scene, then glanced curiously at Ramnes.

"After the first thrill, nothing exciting about it, eh?"

"Not in this weather," said Ramnes frankly. "A lot of poor devils fighting, and dying in rain and mud—for what? I'm glad I'm out of it."

Pelargos broke out laughing.

"Comrade, I salute your honesty, and say the same for myself! You'll see the difference soon enough. Take orders, fight, live or die—for what? An abstract cause. That's one thing, and to hell with it! Another thing entirely to fight for your own cause, to get to grips yourself.... Lars! Come along."

"Eh?" Lars scrambled up. "Whither?"

"To Umbria and destiny! On to the camp, comrade. The horses are waiting there."

Ramnes swung into step. "But you, Pelargos? Your absence—"

"Bah!" Pelargos snapped his fingers. "In the moment of victory, who knows or cares? They'll think I lost my head, got into the fight, and was killed; will they search thirty thousand corpses for me? Not much. There goes Rome, on the whirlwind! And here go we—to our hearts' desire."

In the deserted, empty camp, they came upon a slave waiting with three horses. Pelargos gave him a coin. The three men mounted, walked the horses out of camp, and headed south, while behind along the Trebia died the senators and knights and common men of Rome.

CHAPTER VI

TWO DAYS of hard riding east and south, along the road to Bononia; war and snow and cold had vanished and they were upon sunny skies and vine-clad towns. Their third night on the road found them in a little sprawling village, with Bononia twenty miles away; there, according to plan, they would turn south to Florentia, through the Apennines, and via Tuscany come to their destination.

With sunrise, Ramnes came into the courtyard of the tavern, realized that he had seen nothing of Lars Masena since their arrival late in the night, and saw Pelargos near the tavern fountain, playing with a child.

"Where's Lars?" demanded Ramnes, ducking his head in the fountain spray.

"Gone upon an errand of mystery; skipped out last night and hasn't shown up yet." Pelargos beckoned the child, who was gawking at him. "Hither, little Ganymede, and I'll toss you up to the bright sky! Isn't she a pretty little trick, Ramnes? Speaks Greek, too—pure Greek type, if you ask me. Here, little love!"

"Ganymede's not my name," she said, approaching him diffidently. "That's a boy's name. I'm not a boy."

"Well said, my little Grecian nymph!" Pelargos stooped, caught her up, and held her to the full height of his long arms. "Don't stare at this bald pate; it's not the rising sun! Look up at the sky and the mountains and the white clouds!"

The child clapped her hands with delight and pointed to massed white clouds above the southward Apennines.

"The gods live there!" she cried joyously, in Latin, which came to her tongue more readily than her ancestral Greek. "Clouds on the hills mean the gods are at home!"

"No more, my sweet, no more!" declared Pelargos. "The gods are scattered, chased away, gone forever. I, Pelargos, affirm it!"

"Oh!" She stared into his face, round-eyed. "Gone? All the nice gods?"

"All of 'em, every one!"

"Did you chase them away, Pelargos? Or was it the bad Africans?"

He burst into a laugh, tossed her up, caught her and set her down safely.

"Pelargos—that means *stork!*" she said, proud of her Greek knowledge. "You're not the Stork that Roman officer was talking about?"

RAMNES, LISTENING, started slightly. He caught a lightning-sharp glance from Pelargos; the laughter died out of that long-nosed face.

"What Roman officer, little nymph?"

"Oh, the fine soldier who was here two days ago! He was talking to the elders of the town about someone called the Stork, a bad man; anyone who kills him will get a lot of money. That's all I know about it."

"And more than enough," said Pelargos soberly. He was fumbling in his pouch for money. "Hercules be praised! Like you, I changed names among the Alps," he said to Ramnes, "taking the Greek instead of the Latin. Old Scipio must have missed his Ciconus badly. Ah, here we are!" He brought out a coin and pressed it into the child's palm. "Here, nymph, take this and get a dress for that poor little naked doll—"

He came erect and stared hard at Ramnes.

"By Hercules! What magic is this? A Roman ahead of us— laying traps? It's impossible!"

"Nothing's impossible," Ramnes said bluntly. "What's the mystery about Lars? Why didn't he share the room with us last night? I'm getting tired of this nonsense."

"I'll tell you over our bread and wine. Come on."

They tramped into the serving-room, settled at a table, and ordered breakfast. Alone, Pelargos leaned forward.

"He'll not mind my telling you; said he meant to do it himself. As a young man, before being dragged off as a slave by some accursed Roman, he joined the Friends of Hercules. That's the Greek for it; there's some Etruscan name that'd break your jaw. A secret society—one of the mysteries. It extends all over central Italy. Once a member, always a member; but Lars wasn't sure that it still existed."

"Why not?"

"Anti-Roman. This was the first place he could learn definitely about it, for there's a lodge in town. He disappeared last night. And— Hello! Here he comes now."

He called. Lars, who was in the courtyard, turned aside and joined them. He pulled up a stool, breathing hard.

Pelargos spoke.

"We've news for you. By the way, I've told Ramnes about the Friends of Hercules."

Lars nodded. "Good. And I've news for you; we'd better get out of town fast. There's a reward out for you, and Roman orders to catch you at all costs—which means us too. By good luck, you didn't attract much attention last night; got in too late."

"We've just learned the astonishing information," said Pelargos dryly. "Apparently I'm wanted under my Latin name."

"Right. I know all about it. That's what delayed me—I had to find out. First, we'll have friends and help anywhere. The Friends of Hercules are stronger than ever. Second, the reason Rome wants you: There were spies in the camp at the Trebia. One had been with Scipio in Gaul, and recognized you. A deserter, now a great man among the Africans!"

"But how," put in Ramnes, bewildered, "could it be known Pelargos headed south?"

"Never mind that," said Pelargos hastily, with a confused air. "It's of no great—"

"Wait!" struck in Lars Masena, an imperative ring in his voice. "Remember the night after Lotus Ear died, in camp? And you insisted on cheering me up, and refused to mix the wine as usual, and we had several drops too much?"

Pelargos uttered a subdued groan.

"Oh, I suppose I must admit it," he said, with a grimace. "I did have a vague memory of having done a lot of talking."

"Too much," Lars said severely. "In brief, you were drunk and you bragged. About taking the road to Umbria, about golden treasures and other things."

"Damn it, I'm sorry!" Pelargos exclaimed contritely. "Actually, I was trying to get you out of the dumps. I didn't think any of those Numidians knew what I was saying."

"That spy did." Lars leaned back and spread his hands with an expressive gesture. "And here we are, with the word put ahead of us. Didn't you say something, that night, about catching that fellow Mancinus down in Umbria, and flogging him out of his skin?"

Pelargos gave Ramnes a sheepish glance. "Looks as though I had been indiscreet, yes."

"You can't possibly disguise yourself. You two don't know, as I do, how thorough is the Roman organization in Italy. All these districts and cities ahead of us, even if they're merely allied with Rome, are full of Roman officers and representatives; couriers spread news rapidly. What shall we do about it?"

"Get breakfast, get the horses, and get out of town," said Ramnes. "Talk later."

His words clove through the hesitation and cleared the air. The others nodded.

CURIOUSLY, THESE few days had reversed the position of the three: they had left the Trebia with Pelargos radiant and assured, his sun in the ascendant; with Lars a mere cloaked shadow; with Ramnes silent and unassertive.

Today, as they rode out of the little town, the change was to be definitely noted. Ramnes had come into the ascendancy, his driving urge to the fore, his eagerness to reach the Villa Veturis lifting his Roman spirit into gradual command. Lars Masena had become talkative, gravely wise, a shrewdly alert man. Pelargos, who had been drinking hard, had relapsed into the old careless, gay, sprightly fellow Ramnes had first known. Now, as they came clear of town and headed stirrup to stirrup along the country road, Pelargos swore a great oath.

"Comrades, I've had my lesson for the last time. Ever in my life, wine has ruined me again and again. Now, and I swear it, Bacchus shall go the way of all the other gods! I'll not taste a drop of wine until we reach Reate and the Grotto of the Sybil. I swear it!"

"By what god?" demanded Ramnes dryly. "On what altar?"

"On my sling!" Pelargos exclaimed.

"It's high time," put in Lars Masena. "We're no longer three good friends riding to destiny. We're hunted men, or one of us is; and he's too well marked to be mistaken. Before noon we'll be in Bononia, and there we'll find Romans and trouble. What to do?"

"Halt," said Ramnes, and drew rein. He reached for the buckles of his gorgeous breastplate, removed it, and thrust the armor at Lars. "Ride ahead of us, and ride fast; no couriers have passed us, no one knows the news yet. Proclaim a great Roman victory over the Africans, show this as part of your spoil, and trade it off for Roman armor of any kind at all. Then ride back

a little way and have it ready for me, before we enter Bononia.
Eh?"

"Understood." Lars squinted at him alertly. "To what end?"

"If we're stopped, I'm a Roman soldier taking Pelargos as my
prisoner."

"Ha! Excellent!" cried Pelargos lustily, and smote his long
thigh in delight.

"Wait; we're not finished." Ramnes eyed Lars thoughtfully.
"From Bononia our way lies due south through the Apennines
to Florentia and on through Tuscany. Right?"

"That's the most direct, certainly. Only, as things now stand—"

"Precisely! Rome wants to nip the Stork, knows he's heading
for Umbria, and is ahead of us. What's another way to our
destination?"

Lars brightened. "Ah! Cross the Apennines at the end of the
journey instead of now! Go straight on through Bononia to
Ariminium on the Hadriatic; that's ninety miles. Then along
the coast to Fanum Fortuns, another thirty; there we'll pick up
the great Roman road, the Via Flaminia, and will have something like a hundred and fifty miles to Reate."

"That's our road. And, once past Bononia, we'll probably
have no trouble—they'll be looking for Pelargos along the other
route."

"They'll be looking everywhere," struck in Pelargos gloomily. "Remember, I was known to be the friend of old Veturis!
That damned Scipio is a thorough fellow."

"All right. Off with you, Lars! We'll follow at leisure."

Lars pricked in his spurs and vanished among the olive-
groves ahead.

THE OTHER two rode on slowly for a little, and silently.
Ramnes was mentally weighing the possibilities of this mis-
chance. They were not, after all, very alarming; once past
Bononia, there should be no immediate peril. Ahead in Umbria,
it would be different, but even there danger would be nicely

balanced. It was only fifty years since Rome had conquered the
Sabine tribes of Umbria. There as elsewhere she was well hated.
It was significant that the Friends of Hercules were more pow-
erful than ever. This secret brotherhood, working everywhere
to nullify Roman rule, began to bulk large in the mind of
Ramnes.

"Well, comrade, you're in command," said Pelargos suddenly. "I know the voice of authority when I hear it; you're the
captain of our destiny."

"As far as Eryx, you mean."

"Oh!" The other looked disconcerted. "Who told you that?"

Ramnes laughed. "The Lamnian Sybil, perhaps; a revelation
from the gods, perhaps! You big rascal, why didn't you tell me
everything about yourself, that your family was at Eryx? You're
glib enough in spilling your secrets to the world when in liquor!"

"I know it, comrade; no need of rubbing things in every
minute like a damned nagging fishwife!" complained Pelargos.
"For that matter, I have other hopes that won't bear telling, at
least till we reach Eryx itself. You to Reate, Lars to Asculum, I
to Eryx—eh?"

"Right. He wouldn't tell me why he's so devilish set on
Asculum."

Pelargos began to laugh. "No. And if I were to tell you, I'm
afraid you'd regard the whole thing as childish nonsense. Wait
till we get Lars in his cups, and you may believe him. Didn't I
tell you he'd be valuable? With his pull at this secret society to
aid us, he's better than a legion! Do you expect trouble at
Bononia?"

"Of course. It's the chief city of the district, isn't it?"

"Then had I best get rid of my arms?"

"No; leave them. In case of trouble, I'll take your sword. Do
you know Hannibal's plans—will he march on Rome?"

"Not in the dead of winter, not across the Apennines! He'll
winter where he is, build up his army, make the north of Italy

"Do you know my authority here is absolute?" he rasped.

secure. With spring, Rome will have new armies ready to pounce on him; he must be ready for them."

"Then we're marching slap into Roman territory."

"Pulling out a golden hoard and a lovely woman from under the very nose of Rome!"

"Don't be so glib about it; no telling what's happened in the south. That fellow Croton, that horse-doctor, can't be so far ahead of us—not more than a couple of days at most. I made good time from the north. Do you know what legions were at the Trebia?"

"No. The third was one of them."

"Good enough. Let's get on."

Noon saw the walls of Bononia ahead, through a grayish mist of olive trees. A quarter-mile from the gates, Lars came riding toward them, a bundle across his saddle. He greeted them with a grin.

"The city's in an uproar of joy over my news! And here's your Roman armor, Ramnes."

"Good. Now get along back and we'll meet on the other side of town."

Lars pricked away at speed. Ramnes donned the Roman armor, took the sword of Pelargos, left his steel cap swinging beside the saddle, and rode on with the tall man at his side. The usual crowd of country folk was about the gates, with a squad of Roman soldiers, but apparently no attention was given the two; they passed on and in without question.

TRUMPETS WERE blowing, voices were ringing exultantly; the news of victory brought by Lars was spreading rapidly through the city. Ramnes began to think they would get through the place without trouble, until he rode into the central market-place. Here was a crowd of all sorts, many a Roman among them, and a squad of soldiers clustered about a whipping-post, where a figure was triced up for flogging.

"Halt, there!" rang out a voice. A decurion, or corporal, leaped into the path of the two, with other Romans behind him. "Halt! By the gods, comrades, if this isn't the very fellow we were warned to get! Look at the lean length of him, look at the stork's beak! Look—"

"Suppose you look at me for a change," snapped Ramnes angrily. "You damned rascal, don't you know senatorial rank when you see it?"

The decurion fell back under the lash of those words. "Pardon, lord. This man—"

"Is my prisoner. Taken in the battle at the Trebia, sent to Rome with me by order of the consul."

"The battle! Is it true, this report of victory?"

"The whole Punic army destroyed," said Ramnes, and a howl of delight arose. By his armor and face and tongue, he was so obviously a Roman of rank, that the soldiers fell back. All but the decurion, who hung irresolute.

"Lord, if this be true—"

"If?" barked Ramnes. "*If?* The gods help you when I reach Rome! You'll regret your impertinence to Quintus Curtius—I'll get you transferred into the third legion and make life hell for you! Out of the way."

That settled it; cold Roman pride was absolute. Before Ramnes could pass on, however, a cry from the flogging-post reached him. A hoarse cry in Greek:

"Pelargos! Ramnes! Help me!"

Jerking his horse around, Ramnes eyed that triced-up figure amazedly, and recognized the wizened, blear-eyed features. He beckoned the decurion, and questioned curtly:

"What are you doing to this man?"

"Lord, he's obviously an escaped slave, from his collar; further, he had a passport written in Punic. He can give no good account of himself—"

"Well, I can," broke in Ramnes. "He belongs to Lucius Mancinus, was captured at the Ticinus fight, and no doubt Mancinus has purchased his freedom from the Africans."

"Do you vouch for him, lord?"

"Absolutely and entirely! Let him go free." And Ramnes held up a hand. "You, Croton! You heard my words. Get south to Reate and report to your master at once. Do you hear me?"

"At once, lord, at once," cried Croton, as they loosed his bonds.

"Have you need of money?"

"Not if my property is returned to me." Croton glanced at the soldiery.

"See that it's done," said Ramnes to the decurion, and rode on.

They left the marketplace and forum behind, heading on through the wide streets.

Pelargos pushed up close.

"Why didn't you bring him with us?"

"Too risky. A Roman would not have done so."

*The legions reeled; for one
moment, the whole Roman
line was swept away.*

"Right. You played the part; I'd have sworn you were a knight at least! Well done."

They hastened on, passed the eastern gate without question, and fronted the open road once more. Ramnes, startled by this meeting with Croton, was suddenly anxious at thought of Drusilla, of Lucius Mancinus, of what might be happening down there in Umbria. The way was so long, so long! But Croton, going direct, would get there ahead of him, and would bear word. How would she receive that word? Had she forgot the bearded young ruffian beyond the Alps?

*Maharbal's cavalry,
sweeping around, came
in upon the flanks—but
they did not retreat.*

"Ha! There's Lars. All's well!" The voice of Pelargos scattered his musings and brought him back to the present. "Now we can make time—a hundred miles to the sea, or less!"

LARS WAS waiting. Reunited, the three pushed the horses hard and dropped the long miles steadily behind.

"You might have waited," said Lars, on hearing what had passed, "to make sure Croton was freed."

Ramnes smiled thinly. "No Roman would admit the least doubt of his orders being obeyed, my friend. It would have been a false step."

"Right! Ha! You should have seen his cold and imperious Roman mien!" exclaimed Pelargos lustily. "A patrician to the very life! No fear; Croton's on his way south."

TWO DAYS; three days. The bright valleys of the Po fell behind them as they coasted the rugged southeast line of the mountains, crossing countless little rivers and streams. Danger seemed well put behind, but they took no chances. When they sighted parties of foot or horse, the keen vision of Pelargos scented peril afar and they took to the woods until it was past; this eyesight of his, indeed, was something most remarkable.

"It'll be of use when the time comes," he said, to the comment of Ramnes. "When we reach Umbria, I'm like to be in perilous places; but one gets nothing by risking nothing."

The glint of the far Hadriatic upon an afternoon of sun; with its last light, the white buildings of Ariminium squatted beside the sea, the long walls and bridges, the high towers. A Roman garrison here, the northern tip of Roman rule along the Hadriatic.

The Roman armor and tongue of Ramnes, and an assumed Roman name, passed them into the city unquestioned. There Lars disappeared on his own errands. The horse of Pelargos was lame, a fresh beast was needed; they arranged to spend next morning in the city, meet at noon, and be off along the coast to Fanum Fortunæ.

Mid-morning: Ramnes, with a groom, was inspecting the horses when Pelargos appeared, accompanied by a horse-dealer and an enormous gaunt gray mare, for which the lame beast was exchanged. As the deal was concluded, a swarthy, bearded man came walking into the inn yard, asking for Pelargos. The latter flung a swift word at Ramnes.

"Quick, comrade—turn away! We're strangers. I've got this rascally priest of Hercules on a golden hook—"

He hurried off, greeted the swarthy fellow, and the two began to walk up and down, chattering Greek at a great rate. Ramnes stretched out in the sun by the fountain, amusedly wondering what Pelargos was up to now. The priest seemed a shrewd, capable fellow, and not too scrupulous, to judge by his looks; he stowed away a purse Pelargos gave him, and as the two paced within earshot, Ramnes caught his words:

"Well, I'll go to Eryx, I'll tell your vision, but I'll take no responsibility. By all the gods, it's a ticklish business! Either you're a madman or you're up to something."

Pelargos grinned. "Gold, my friend, is eloquent!"

They drifted out of hearing and presently separated. When the priest had gone, Pelargos came over to the fountain, and met the inquiring gaze of Ramnes.

"Comrade, that rascal takes a message to Eryx."

"Oh! To your family?"

Pelargos rubbed his long nose. "Not exactly. Look! Trust me a little while. I'm gambling largely on destiny; if all schemes fall through, no harm's done."

"Right." Ramnes shrugged. "Do you know what's worrying me?"

"No. What?"

"Suppose we find the treasure you talk about. How much of it do you think three men can transport anywhere?"

Pelargos met his whimsical glance, and the birdlike eyes twinkled.

"Ha! Practical fellow, aren't you? Well, I've an answer for everything—but that, too, depends somewhat on destiny. Now I'll tell you something, give you a mere clue. Do you know that thirty years ago Metellus gave the Africans a bad drubbing in Sicily?"

"So I've heard," Ramnes said drily.

"Right. He captured over a hundred elephants. He built a mammoth raft and ferried those elephants across the straits into Italy."

"Yes? What became of them?"

"That," said Pelargos, "is precisely the question. If rumor, gossip, army talk, should be correct, the dice will turn up a double six for us. Content to trust me?"

"Yes. If we— Hello! There's Lars, and in a hurry. Something's up."

LARS MASENA appeared, walking fast, his face gripped by excitement. He came up to them with eyes ablaze.

"You've a room here? Come along, come along! Take me to it. News! Wine first. I'm dry as the dust of hell!"

He snapped an order at a serving-man, received a flagon of wine, and gulped it.

"No pause to mix it, d'ye notice?" said Pelargos admiringly. "Ha! A fury's on the man! Here's the real Lars emerging, comrade—"

"Stop your mockery and take me to your room," broke in Lars.

He was, indeed, a different person; the last vestige of the disconsolate elephant-trainer had vanished. Now there was a light in his eye, a firmed vigor in his face, a brusque energy in his voice; he had suddenly come all alive.

When they were in the room with the door closed, he faced the other two.

"There was a man from Asculum—he knew her, he'd seen her!" he burst out.

"Who?" demanded Ramnes.

"Rhea! She's not in Asculum at all. We'll not have to go there!"

"May I ask who the devil is Rhea?"

Lars looked blank. Pelargos took up the word, looking cynically amused.

"Right. You've never told him, Lars. Comrade, the dream and heart's desire of our honest Lars, is to find a woman named Rhea. They were in love thirty years ago; he's never been able to return and claim her. Oh, it's no use giving him any practical advice! I've told him she's probably dead, or married and surrounded by brats—a grandmother, in fact! He won't listen to me—"

"And I was right, right!" blared out Lars exultantly. "I told you we had taken oaths to Minerva and Aphrodite the Cyprian, that she'd sworn to wait for me, that I'd sworn to come back some day! I told you! And I met this man from Asculum who knew all about her. She's never married. The family has left the old town, in fact. I tell you, Rhea believes in me, knows I'll find her again!"

"Oh!" said Pelargos, looking blank in his turn. "And you want to take horse and leave us and find her—is that it?"

Lars drew himself up. "Have I not sworn oaths to you, Pelargos? We go in company—first your errands, or those of Ramnes, then mine," he said with a stern dignity.

Ramnes struck in, smiling:

"Come, old friend—this is the secret you never told me? I'm glad, for your sake. Why, you look twenty years younger! Congratulations."

"I—I didn't have the heart to talk of it," stammered Lars, flushing. "I hoped against hope, prayed to the gods; all these years, in Sicily and Africa and Spain and Gaul! Besides, Pelargos hurt me cruelly with his talk about what might have happened."

"Confound it, man, I only spoke the truth!" exclaimed Pelargos. He took the hand of Lars and pressed it warmly. "Yet I was wrong; and I've never been so glad to be proven wrong. Where is she now, this Rhea of yours?"

"They've got a farm," said Lars Masena, giving him a strange look. "Where, you ask? You may well ask, you who sneer at the gods! It's just outside Eryx."

Pelargos took a step back. "Eryx!" he repeated, and swallowed hard. "Eryx!"

SILENCE FELL on them. Ramnes, looking from one to the other, felt a thrill, a prescience of strange unseen forces—the workings of fate, or the doings of the gods? Why was this unknown town of Eryx apparently tangled in the destiny of them all?

Pelargos rallied. He sighed, stirred, shook himself like a dog, as though to be rid of some superstitious chill.

"For you, at least, the dice turn double six!" said he. "Let's saddle up and get out of here. We can reach the Via Flaminia by night and be on the last leg of the journey."

"And you'll no longer doubt the gods?" cried Lars Masena joyously.

*"Those legions aren't yielding," said Ramnes.
"No," said Pelargos; "they're dying."*

Pelargos gave him one cynical look, and tapped his breast.

"My friend, here are the gods—if we could only visualize them," he said, and strode out, lifting his voice at the grooms and hostlers.

CHAPTER VII

FANUM FORTUNÆ and the sea lay behind; southward, now, on the Flaminian Road, the wide highway partly finished, partly still under construction, by which the hand of Rome lay upon Umbria and the Gallic tribes to the north.

Road-workers, parties of soldiers, sutlers' wagon-trains with supplies, levies of men and horses, recruiting officers tempting the hill-folk to take the Roman penny—here, abruptly, the three found themselves riding amid farflung echoes of war. Of actual Roman troops, there were very few, all detachments having long since been called in, but the occasional colonies provided veterans or reservists who had taken over all administrative functions for the republic, and the Latin allies provided masses of recruits.

Another night found them at the Metaurus river, in a tiny hill town, with the chasm that pierced the shaggy Apennines ahead. Pelargos, only too conscious of possible danger, had discarded his armor and donned Greek dress, shortening his stirrups so that his great height did not readily appear except when he was afoot.

They had turned aside, now, from the road to Eryx, which lay somewhere down the seacoast. South lay their way into the heart of Umbria; then, if all went well, eastward to the sea again, to Eryx.

On, now; a Roman citizen riding with his two freedmen to join in the war, a likely story.

"About the time we get there," said Pelargos, "they'll have the news from the Trebia. So far, we're ahead of it."

They rode hard, pushed fast, plunged along the fertile Umbrian valleys, then up into the heights once more. Twice they ran into trouble, meeting agents of Lucius Mancinus who tried to impress their horses for the service of the state, for hereabouts horses such as these three were hard to come at. The cold caustic Roman tongue of Ramnes sped them on each time, but as Lars muttered, the portents were bad.

"Look for trouble at Spoletium," said he darkly. "A Roman colony was established there twenty years ago. Once past, all's well; thirty miles farther to Interamna, then we leave the Via Flaminia and cut across the same distance to Reate. The mileage is approximate, but the peril at Spoletium is not. At a pinch, we could get there by midnight."

"No pinch," said Ramnes. "Make it tomorrow morning and get it behind us."

Pelargos, that night, oiled his sling and rearranged the contents of his two pouches. He had halted, at every mountain torrent, to seek out a few pebbles to his liking; now he had a goodly lot of them, smooth and round, and also a stock of his jagged iron missiles.

"I did a lot of forge-work while we waited at the Trebia," said he. "Now my fingers are itching for the sling; there's killing ahead."

"Why not three slings?" asked Ramnes, remembering the battle.

"Bah! For an expert, one's enough." Pelargos cast an envious glance at the flagon of wine before Ramnes. "My throat's parched for a drop of that juice of the grape! I'll be a glad man when we reach Reate and my vow's ended. Suppose we get blocked in Spoletium?"

"I was thinking of that." Ramnes turned to Lars Masena, who by this time was aware of their whole errand. "In case of trouble—"

"The Friends of Hercules are strong," broke in Lars.

Ramnes shook his head.

"I don't mean that. Ride ahead and reach the Lady Drusilla at the Villa Veturis, somewhere near Reate. We'll meet there, if separated. Tell her you're from me."

Pelargos chuckled. "You're taking a lot for granted, comrade! Remember her pride."

"And her warm eyes," said Ramnes.

The Stork gave him a curious glance and said no more.

Lars shrugged and assented.

ON WITH morning, until the warming sun found them looking up toward the high pass where Spoletium sprawled all up and down its rocky hillside, and on farther where the road left the fertile valleys and wound snakewise toward the summits. It was close to noon when they rode in at the eastern gate, unchallenged and unnoted. As they headed across the narrow streets of the hill town, they laughed together at their fears.

"Laugh not," said Pelargos, sobering. "It's never the expected that crops up to hit one behind the ear!" A sudden torrent of low oaths broke from him, as he stared at the gate ahead.

Ramnes eyed him, startled.

"What is it?"

"A man I knew in Sicily, a damned Cretan archer—ride on, ride on! He may not remember me. Of all the tricks of malignant fate—"

He drew his wide-brimmed Latin hat down over his eyes. Ramnes made a gesture to Lars Masena, who rode on well ahead of them. A cluster of soldiers were about the gates; a Roman centurion and several auxiliary officers were standing in talk. Lars saluted, spoke in the Sabine dialect, and without being halted, passed on outside. Ramnes followed; the men eyed him curiously but asked no questions. Behind, he heard a shout, a commotion. He flung Lars Masena a curt word.

"Ride!"

TURNING HIS horse, he saw Pelargos on the gray mare, in the gateway. An officer, a Cretan by his broad accent, had halted him; two of the soldiers had lowered spears to block his exit.

"By Jupiter, it is! The same long-nosed rascal!" cried the Cretan, who carried slung at his shoulder a powerful horn bow. "The champion of all slingers—well met, Stork, well met! You've not forgotten me?"

"The lion never forgets the jackal, Cretan," growled Pelargos. "What are you doing here?"

"Detached duty. Why aren't you with the army, you loud-mouthed son of iniquity?"

"On my way to Rome, to join up, now," snapped Pelargos. "Give passage, there!"

"Not so fast; I owe you a few scores, my honest Stork," began the Cretan. "You and your blasted bragging about a slinger being worth three bowmen—"

"Here, what's all this?" The Roman centurion broke in upon

the scene with brusque authority. "Stork, did you say? By the gods, you're right! The fellow's a good seven feet long—ha! The very man who's wanted—the Stork, sure enough! Off that horse, you; take him in charge, men—"

Pelargos loosed reins and drove in spurs. The gaunt gray mare reared up, screamed with mad pain, and knocked the soldiers right and left in the wild forward leap. Next instant Pelargos was roaring at Ramnes to ride on.

Instead, Ramnes joined him; stirrup to stirrup, the two horses went along the road at a gallop, scattering country-folk, and reaching at last an open space.

"Ride ahead, leave me!" Pelargos looked back, and cursed hotly. "Horses. They're after us. I'll stop them. You go on."

"Lars has gone on; I stay," said Ramnes, seeing that Lars Masena was indeed out of sight.

Pelargos flung a furious oath at him.

"I can stop them, I tell you! This means fight. It's my affair."

"Don't waste breath."

The northern valley lay behind them now; ahead, the road twisted and wound along hill flanks above a brawling torrent. Lars must have gone on full speed, for they saw no sign of him.

Twisting from time to time in the saddle, Pelargos vented a grunt.

"Not so bad. That damned Cretan, the centurion, and five others. They're gaining on us. Faster!"

"No," said Ramnes coolly. "Slower. Let 'em gain. Pick your spot, and save our own horses. We've a day's hard riding ahead of us, and more."

"As you say. Five bowmen, and the Cretan; he used to be a great hand with the bow. I'll take them. The centurion to you. The road mounts—excellent! There's our place, a half-mile farther on; it was made for us."

The road was mounting toward the crest of the pass, twisting and winding as it rose. All was clear ahead, with the emptiness of high noon. Pelargos quickened his pace, pushing on well into the lead, Ramnes refusing to hurry.

Here the road circled deeply about a hillside spring, mounted beyond in a sharp twist, mounted still farther till it was directly above the spring and the circle. Here Pelargos had dismounted and stood smoothing out his sling.

"No hurry," said he. "Best tether the horses."

Ramnes obeyed, tying the horses among the trees. He rejoined Pelargos, who was taking his iron bullets from the pouch, filling his mouth with them.

"Sword out," mumbled Pelargos; "here they come. Best try a pebble for distance—hard to judge angle fire like this."

He slipped a pebble into the sling, whirled it, loosed it at the road below, and nodded with a satisfied air. He had picked a spot free of trees, giving clear view.

Swiftly, with a rush and a clatter of hooves, a stream of figures pulsed into sight below—the Cretan in the lead, five bowmen strung out behind, the centurion last of all, a light javelin in his hand.

The sling whirled. Pelargos set another missile in place; one of the bowmen pitched forward in the saddle. The sling whirled again. The iron pellet, unseen, drove home just as a startled yell rang up. A second man threw out his arms; Ramnes could see the blood springing on his face as he fell over. A burst of yells, of wild voices. Pelargos swung around. The horsemen were pressing up the steeply pitched curve, their backs to him, unable to stop their horses or realize where he was.

The sling whirled again, and a shout of delight pealed up from the slinger.

"Take that, Cretan! Take that from the Stork! Fair as you please, slap in the temple—ha! *Back,* comrade! Across the road and among the trees! They're afoot and scattering to get at us!"

Under the urge of hand and voice, Ramnes comprehended. So quickly had the affair transpired,—with such incredible

precision and rapidity had Pelargos loosed his flitting death,—
that Ramnes had scarce freed his sword from scabbard.

He ran back across the road toward the horses and the thick
trees, Pelargos at his side, chortling with glee.

"The Cretan and two of his men paid out—that leaves three,
and the centurion. We needn't worry about that blasted
Roman—he can't get at us. The others can. 'Ware arrows, now!
Watch those trees ahead, at the curve. They're coming up to nip
us. Show yourself, comrade! Let 'em have a glimpse of you, stir
the brush a bit!"

Pelargos darted a dozen feet away and stood immobile,
watching, eyes fastened on the greenery back across the road.
Should Ramnes show himself—tempt a shaft from those horn
bows that could pierce the best armor at a hundred paces? Trust
the keen eyes of Pelargos? Three archers there, stealing through
the green trees, shafts notched and ready.

Why not? Ramnes reached out, agitated the brush beside
him, showed himself, ducked quickly behind a tree. Well that
he did. A bowstring twanged, an arrow came slanting down
the sunlight—another—a third. The deadly shafts searched out
where he had been an instant before.

Then lifted a scream. Pelargos had whirled the sling, loosed
it; the scream replied—a piercing, reiterated scream, a man
there gasping out his life, unseen. The gut twanged and twanged
again; arrows flitted vengefully. The preternaturally tall shape
of Pelargos doubled, unfolded, doubled again. The death he
wielded was silent, terrible, unseen.

A piercing cry, an incoherent, yelping moan, and Ramnes
stared in horror as a flopping thing broke cover—a man, twisting over and over, clutching at his neck, rising, falling again.
Pelargos grunted, and the sling whirled. The man fell limp and
sprawling to the merciful cast.

"Two!" cried Pelargos. "Now for the other…. I have him, I
have him!"

The sling was loosed; the vibrant note of a bowstring hummed

at the same instant. One low, gasping cry from the trees opposite. A man fell forward into view, arras outflung, motionless.
But Ramnes, aware of a startled grunt, turned to see Pelargos
pitch over and crash headlong into a tree bole, and lie still.

"*Habet!*" lifted a voice. "He has it!"

IT WAS the centurion, breaking cover, coming at a run,
javelin ready to cast. Ramnes took a step forward, into the
sunlight. The staring, furious countenance fronted him; the
javelin leaped at him. He avoided the throw, and the centurion
had his sword out as he followed—steel glittering, hot oaths
panting, himself hurtling forward in utter ferocity.

Instead of recoiling, Ramnes leaped at him, met him breast
to breast with a crash of corselet against corselet. His father
had taught him this shattering body-blow. The other blade
slithered on his armor. His own steel hewed at the neck, bare
and sweated, and blood leaped to the stroke.

The centurion, recoiling from that crash of bodies, slashed
terribly by the sword-edge, rocked on his heels. Against that
solid, massive body-bulk, his own lesser weight had failed
utterly. The blade fell from his groping fingers; he stared at
Ramnes with fright, horror, agony fleeting across his face as
the blood spurted over his armor. Ramnes, set for a second slash,
checked it. Death was in this man's eyes.

"Trick—damned trick!" gulped out the centurion. "Marcus
Mancinus taught us that—the Fourteenth Legion—you devil!
May the gods drag you down to hell!"

He sighed and bowed forward, and fell. Ramnes, with sudden
pity, sprang to him and turned his face to the sky. The eyes of
the dying man rolled; his voice came faintly, wildly:

"She was right. She cursed me—the Lady Drusilla cursed
me by the gods—When we burned the villa—cursed me—
within the week—"

The faint voice died away; the head lolled; the centurion was
dead.

Ramnes knelt, staring down at the pale face, surmise and

conjecture hammering at bis brain, all else forgotten. This man had been in the Fourteenth, had served under his father, who had taught all his men that trick of meeting the lighter enemy with the body. Odd! But the curse! Drusilla had cursed him—a week ago the Villa Veturis had been burned! By Roman hands? By Lucius Mancinus of the wild boar's heart?

Then, remembering the prostrate figure of Pelargos, Ramnes leaped to his feet and swung around. A sudden breath of relief escaped him. Pelargos was sitting up, waving a hand at him, speaking.

"Well done, well done! Now come here and give me a hand. Lucky it was close quarters—the blasted shaft went clear through, almost. Can't reach it myself."

"You're hurt? Hit?"

"Hit, and banged my head against a tree," Pelargos said, as Ramnes came on the jump. He bared his thigh; the arrow had gone nearly through and was hanging. "Pull it through—jerk it! That's right. Hercules be praised, it missed the bone! Now it's a matter of doing a good job with the bandage. Get a shirt from that rascal in the road. That was sweet work, with the centurion! Do you know you're a very Hercules? Well, hurry up with the shirt—"

Ramnes was back quickly, the archer's blouse torn in strips. Pelargos investigated his own wound with deft appraising fingers, wiped away the welling blood, grunted.

"No black blood; that means no particular danger. Tighter with that bandage! We must get out of here quickly, before any others come. Luckily, that centurion wasted no time in talking to others—he mounted and came, and died. So the Stork's safe, for the present."

"He talked as he died," said Ramnes, "Less than a week ago, Drusilla cursed him."

Pelargos heard, and whistled softly.

"Didn't I say that young woman was intimate with the gods?" he observed. "Something's happened, there at the Villa Veturis;

no telling what. Mancinus, depend upon it! We'll find out at Reate, or you will. This damned hurt is going to cripple me for riding, once the wound gets stiff. Clap on that last strip of cloth…. Good! Now, your hand."

He came to his feet, grimaced, and waited while Ramnes brought the two horses. Once in the saddle, he shook his head and surveyed Ramnes gravely.

"Not so good; I'll stick while I can, but I'll have to keep at a walk. And you're on fire to get ahead, after what that centurion said."

"Never mind; come along. We'll have to walk the horses anyway, up this road to the summit."

ON FIRE? That expressed it. Ramnes, with an effort, fought the savage anxiety, the burning desire to strike in spurs and ride on like mad. With a spare horse, he could keep going day and night, could reach Reate by tomorrow noon. But he had no

It was the centurion coming at a run—steel glittering, himself hurtling forward in utter ferocity.

spare horse, and he had a wounded comrade. He choked down impatience. A week ago or less! Croton would hardly have reached Drusilla.

"I can't quite credit it," said Pelargos thoughtfully. "That Mancinus should lift a hand against a Roman lady of rank—it's rather preposterous. That soldiers should use any force against the daughter of a veteran officer of consular rank—no, no! Well, we'll find out in due time. Ah! This cursed hip hurts."

THEY RODE on. As far as they could make out, there was no further pursuit, no body of men on the road from Spoletium. It was doubtless thought that seven were plenty to catch two men.

"Now you perceive the beauty of my bullets," said Pelargos, with an air of satisfaction. "Take a stone: it may or may not do the work. But when that jagged lump of iron hits and cuts home—it does the job once and for all. True, it needed two to finish off that man who floundered out like a dying fish, but that was because I didn't get a good crack at him the first time.

Probably would have finished him eventually, but to see him flopping in the road irritated me."

"Oh!" said Ramnes dryly. "I thought your second shot was an act of mercy."

"There's no such word, comrade; I believe in efficiency, and that excludes mercy," said the other coolly. "This was a rather sloppy performance, and I'm ashamed of it. On such an errand as ours, with play for high stakes,—and higher, by Hercules, than you're aware at present,—the most vital thing is efficiency. You showed it when you met that Roman. Give the other fellow the help of all the gods on Olympus, and give me efficiency, and I'll make a fool of him. Better luck next time."

"Perhaps," Ramnes suggested, "you'd better take occasion to explain your various hints and ambitions. Higher stakes than I'm aware? Then what?"

Pelargos grimaced. "Not yet, comrade. I'll have information at Interamna; Lars will get it there or elsewhere. If rumor hasn't lied, if I find things as I hope, then I'll lay all bare to you. No use stirring up false hopes or planning on what may not come true. Hello—here's trouble!"

They had gained the summit. Ahead, the road ran straight between high forested walls. And in the road, coming toward them, were two horsemen and four men afoot, with a glint of steel. Pelargos shaded his eyes and squinted afar.

"Four men on foot are rustics, countrymen, but all armed," he declared, though Ramnes could distinguish nothing of the figures. "The riders are soldiers. Not Roman armor, though; looks like Sabine cavalry equipment, from the long swords and flared helmets. They've got a damnably businesslike air about 'em."

"We'll have no trouble," said Ramnes.

"Hm! We can't afford to have any. I couldn't bear trot or gallop for two minutes. In fact, I can't bear even a walk much longer—must soon get out of the saddle altogether," Pelargos rejoined. "Confound it! I tell you they do mean trouble! They're pointing at us and coming on faster, as though they recognized us. But that's impossible."

He drew rein, and drew a breath of relief as the horse halted. His face was twisted and gray with pain. Ramnes waited beside him.

The approaching group were, indeed, coming forward with intent and hurrying air. As they drew closer, Ramnes was amazed at the exactitude of the slinger's description; every detail was as Pelargos had said. One of the two horsemen trotted on ahead and flung up his hand in greeting, as he drew rein, eying them.

"Hail, friends! We were expecting you."

"Indeed?" said Ramnes grimly. "And who may you be?"

"My comrade and I are from a detachment of guards, these others from workers; road-work on ahead. We were sent back to help you—the description was exact. Your comrade, Lars Masena—"

"Ha!" ejaculated Pelargos lustily. "Friends of Hercules, comrades! Lars sent 'em back!"

"Precisely." The leader smiled. "I'm glad you've had no trouble with the accursed Romans—"

"No trouble?" said Ramnes. "A dead centurion, six Cretan archers dead, back there. And my friend here got an arrow through his hip; he can't sit the saddle."

MEN CROWDED around. They were earnest, rude, uncouth Sabines, and they hated the Romans with all their hearts. Tongues clacked rapidly. Two of the men set off at a run to despoil the dead. The leader, getting an understanding of the situation, turned to Ramnes. It appeared that Lars had met them, had found himself among friends of his secret order, and had gone pelting on for the Villa Veturis.

"Now," said the Sabine leader, "suppose your tall friend dismounts and waits here; we'll bring a wagon, and can send him on to Interamna tonight. There, we'll turn him over to others of the society. He'll be safe, I promise you."

"Good, good!" blared out Pelargos eagerly. "Comrade, it fits in! Take my horse and your own, and gallop your heart out! I'll be along in a day or two. Meet you at the Villa Veturis. Agreed?"

CHAPTER VIII

RIDING AT full gallop, shifting from horse to horse each half-hour, Ramnes was certain of overtaking Lars Masena before reaching Interamna. Here he underestimated the time he had consumed in the pass above Spoletium. It was late afternoon when he rode into the city above the pleasant valley of the Nera, and he had seen nothing of Lars.

Far from offering any peril, Interamna ignored him completely. The city was in a boil, a yeasty ferment of wild excitement. Five thousand cavalry, from the great training-camp near Reate under Mancinus, were jammed in the streets; they were leaving at once for Rome. News of the Trebia had arrived at last. Ramnes, listening to the talk as he walked his two horses through town, heard that the entire Roman army had been wiped out, except for a few thousand men. He was not surprised, but Umbria was delirious. The anti-Roman feeling was by no means concealed. Those of the Roman party were stern, silent, downcast.

To get through the packed forum was impossible. Cursing the crowd, Ramnes sought information on the road to Reate and from a roadside merchant bought wine and cheese. As he was asking his questions, he became aware of men closing in on either side of him, then caught a voice at his ear.

"A great day, friend, for those who do not love Rome! Where's Pelargos?"

Ramnes turned, to see Lars Masena grinning beside him. A glance at the others, and he perceived that Lars had found friends.

"Thanks be to the gods!" he exclaimed in relief. "Pelargos? Being brought by wagon; those Sabines you sent back to help us have him in charge. An arrow through the thigh. How can we get out of this accursed town?"

"I can't, but you can," said Lars. "I just got here; the fact that I saw the Trebia battle stops me. They all must hear about it at first hand. It means something, let me tell you, to these men under Rome's yoke! Is Pelargos badly hurt?"

"No; a flesh-wound. He can't ride at present."

"Come along with us. Here, let one of my friends take your horses. We're having a look at the propraetor, your friend Mancinus—"

"Wait! You don't know what's happened at the Villa Veturis!" struck in Ramnes.

"I do; more than you, perhaps. But we can't talk here. Come! We'll be on our way again in an hour; the horses will meet us outside the gates. Ha! There's the speech now."

Ramnes let himself be swept along. To talk in this crowd was impossible. Trumpets were ringing a clarion call from the forum. A bedlam of shouts were going up: "Hail, Mancinus! Hail, propraetor!" Curiosity seized Ramnes to see this man. Besides, Lars evidently knew more than he about the Villa Veturis happenings.

The crowds yielded passage to the group. They came into the forum not far from the high stand with its curule chair and six lictors and surrounding guards. A slim, powerful figure stood there—not in the purple-edged toga of his office, but in dusty armor. A long, aggressive, lean face with undershot jaw, a voice curt, incisive, challenging. So this was his cousin—unknown, accursed!

"For the love of the gods, wipe that look off your face!" grunted Lars, tugging at the sleeve of Ramnes. "Come; we've heard enough. Ranting about the glories of Rome. Come!"

THINKING OF his dead father, of how the man before him had mounted upon injustice to wealth and power, Ramnes felt savage, hackled fury rise within him at sight of this Mancinus. His pulses were throbbing as he tore his gaze away and

*A woman's voice
said: "It is good
you didn't kill
him! Mancinus
would bring fire
and sword here!"*

went along with Lars and the others, dodging into a courtway close at hand and then into a house, and so into a large and empty room. A slave brought wine, cups, food; then the doors were locked.

"We're safe here; speak freely!" said one of the group.

Lars introduced himself and Ramnes, who told of Pelargos and the killing on the highway. The Trebia? Aye, he had seen that also; it was Pelargos who was largely responsible for the Punic victory. One of the local men laughed harshly.

"We know all about your Pelargos—under his Latin name. Reward notices are posted in the forum. Umbria is being searched for him. A deserter, eh? One who became a captain under the Africans? They'll never forgive that in Rome! Well, trust us. Your Pelargos will get safely to Reate."

THE VILLA Veturis? This was hearsay, but reliable. Four days ago, the propprætor had been there with some officers. Trouble arose over a slave, it was said; the household slaves attacked the officers, there was killing, the villa was set afire and burned. Mancinus and his party had departed hastily at full gallop.

The Lady Drusilla? Oh, she had been away at the time. She was but recently home from Farther Gaul. She was not concerned in the tumult. It was no secret, however, that she had no sympathy with Roman oppression and misrule. Probably Mancinus would not dare molest her, thanks to her rank and her father's name. Still, who could tell? He was a hard man, bitter hard, and loved cruelty. He had flayed two men alive at the gate of Reate a fortnight since. But what of the great battle? The Africans? The elephants? Were they like the Monster of Heracles?

Lars told about the happenings on the Trebia, and Ramnes sat lost in thought. So there was no crisis, no need of haste. Trouble over a slave, eh? He started slightly. Could that slave have been Croton, home again? And she, of the warm blue eyes—she was there, there, a day's ride away!

He stirred uneasily, was caught by a name, listened to the talk. Lars broke into a peal of laughter. The Monster of Heracles, eh?

"That's a good one!" he said, turning to Ramnes. "It seems that there's a little place settled a long time ago by Greeks, the other side of Reate; nothing much there except a temple to Hercules, and the Greek name of Heracles is kept. Well, about thirty years ago,"—and he broke off, pausing an instant, at bitter memories,—"at the time I was dragged off to Sicily, the Romans captured a lot of elephants down there and brought them to Italy."

"Eh? Oh, I remember!" Ramnes exclaimed. "Pelargos was telling about them."

"So? Well, these priests of Heracles got one of those elephants, somehow, and kept him, built a special place for him. These tribes had never seen such a beast; he became known as the Monster of Heracles. He's still there; probably getting on in years, too. People come from everywhere to see him, and the priests make a fat thing off it. Where did Pelargos hear about those elephants? Well, no matter. Here, try some of this Venafrum—the real wine of the gods, liquid gold!"

Ramnes ate and drank, but frowningly, lost in conjecture. Ah! That priest of Hercules, who was worshiped as a god everywhere in these parts, back at Fanum Fortunæ! The priest whom Pelargos had dispatched with some mysterious message to Eryx! It was just afterward that the Stork had spoken about those elephants. And this Monster of Heracles was kept by the priests of Hercules! Well, there was plainly some connection. No wonder Lars Masena was so uproariously amused by the name of this poor ancient beast, and the veneration paid him by the hill folk. Elephants would soon be no marvel in Italy, unless those of Hannibal were all dead by now.

"I'm off." Ramnes came abruptly to his feet and made his farewells to their hosts. "Lars, why not stay here, await Pelargos, and bring him along in a day or two? Apparently there's no hurry on your account. I can go ahead alone."

Lars assented. One of the Sabines undertook to guide Ramnes to where the horses would be waiting, outside the gates, and to show him how to reach the Villa Veturis without going through Reate. By morning, it seemed, he should be there.

SO, WITH his guide, Ramnes departed. The assembly in the forum was ended, the cavalry had departed for Rome, the people were streaming away in all directions. Ramnes got his directions. But, as the two of them passed beneath the arch of the city gate, a sharp exclamation of dismay broke from the Sabine:

"By Hercules! The proprætor himself!"

Mancinus, there in the saddle, a group of officers around

him—angrily questioning the man who held the two fine horses.

"Hand over those beasts, d'you hear?" lifted the proprætor's voice. "And answer me. Whose are they? Answer, you Sabine dog, or I'll have you flogged!"

"The horses are mine."

Ramnes stepped forward, took the reins, and swung up into the saddle. Roman tongue, Roman eye, Roman armor—the effect was instant. Eye to eye with Mancinus, now, he was more fully aware of the hot sneering cruelty in that lean face and ugly undershot jaw, and the dominating, unscrupulous character behind the cruelty.

"Who are you?" rapped out Mancinus, startled. "Are you one of my men?"

"The gods forbid!"

The hot eyes narrowed. "Your name?"

"A better one than yours."

A RIPPLE of delight shook the listening crowd. Roman against Roman—ha! Something rarely seen! With an effort, Mancinus reined in his anger.

"Are you aware," he asked coldly, "that I am proprætor here, that I've confiscated those horses to the use of the republic?"

"Try to get them," said Ramnes laconically.

Despite his blazing eyes of fury, Mancinus took warning. An enemy, no doubt of it; a Roman, no doubt of it; if a Roman of rank, have a care! But the open appreciation of the country-folk rubbed him on the raw.

"Do you know my authority here is absolute?" he said raspingly.

"No." Ramnes was icily impassive, to all seeming. "A proprætor has military rank only; you assume civil power and the lictors of a prætor, but you say you're only a proprætor. Perhaps you are a consul or even a dictator in disguise. One would think so, from the reputation you have in these parts, Lucius Mancinus."

The deliberate words bit deep, planted alarm of the unknown.

"I lack your name," snapped Mancinus.

"Continue in the lack. I'm a Roman citizen, which is all you need to know."

Impassive, indifferent, Ramnes turned his horse with total unconcern and rode off, leading the big gray mare. He had played the part of patrician to a nicety. The laconic insolence, the incredibly cold hauteur, left Mancinus biting his lip with fury, yet baffled. That he had exceeded the powers of his purely military rank, was all too true. If this were some emissary from the Senate, it might mean trouble for him.

Once well away, Ramnes struck into a swift pace, livid with emotion; that effort of repression had taken all his willpower. More than anything in the world—almost—he wanted to come to grips with this man who had mounted upon the ruin of his father, and he hated to dissemble. Well, at least they knew one another—would know each other better when they met with the mask off!

He sent the horses on at full gallop. The sun was already down behind the western peaks, there was no particular need of haste, but he wanted to get away from Mancinus, who was apparently going back to the camp at Reate. With darkness his pace must slow, for these were country roads.

What lay ahead? What could he expect at Villa Veturis? This question began to loom more largely and darkly, now that he was close to journey's end. Or was he? That he must go on to Eryx had been more than implied. All this way from the sea he had traveled along one arm of a V, with Reate at the apex; now turn and go back along the other arm, a hundred miles to the coast, farther to Eryx—by the Via Salaria, a road only partly laid out and begun; Eryx was beyond Roman jurisdiction. Only a little, but still beyond.

What of Drusilla in all this? His errand to her began to seem tinged with madness, as he reflected on it, and night drew down along the hills, and the cold stars brought reason. She had been like a vision, that day. He had fancied invitation kindling in her eyes, as with the same thought springing in his brain; he must find this woman again! But how far had fancy outrun probability? He could not tell her such things. The very idea made him shiver.

"I can use Pelargos as excuse; she knows him," thought Ramnes. "But that, damn it, will be a lie. Tell her the truth, as her eyes command—and see her laugh at me for a fool? Tell her of treasure, and have her shrink from me as one accursed? Damned if I know what to do, what to say!"

He rode on into the night, tormented. Another man would have halted at the first wayside shrine, sacrificed to the gods, and prayed for direction. Ramnes had seen his father act thus too many times, without result.

IT WAS an hour past midnight, when he came to the forks in the road. By his information, the right-hand road went to Reate; that to the left, would take him to the villa, in its long valley. He turned, and dogs at some near-by farm gave savage tongue as though to greet him. A little farther on, he tethered the horses among trees and rolled up in his cloak for an hour or two of sleep. No use getting there at untimely hours.

He was, in fact, beginning to shrink in alarm from getting there at all.

With the first streaks of dawn, he was riding on, having finished his cheese and wine. His road was well defined, much traveled. It led into the long, rising valley described to him. Those gullies coming down from the high hills all along the right—some one of those must hold the secret of the sybil's grotto. The villa was somewhere ahead, by a stream that issued from the hills. Vine-stalks dotted the slopes, clumps of trees here and there were gilded at their tips by the rising sun.

Conscious that his heart was beating fast with expectation, Ramnes broke into a laugh and slowed the horses. Here was a stream, he had a razor—why not? He passed a hand over his chin and decided for it.

With this he was off, dousing his head in the icy water. He fell to work briskly, and if the job was not neatly or painlessly done, at least he was cleaner for it. Laughing again at his own conceit, he paused to unsling his steel cap and jam it over his hair, which a barber at Fanum Fortunæ had clipped short. What with shaven jowl and armor, he flattered himself that he made a very different figure from the uncouth barbaric Mancinus of the Alps.

He turned to the horses, and put out his hand to the saddle.

Whack!

Something missed his ear and smacked into the horse. The beast reared, gave a squeal of pain, and went away with a leap and a run. The other horse plunged, whirled, and dashed away. Ramnes swung around, bewildered.

Crash! Something hit his corselet with such force as to knock him backward. He lost balance and fell, then came to one knee. A blow struck his steel cap—a ringing, blinding concussion that dazed him. Almost at once, another. A stone glanced from his corselet. Stones! Slingers!

He wavered there, unable to rise, all but sprawled senseless by those shocks. Hoarse voices came to him; his eyes cleared; he saw men running forward from the nearest trees. Shaggy, skin-clad men, shepherds, slings discarded now for clubs. Four in all, plunging in to finish him. They thought him down for good. Sabine shepherds, men of the hills, their speech meaningless to him.

He slumped a little in a swirl of dizzy pain, head hanging. In the nick of time, his brain cleared; muscles and nerves responded to his frantic thrust of will. The foremost man was rushing at him, swinging the massive club, bearded face and wild eyes alight with exultant ferocity.

BARELY IN time, Ramnes moved, sprang, propelled himself up and forward, ducking the club and ramming the shaggy figure headlong, steel cap to belly. If the crash sent him all asprawl, it did worse to the other. The man dropped his club

and doubled up in a nerveless, helpless mass, kicking spas-
modically with one foot.

Desperately, Ramnes scrambled aside as the others rushed
in. The fallen club touched him; he caught at it, gained his feet,
swung the knotted stick and felt it smash home. A leap, and he
was in the clear. One man kicking, one down with bloodied
face, two coming for him and snarling like dogs as they struck.

Vaguely, he was aware they must have taken him to be a
Roman. No stopping to think, however. Here the work was fast
and furious—blows coming in from either side, the massive
club swinging in his hands, answering his output of strength.
It met those blows with shattering force, slapped into one
bearded face and sent the owner staggering. Ramnes whirled
upon the second man, knocked the club aside, swept in a low
stroke for the legs, felt it go home, saw the man lose balance
and go down.

Clear? Not yet. Bloody-face was up and shambling in with

long club aswing. These weapons did brutal damage, but killed not. Ramnes loosed his voice at the fellow in hot haste, crying that he was no Roman, and mouthing the name of Drusilla; but the shaggy man heard nothing, understood nothing. He hurtled forward, lashing in a blow. One of the others was up and plunging. Desperate, Ramnes flung himself at them in an effort to knock them aside and win clear. He comprehended only dimly that his tremendous and unexpected strength was beating down all four of them, that they were in wonder and frantic awe and fear of him.

He ducked a terrific swing from one club, sidestepped to avoid the other—and the first man down, who was still down, caught his ankle in one swooping hand. He dragged himself clear, but the effort lost balance for him. He went staggering, arms outflung, weapon useless. The two were upon him like wolves.

A glancing crack knocked away his steel cap and sent him

down. He saw the finishing blow coming, tried to ward it off with his arm—and his last memory was a shower of blinding sparks.

He struggled back to consciousness through queer zones of fancy.

An orator was speaking—Lucius Mancinus, it seemed, in that dry rasping voice which stirred him so disagreeably.

"You fools, who else could it be but Hercules come to life? Look at this steel cap, look at this armor—battered, crushed, dented! No ordinary man could have withstood such blows. No ordinary man could have beaten you four giants. A god, I tell you! Hercules himself, by his looks, or some other god."

DULL, CONFUSED voices in the strange clacking Sabine tongue. Then nothing for a while. Then a cool, serene voice that wakened echoes in the memory—a woman's voice— said:

"It is good that you didn't kill him! Kill a Roman, and Mancinus would bring fire and sword here! Wash the blood from his face, Caius. You say there's no great harm done him? Very well. Put a wet cloth over his head. Apparently he did more damage to our four heroes than they did to him. Catch his two horses, you four, and bring them here, then get back to your flocks and don't lift hand against any other Roman, or I'll have you punished."

Drifting, again; grateful coolness and wetness on his head. Presently his eyes flickered open. He was sitting propped against a tree. His gaze focused on the only thing in front of him—the valley, a group of fire-blasted trees close at hand, among them the blackened ruins of what must have been a great house. Memory returned. The villa, of course! It was her voice he had heard!

He twisted his head. The effort hurt, sent stabs of pain through head and back. But he saw her standing there in the sunlight, directing a group of slaves and freedmen. Starting the day's work, no doubt, in the fashion of Roman matrons. Seeing to everything about the place, even if the house was gone. A cottage close by—no doubt it was some freedman's house that she was now occupying. Croton! Where was Croton?

His eyes strained upon her. Now her red-brown hair was coiled about her head, and she wore a white gown caught in at the girdle. A slim and slender woman, very proud and poised, filled with youth and loveliness like the morning sunrise about her.

Ramnes put up a hand and shoved the wet cloth from his head. He tried to speak, but blood was in his throat. He spat it out, and she turned, and saw he was awake. Catching a cup of wine that a slave held, she came swiftly toward him and sank down at his side, her anxious eyes upon him. The same eyes, blue, lively, filled with glinting lights.

"Drink this," she said gently, and put the cup to his lips.

"I'm sorry, dreadfully sorry," she went on. "They would have killed you, had not my freedman Caius seen them and rescued you. They're poor, wild fellows—"

"Oh!" said Ramnes. "Don't apologize. It's the other way around; I got what I deserved, perhaps. That makes us even. You see, I've owed you apologies for a long time."

"You?" Her blue eyes searched him. "Impossible. I've never seen you before."

"We exchanged words. You were tender and kind; I answered like a boor."

"I don't remember it at all," she rejoined slowly. "I'd certainly know if we'd met before today. You're not a person to be forgotten."

"Nor are you," he said, and laughed shakily. "No man who has ever looked into your eyes—who looked into your face as I did, that morning—could forget it through all his life."

A touch of color came into her cheeks.

"Where was this? Who are you?"

"Is Croton here? Did he come?"

"Croton!" The word was jerked out of her. "Croton was killed some days ago. Yes, he came. How did you— Ah!"

The blue eyes widened. She put one hand to her mouth in a gesture of alarm, of wild surmise. "No, *no!*" she broke out sharply. "You—it's impossible!"

"I must find that woman again!" said Ramnes in a low voice. "That was the message I read in your eyes, if you want the truth of it. I can't lie to you, Drusilla, or utter pretty phrases. I obeyed what the look in your face commanded me. I could not help it. Yes, I'm the same person. You remember now!"

"Yes, I remember now," she breathed, staring at him. "That morning with Scipio. And Croton told me of you, gave me the message—oh, it's like a dream, an impossible dream! Why on earth are you here?"

RAMNES LAUGHED, struggled to rise, and a groan escaped him as the movement brought a swirling eddy of fire across his brain. He dropped back again and lay unconscious.

CHAPTER IX

"DID CROTON give you his warning about Mancinus—about the dagger of Eryx?" asked Ramnes.

Drusilla nodded, a swift anger springing in her face.

Four days had passed since Ramnes' rough reception, and he, his bruises healing, sat watching her working over the fine washed wool and making it ready for the spinning-wheel. Odd, he thought, that she who was so thoroughly the Roman matron of rank, personally supervising everything on the estate, should have so little Roman in her character.

She held up a bit of the fleece.

"See how it glints and sparkles in the sun? That's a sign of the finest quality wool. My grandfather imported some Phrygian sheep, forty years ago."

"Afraid to talk or think about Croton, are you?"

She flashed him a look.

"I hate being angry, and all this makes my blood boil," she said. "But I suppose we must talk it out sooner or later, so let's get it done."

"You've evaded the issue every time I've brought it up."

She assented with a cool gesture. "I'm none too sure of you, Ramnes; of why you're here and what you want. You've evaded, too. Mention the future, and you shy like a frightened horse."

He laughed. "Why not? I've told you what's planned, so far as I know it."

"Nonsense! You and that man Pelargos and the elephant-man—looking up long-lost families and loves?" Scorn flared in her voice. "Yes, that sounds like Pelargos; a cynic mouthing many words, jeering at the world."

"How old are you, Drusilla?"

"Twenty-three."

Not sure of him, no doubt divining his reticence. He had not mentioned the supposed treasure. No word had come from Pelargos and Lars Masena.

"I've been afraid of the truth; I still am," he said. "Do you know where the grotto of Lamnia the Sybil lies?"

"The place accursed? Yes. Three miles from here. All the world shuns it."

"That's one reason I'm here. You're the chief reason. Let's risk the truth! First, tell me about Croton. He expected that you would protect him and obtain justice for him."

She winced at this. "Mancinus had behaved shamefully here, after I went hurriedly to join my father in Gaul," she said, her blue eyes sultry with anger as they looked out across the valley. "He hated us, you see; for reasons. He took what he wanted, made a slave of Croton—all for the service of the republic, of course. The day after Croton came home, I went into Reate. Two senators from Rome were there, a commission sent to establish a war-supply service and to arrange new treaties with

the Latin tribes. I appealed to them for justice and demanded
that Mancinus be punished. They—well, they were very Roman."

She broke off, her voice bitter.

"I threatened to go to Rome and get justice from Scipio,
who's consul now," she went on. "An excellent plan, they agreed;
but he's with the army. Oh, they were smooth, polite, ironic!
You see, I've no family in Rome; my father's friends are in the
army. Better, they said, to make sacrifices for the good of the
republic, in this time of crisis. The truth is that my mother was
Sabine, not Roman; they even flung that in my face and advised
me to marry a Roman."

"Oh! Mancinus?" put in Ramnes, and she nodded. "Evidently, our good cousin has high-placed friends. But go on."

"While I was in the city, Mancinus was here, looking for me. He found Croton. He and some others were drunk. They killed Croton, the slaves and shepherds attacked them, the villa was burned. I got home to find one officer, a centurion, still here, looting."

"And you cursed him, and he died a few days later," said Ramnes.

"Oh!" Her eyes went to him, wide and startled. He had not told her of that affair near Spoletium. "He died? How?"

"By my sword. Come, let's have it out!" Ramnes faced her, gravely intent. "I'm not here to make peace, but war. You know

*"You're not afraid
of the curse?"
exclaimed Ramnes.*

I was with Hannibal; I may be with him again. I've turned my back on Rome. But you, Drusilla, may hate me for this."

"Hate you?" She looked at him steadily. "Did I seem to hate you, that day we first met in the shadow of the Alps? You, whose father saved my father's life?"

"No, you did not; but I was no open enemy of Rome, then. You gave the only words of sympathy ever granted my father. Yet you're Roman in blood, in education, in all that you are; the sort of woman typical of the republic's traditions, the finest and noblest—"

"Ramnes, for those words I could almost hate you!" she broke in, low-voiced, tense. "So that's why you've so closely guarded your tongue! You forget that the women of the oldest families in Rome came from Sabine stock. You forget that I'm more Sabine than Roman. What have I to do with those cold, callously cruel, deadly practical Romans? For twenty years the Sabine people have been ground down and oppressed by such men as this Mancinus. If a Roman has such vision and warmth and nobility that he cannot conform to their barbarous virtues, they kill or exile him; your father was that sort of man, as I've heard my father say."

THE TORRENTIAL words rushed from her in a blaze of emotion. Ramnes half sprang to his feet, then relaxed abruptly.

"All very well, Drusilla; but Rome, to your spirit, is still Rome."

"Yes," she said passionately. "A state that crushes out every spiritual factor, that grinds the individual into the common mold; a state whose ideal is a relentless efficiency for the common good—no, no! People don't exist to serve the state like slaves! Rather, the state exists for the people, for humanity, as in the Greek democracies. There's a higher, nobler force than mere brutal might! Rome may grow great on brutality, but in the end she'll perish and contribute nothing to the world!"

"Slightly exaggerated, I fear, but in the main well said!" With a laugh, Ramnes was on his feet, his face alight, his eyes shining and eager. "I never suspected this; I thought you a woman, I find you a goddess! Magnificent!"

"A goddess? Don't talk like a silly shepherd boy," she said with new bitterness. "I'm merely a woman—prey for the strongest. A woman, to be dragged down by Mancinus the propræ-tor to gutter level; to be defiled and shamed and mocked—eh? What is it?"

She looked up suddenly, as he reached out and touched her, putting his hand on her shoulder, smiling down into her eyes.

"You've made me realize something, Drusilla. The broken and the helpless, the exiled and friendless, the outcasts who have nothing to follow except the gleam of heart's desire—why, that's what we all are! You, I, Pelargos, Lars—and by the gods, four strands to a rope make it stronger than three!"

His voice leaped up, vibrant, ringing. "What's to do for such as we? Rage against the world like mad dogs, destroying, tearing down? No! Come, follow the gleam with us, find our heart's desire and build upon it, grow strong in it!"

"So?" Her blue eyes kindled. "You've guarded your tongue well. What, then, is your own heart's desire? You've told me what the other two seek. What's yours?"

"You."

The one word—finality, decision, laconic strength, and gaze unfaltering. Her breath came more swiftly. She opened her lips to speak; then her eyes flickered away, her face changed, she came abruptly to her feet.

"Not now. Who's this?"

Ramnes turned, in startled surprise. Neither of them had observed the approaching horseman, until an irruption of dogs with full-throated alarm revealed his presence. A shout broke from Ramnes, a shout of mingled greeting and laughter, as the strange figure swung from the saddle, and Drusilla hastily called off the dogs.

Pelargos—but what a Pelargos it was! That long shape was

cloaked in woman's garb, with floating woolen mantle tucked tight under the chin, and heavy braids of dark hair issuing from below the wide-brimmed Umbrian hat. A strange, gaunt woman of some hill tribe by his looks. Not until the name reached her ears did Drusilla comprehend who it was.

"Laugh, confound you!" exclaimed Pelargos. "Laugh, split your sides. Make a joke of it all! But I tell you they've got every road patrolled, they're combing every nook and corner; that business near Spoletium has put the hounds out after Pelargos in full cry! If I hadn't ridden most of the way here with a dozen country-folk supplied by the friends of Lars, I'd never have got through! Lady Drusilla, salutations. You remember me?"

HE TORE off hat and wig, ripped away the woman's gown and mantle, and grunted angrily to the roars of laughter from Ramnes. Drusilla conquered her mirth, greeted him, and spoke to the slaves and servants who came running and staring. The bald head and incredibly lanky figure emerging from this woman's costume brought fresh laughter from Ramnes, and with a sheepish grin Pelargos joined in it.

"Oh, the hurt's doing well enough," he said, when mirth settled into questions. "Lars will be here tonight, if all goes well. Lady, it's a long time and a long road since we laid your father to rest in Farther Gaul; my service to you. Perhaps you have a trifle of wine to spare a thirsty soul? My vow's ended, comrade, and I've kept it till now."

A table was brought, wine and fruit arrived, and when the three were alone Pelargos stretched out comfortably, his birdlike eyes seeking Drusilla.

"Did this grinning rascal tell you of the flea he put in the proprætor's ear?"

"No," said Ramnes hastily. "We've been getting acquainted ever since I arrived; in fact, I've just now reached the point of talking freely. Some of the local shepherds took me for a Roman, greeted me with slings and clubs. Hang it all, Drusilla is one of us! I was a fool not to trust her from the start."

Pelargos gulped his wine and stared.

"I don't know what you're talking about, but let it pass. Your brush with Mancinus had results; apparently he's discovered that you were no emissary from Rome, for he's got rewards out for you, also. The roads are hot with cavalry. Haven't any been here?"

"No. My people are on watch," Drusilla said. "They must have taken you for a woman, since they gave no word of your coming. Now, suppose you let that tongue of yours have free rein, and make up for the silence of Ramnes! Tell me everything."

"Gladly. Do you go to Eryx with us?"

"Why should I?" she said, with her level look.

"You'd better. Mancinus has got you appointed a ward of the state, is coming here to see you. If the deviltry is as Croton said, you'll have to jump fast! Lars said last night that Mancinus is boasting you'll be his wife in three days."

He went on, talking fast and furiously as the wine flexed his tongue. He told Drusilla all that Ramnes had not, and spared himself no glory in telling of the Trebia battle. She made caustic comment, with a lift of her brows.

"You were always rated a braggart, Pelargos. Need you boast now, when you're at the end of your rope?"

His bright eyes searched her face for a moment.

"Sometimes my boasting has a purpose, lady," he said gravely. "The man who thinks well of himself, is thought well of by others; when there's great work to be done, swaggering lends confidence. Look how the Romans boast about their work at sea, spreading the story that a wrecked Punic galley taught them to build ships, and eventually to scatter the navy of Carthage! That's pure brag, to build up the Roman name."

"Isn't it true?" asked Ramnes curiously, and Pelargos snorted.

"Shipwrights and seamen aren't made in a day. Ancus Martius, the fourth king of Rome, had great shipyards. Two hundred years before Duilius beat the Punic fleet, a reach of the Tiber was expressly set apart for ship construction. Immediately after the Tarquins were expelled, a treaty with Carthage assigned limits for the Roman fleet. Why, the earliest Roman money bore the image of a ship's prow, to show sea power! No, no, lady. I, who war against the gods, am hoping now to create a god, so let me strut and swagger as I will."

"Your windy words seem to hide some sense," said Drusilla, frowning, "but I don't like vague allusions. Just what do you propose?"

"Aye," said Ramnes. "Let's have definite plans."

Pelargos dissented. "Not yet; don't flourish the palm before you win the race. All our future depends on certain elements; tonight when Lars arrives, I'll know the best or the worst, and lay everything before you. Fair enough?"

"So it seems," Drusilla answered. "But why should I go to Eryx?"

"For friendship and safety. You've none here."

"Mancinus can't harm me. That silly story about using the dagger—"

"BY HERCULES, it's not silly! It's true!" exclaimed Pelargos vehemently. "In Reate and Interamna were three men, powerful leaders of the people, who hated Rome, distrusted Mancinus, and set the people against him. I don't know their names, but Lars does; he got the whole story. Where are those three leaders today? Half-imbecile, servile sycophants of the proprætor, their wealth and power turned over to him. A judgment of the gods, says Mancinus! No, lady, that accursed weapon is an actual fact. Let him but prick your arm, as by accident, and you become his slave."

"I don't believe it. I'm not afraid of him!" she broke out.

"Well, I am," said Pelargos. "But Ramnes isn't."

"For the last time, will you give some definite reason why I should go to Eryx? You have more in view than merely finding your family again?"

"Yes." Pelargos rubbed his long nose. "Go, then, because we go. Eryx is beyond the present reach of Rome. The first need is money; ours is about used up. If all goes well, I hope to leave here tomorrow evening—and we'll go like gods! Ramnes, did you tell her the secret that her father told me?"

Ramnes shook his head. Pelargos gestured irritation.

"You've certainly wasted time! We must find that treasure, or give up the idea, this very day. Talk about destiny! It's driving us like a millrace—you don't know our friend Mancinus has his eye on Eryx? Aye; plans to get its wealth and man-power for the use of Rome—"

"Pelargos," cut in Drusilla gently, but with a sweetness that tokened danger, "either abandon your vagueness this minute, or I leave you. What secret did my father tell you?"

Suddenly blunt and direct, Pelargos told of the treasure. Ramnes watched to see how the story affected her; a breath of relief shook him, delight seized him, when her blue eyes kindled and color rose in her cheeks, and she came quickly to her feet.

"Good! We'll get horses, and prove or disprove these words, without delay."

"You're not afraid of the curse?" exclaimed Ramnes.

She gave him a level look.

"I fear the gods, Ramnes, and reverence them; but I neither fear nor reverence Rome. Luckily, we have your two horses and that of Pelargos. I'll be ready in five minutes."

She turned toward the cottage, calling the slaves. Pelargos looked at Ramnes, and chuckled softly.

"All's well, comrade. Never blurt things out to a woman till the right moment; make her force the issue, and she's yours. Once you know the trick, it's easily done."

"Oh, you're a human marvel," Ramnes said dryly. "Is it true Mancinus is coming here?"

"Yes." Pelargos knit his brows. "And, if everything else works out, you'll have the hardest job of all as your contribution to the common good! One I don't envy you by half, either. But let it wait—depends on the treasure, on Lars, on Drusilla. Here she comes."

The horses were brought; Drusilla mounted; the three went riding off.

They cut away from the long valley, following the stream that wended back through the hills, where sheep grazed beneath towering chestnuts and massive oaks. In half an hour they reached what Pelargos declared to be the spot, Veturis having mentioned certain landmarks; but finding any cave entrance was another matter.

NOON WAS near when Drusilla, pushing through a tangled thicket, lifted a call that brought the others. There, under an overhang of rock, showed an orifice dark and jagged, completely hidden away.

"Veturis killed a wolf here," said Pelargos. "Smells clean. Fire, comrade?"

"Wait here," spoke up Drusilla excitedly. "I'll ride back—we have torches ready for use. I'll bring them, and something to eat, and fire."

She was gone with a leap for the horses, running lightly, her briar-torn robe fluttering.

Pelargos gazed after her.

"What a woman!" he ejaculated. "There was never a goddess equal to that flesh and blood and brain! You're lucky, comrade. Well, this looks as though we'd see Eryx and no mistake. When we fell in with Lars, I knew the fates were weaving their web for us! By the way, I neglected to mention that the son of Marcus Mancinus is even more badly wanted than I am."

Ramnes started. "What? You mean they know who I am? Or rather who I was?"

"Precisely; Romans aren't fools. I didn't tell you in front of Drusilla, for the words have an ugly sound. That fellow Alimentus talked a lot; the officers who were with Scipio, when you met Drusilla, have talked. It's known that a real Roman was with Hannibal. It's one thing for a hireling like me to turn against Rome, but for a Roman-born to do so, puts foam at their lips! Add to this, the natural hatred of Mancinus for his relative. In short, the man who kills you and brings in your traitor's head gets wealth and rank."

Ramnes laughed harshly. "Very well! My head will cost them something."

"I trust so; but gold's the first and most loyal friend in case of need. And if we find this Roman gold and make it fight for us—ha! Beautiful irony! I'm going to take a look inside there, to make sure we're not on a false lead."

He rose, made his way through the close thicket, and vanished through the opening, which was large enough to admit him when doubled up.

RAMNES SAT in tumultuous thought. They knew him? Let them! It was of small account, beside the astonishing revelation of Drusilla, of all that lay in her heart and mind. When Pelargos came scrambling out, grimed and cursing, to report a certainty of caverns, Ramnes scarcely heard; he told the other all that had passed, all that had been said.

Pelargos rubbed his nose, scratched his bald pate, shook his head doubtfully.

"Comrade, you and she alike are idealists, of a sort. I'm not. I don't comprehend just what all your fine words are about; but my family's in Eryx, Lars will find his heart's desire there, you'll find—what? A future, if things work aright. Did Croton tell you the origin of this dagger Mancinus now has?"

"The dagger of Eryx?" And Ramnes frowned. "Something about the gods; I don't remember."

"The gods, aye. Those Greeks are superstitious."

"How do you know so much about Eryx, anyhow, Pelargos?" demanded Ramnes bluntly. "You said your father was a Greek. You were born in Spain."

Pelargos grinned. "He was a Greek, yes; from Eryx. Chew on that, comrade!" And he leaped up. "Ha! Here comes our fire and light; now for the loot of Rome! You'll be more likely to see it than Hannibal will, if I'm any judge."

AS DRUSILLA arrived, her horse blowing, Pelargos seized one of the torches she bore and lit it at the pot of embers; fanning it into flame, he went plunging for the cave entrance. Ramnes motioned Drusilla to follow, and himself brought up the rear, with extra torches.

The opening admitted them freely. Inside, the ruddy light of Pelargos guided them along a fairly large cavern which ran endlessly, it seemed. Bones littered the floor but there was no token of human visitation.

Suddenly the light ahead disappeared. Darkness enveloped them. Drusilla uttered one low gasp; then Ramnes caught her hand.

"Come along—the passage has turned, that's all."

Her fingers gripped his; something was born between them on the instant, as though this touch of the hand demolished some final barrier. Their voices rang with hollow echoes from the cavern roof, a foot or two overhead. They caught up with the light around a turn and saw the stooping shape of Pelargos on ahead. Then they heard his voice, in a wild, exultant, incoherent yell of excitement.

They hastened on, for the light lessened once more. The passage opened into another; Pelargos was standing in a large but rather narrow chamber with high roof, the torch held high. Its spluttering ruddy flames lighted up everything. The three stood staring, silent.

From this chamber various passages led away into obscurity. At one end were piled a curious lot of objects—stools, crude stone images, a huge bronze tripod, a litter of old clothes and weapons, evidently left from ancient occupancy. But piled in the center of the place, filling the floor, were the treasures of pristine Rome, of the city and temples destroyed by the Gauls nearly a century ago.

It was a queer hodgepodge of intrinsically worthless objects,

*"I want for myself this little casket.... Only the
priests know that these treasures are lost!"*

no doubt venerated relics of temples and shrines, and glorious
eye-filling riches in massy gold and gems. Caskets and chests
of bronze and wood and leather; vases, shields, votive offerings
of ruddy metal, old-fashioned weapons and armor of the most
glorious description.

Pelargos moved, went to one of the high leather sacks, and
with an effort broke the rotten draw-strings and pried apart
the stiff leather folds. He scooped out a handful of gold orna-
ments and coins, and let them dribble back. He struck his

knuckles against one of the tall golden vases. The actuality of it was stupefying.

"Well, here it is," he said hoarsely. "Loot of the Etruscan kings, loot of the Latin tribes, loot of the temples and treasury of Rome! Placed here and lost; those who hid it, killed by the Gauls!"

Drusilla approached a small but gloriously worked casket of gold and ivory. As though fascinated, she traced with her finger the letters worked on top and sides. A sudden low cry escaped her; she looked up, eyes dilated, awe and wonder in her face.

"Look! Look! Do you know what this is? Can you read? The books of the Cumean Sybil! The most sacred thing in all Rome, the prophecies which guided and guarded the city! They are supposed to have been laid away for consultation only in the greatest emergencies; no one has seen them for ages, except the priests—"

"And in reality they were put here and lost!" Pelargos broke in with a wild laugh. "Ha! There's Rome for you! No one dared admit they were lost, eh? Well, well, let's have another torch or two. Comrade, you and I will have to move out to the entrance whatever we want to take with us. We'll have to take all we want, for we may not get back here."

"I want this." Drusilla put her hand on the casket. "But, Pelargos! How can we hope to carry much of this treasure with us?"

"I'll answer that tonight," said Pelargos, his bald pate shining in the torchlight. "You know more about the relics of the gods of Rome than I do, lady. Pick out some of these things—sacred images and so forth. Probably these small caskets hold the most precious objects."

DRUSILLA BEGAN to examine the boxes and chests, as Ramnes moved them out.

"Everything's marked," she exclaimed. "See the leather tags on the armor? Oh—it can't be true, it can't!" She caught her breath, staring at a little casket of curious old bronze. "The

sacred image that Aeneas brought from Troy! And that stone
figure—the Minerva that fell from heaven! Those golden arms,
the relics of the kings of Veii—"

Pelargos laughed again. "Plague take your images from
heaven! I've seen 'em in Spain and Gaul, stones that fall from
the sky with fire and noise. Just stones. Funny sort of gods, who
have nothing better to do than bombard the earth with fiery
images! Ramnes, here are weapons, armor, and the good gold
coin that spells power. We'd better get what we want moved
out to the entrance. We can't take too much; let Drusilla have
the heavenly images to play with, and we'll stick to solid worth."

"Wait!" Drusilla intervened, breath coming quickly, and eyes
alight. "I want for myself this little casket with the books of the
Cumean Sybil; but wait! Do you realize what this means? The
choice it offers to us?"

PELARGOS SHOOK his head, frowning. Ramnes
nodded, with a slight smile; he had been thinking of just this
thing. Cool, unexcited by the scene, careless of the heaped metal,
he had been weighing potential and actual values.

"To bargain with Rome, you mean?"

"Of course!" she cried. "Only the priests know these treasures
are lost; they're supposed to have been saved from the Gauls
and to remain hidden in the temples. The priests know. They've
handed down descriptions, everything. And the priests are the
most powerful men in Rome, remember!"

"Ha! I see!" burst out Pelargos. "Hand over this stuff, bargain,
barter! We could have anything we asked. Eh? And then get
our throats cut to stop our tongues."

"Right," said Ramnes calmly. "Who'd trust Rome? Not I.
Rome would go to any lengths to get this stuff, true; and to any
lengths to keep the people from knowing it had been lost.
Would you trust Rome, Drusilla?"

The light died from her face. "No."

"Nor I," said Pelargos. "But I'll not hold you. Choose, then!
If against Rome, be against her; if seeking some way to buy her

friendship, seek it! But not I. The temples at Eryx will go wild to get some of these relics. The priests there will be more valuable to us than the priests of Rome. Drusilla, take what you like of all this pile, and go to Rome, if you wish. Here's your chance. The choice is yours."

"Right," said Ramnes gravely, looking at her. "I don't know yet just what Pelargos proposes at Eryx; but my choice is made. Yours is to make."

"Tonight, then, when your friend Lars arrives," said she, and turned away, cradling the little casket of gold and ivory in her arms.

"All right," said Pelargos briskly. "You hold a light, we'll work. At it, comrade! Two of these leather bags of gold and trinkets, to the outer entrance, and what other stuff we can find of most value."

They worked for a long while. To Ramnes, it was absurd to hope that they could carry away what was dragged out along the passage, yet Pelargos seemed cheerfully confident.

They broke off to explore the grotto's ancient approach, which ended in a blank wall of massive stones, the wall upon which had been laid the curses of Rome. Pelargos roared with laughter over the whole affair. Rome, hiding away here her choicest treasures and securely concealing them under mighty curses— only to lose them when those who knew the secret died! Even Veturis had been bound by his awe and superstition. But as Ramnes said truly, Veturis had not been driven by all the devils of despair and lost hopes and an empty future.

"Here's such armor as you'll never see again," Pelargos exclaimed once. "Equip yourself! You came here a mere man, fugitive and battered; go forth a god, comrade!"

"Oh!" Drusilla examined the leather tag affixed to a glorious Etruscan helmet of bronze and gold. "Ramnes! Here's the armor of Porseria, king of Tusculum, a votive offering to Mars after he was killed! Take it, take it!"

Laughing, Ramnes obeyed; the massive armor was a bit large,

even for him, but the spear that accompanied it brought a grunt of delight from his lips. A tempered bronze point, hard as steel, a heavy shank, adorned with golden grips—a massive weapon, a thing of cruel weight but beautiful balance. Pelargos, decking himself out in fanciful helm and breastplate of Greek workmanship, smiled.

"And to think my little pellets of iron, my strip of leather and cord, would let death and daylight through your bronze at fifty feet! Here, take this shield," and he rolled out a small but exquisitely worked shield adorned with a Gorgon's head. "Not too heavy, and has a good grip. Well, how's the time going?"

THEY SOUGHT the daylight, and were amazed to find the afternoon nearly gone and the sun at the western hills. They had even forgotten to eat, and laughingly made amends. When Ramnes strode off to get the horses, Pelargos nudged Drusilla and pointed.

"Look, lady! There's Hercules come back to earth again; did you ever see a man more fitted to be a god? Not Hannibal himself, I tell you!"

Her blue eyes dwelt upon the glittering armed figure, whose splendid proportions and lithe power seemed so incredible.

"What a Roman he would make!" she breathed, half regret-fully.

Pelargos sniffed.

"What a god he would make, you mean! And by Hercules, that's what I'll make of him! He's only half awake to life and power and his own possibilities; one good blooding, and you'll see a different person there, a man greater than other men, emerging from youth and bitterness. He's wise, cool—all he needs is to feel and know himself. You should have seen him down that centurion, all in a minute. Give him his chance, now, and there'll be one of the old heroes come to life!"

They rode back to the ruins of the villa, Pelargos jingling gold and Drusilla with the casket in her arms; but Ramnes found a fierce delight in the great spear, massive as himself, made as though for his strong hands.

The slaves and servants stared amazedly. Drusilla assigned them a cottage close to her own, one of the outbuildings which had escaped the flames.

"I have writing to do," she said, smiling. "Caius, my freedman, is an excellent scribe. Make yourselves comfortable, and I'll get you to witness some papers when we're through. No sign of your friend Lars, so far. We'll be warned if he or anyone else comes."

Half an hour later a slave summoned them to her cottage. They were shaved and bathed, rested and at ease. They found her working with the freedman, at a table heaped with seals and writing-materials.

"Will you witness these?" she said, pointing to a heap of papers. "If you can't write, Pelargos, make your mark. These are letters of freedom for all my slaves."

"What?" exclaimed Ramnes. "Why are you freeing them?"

"I'm gambling," she said, smiling, looking into his eyes. "The die is cast. I'm gambling with destiny—and you two. I'll have no use for these slaves in Eryx."

So she announced her decision.

CHAPTER X

A N H O U R after sunset, when they were sitting down to dinner in the cottage, came Lars Masena. A shepherd had come in posthaste with word of a single horseman, so they were ready, with a place set at the table and a couch for him.

The change in Lars, of which Ramnes had previously been aware, was now even more pronounced. He was assured, confident, radiant; at first entrance he flung Pelargos one quick nod, one gesture, as though to announce that his mysterious errand had been more than successful. Drusilla greeted him with an appraising quality beneath her cool dignity, but speedily thawed to him. He seemed, indeed, to be consumed by a laughing, eager exultation.

"What news?" demanded Ramnes.

"Oh, the best!" Lars rejoined, beaming. "That is, if you don't linger about here. I hear Mancinus has proclaimed a huge reward for your head—a traitor to Rome and so forth. What about the treasure?"

"Found and ready," exclaimed Pelargos.

Drusilla regarded Lars with a smile.

"I'm told that you're something of an expert with elephants. You should visit the one at Heracles, not far from here—the Monster of Heracles, he's called."

PELARGOS EXPLODED in laughter, and Lars grinned.

"I've just come from there," he said. "Your Monster is an old bull, a big one, flabby with lack of exercise; he was overjoyed to see me."

"What?" said Drusilla. "You talk as though he were an old friend!"

"Lady, he nearly danced for joy when I spoke to him in Carthaginian! He had not forgotten his youthful training—he was captured by the Romans, you know. When I left, he trumpeted after me. The priests were dumfounded. I dropped in as a chance traveler, and departed as an honored magician."

"And can you get him?" demanded Pelargos.

"Easily. He's chained to a huge tree in the temple grove—a long chain. I have only to knock out a staple, and he's free. They'll never know he's gone, till next morning."

"And will probably assign it to the doing of the gods!" Pelargos laughed loudly, caught the look of Drusilla, and leaned forward, his elbows on the table. "All right, all right! Here, comrades, is the game. Tomorrow Lars goes back to Heracles; he steals the elephant and gets here in an hour or so after dark."

"Less," broke in Lars Masena. "He'll travel fast, faster than horses."

"And picks up the load of gold. Ha! You see the point now?" exclaimed Pelargos triumphantly. "You see the millrace of destiny? But only a part. With that elephant and our horses, we get off, travel all night, get past Asculum before morning, and have a clear road to the sea! Hide by daylight, travel by night. On to Eryx, and the fulfillment of the ancient prophecy!"

Ramnes stared admiringly, as everything suddenly dovetailed and came clear—or at least enough to give him an inkling of the slow plotting, and why Pelargos had wanted to make sure of details.

"What prophecy?" he demanded.

"Mine." Pelargos grinned. "Remember that priest of Hercules at Ariminium? The one to whom I gave half my plunder, and sent to Eryx? Those priests, comrade, are smart men, and for gold they'll do much. I told him I was one of Hannibal's captains and was coming to Eryx, with the god Hercules. You see, there actually was some old prophecy that Hercules would return to life and show up in Eryx. Now, by this time, it'll be spread all over the city. No one will know much about ancient prophecies except the priests, and they'll embroider it to suit the cloth. Remember, Eryx is worried over the Roman power;

remember, we've learned that Mancinus expects to gobble Eryx! The prophecy is all set, be sure of that. When Hercules shows up on an elephant—"

Ramnes, who had listened with gathering anger, broke in abruptly:

"Enough of this blasphemy! I'll have no part in it. Shame on you for assuming that I'd lend myself to such a rascally imposition!"

"WAIT, MY noble Roman, wait!" cried Pelargos. "You don't understand! I'm giving you Eryx—the city, its fleet, its territories! I'm making you king, tyrant, dictator, judge, anything you want to call yourself—ruler of Eryx!"

"Are you insane?" demanded Ramnes sternly.

"No. Lars will back up all I say. Here's a city of thirty thousand souls, ruled by a council of elders, and badly ruled; the royal family died out some generations back and the city became a republic, to its sorrow. What happens? In time of crisis, with the hand of Rome reaching out to grab everything, the god Hercules appears riding on an elephant. The prophecies have come true!"

"I'll have none of it!" snapped Ramnes. "I'll not stoop to such pretense!"

"You don't have to do anything; just take what's given you. The more you deny being a god, the more firmly they'll believe you are one. You'll come with gold in your hand—ha! Trust the priests to do the rest! Offer the city only one thing; help against Rome. Be their leader. Send to Hannibal offering alliance and help. He'll make no campaign until spring; then Rome will make a supreme effort, and either crush him or be crushed. Here's the end of the rainbow I showed you on the other side the Alps, Ramnes!"

DRUSILLA TURNED, and her face was radiant.

"Oh, Ramnes! It's as you said only this morning—the chance to build, to create, to effect something great!"

So it was, indeed; her words shook him, and his eyes were opened to the truth. Pretense? Not at all. He need pretend nothing.

Lars squinted at him across the table, and spoke.

"You're the man for it, the man to do it, Ramnes! Come in the likeness of a god; then let your actions speak for you. Eryx is ripe to be plucked. What's more, the Friends of Hercules will back you up. I'll guarantee that five thousand Sabines will be there in three weeks, to fight against Rome! If you don't pluck the ripe apple, Mancinus will."

"You can," said Drusilla softly. "You'll not lose the chance, comrade?"

The word burned joyously in his brain as he stared at her, at the others. Realization came to him. Power! He, the gawky barbarian youth, suddenly caught and rushed down the millrace of destiny, as Pelargos expressed it; shoved into power—could he do it? Could he play such a game?

"By the gods!" he exclaimed slowly. His features firmed, settled into sudden exultant strength. "It's incredible; yet—ah, what a glorious incredibility! Yes, I see it now, what it means, what it might be! Right, Pelargos!" He looked at Drusilla, and laughed eagerly. "And you'll help?"

"If I can, yes. I can see the future, there in Eryx!"

"Then it's settled. But why delay?" The gaze of Ramnes, now all ablaze, struck out at Pelargos. "Why not go now, tonight?"

The Stork palmed his bald head, anxiously.

"We must risk delay. If Lars went now, he'd not get here till after midnight with the elephant. Between here and Asculum, seventy miles, all is danger; we couldn't get past Asculum by dawn, and an elephant is no easy thing to hide. With an early start tomorrow night, we can do it. At least, Lars and I can do it with the elephant; you and Drusilla follow on horseback, and we'll wait for you next day beyond Asculum. Remember, that beast can go like the wind! Then, past Asculum, we're practically out of danger."

"Seventy miles in a night, loaded with gold and two men?" queried Ramnes skeptically.

Lars wrinkled up his face. "I think so; if not, I know a place near Asculum where we'd be safe. But near here or Reate, none. Thank the gods, we're between Reate and Asculum, and have only the one city to pass! That elephant, remember, must be out of this whole district between sunset and sunrise. It'll be a pinch, but we can do it or kill the old bull in the attempt!"

"Very well; then we risk delay." Ramnes met the gaze of Pelargos, and laughed aloud. "You crafty schemer! That glorious armor, the gold, the relics of the gods—yes, we should be welcome enough in Eryx, if things are as you say! We'll find Romans there?"

"Romans are everywhere. Mancinus has spies there," said Pelargos, a question in his eyes.

"Then the first thing to do is to seize every one of them," said Ramnes thoughtfully.

The face of Pelargos cleared. He exchanged a glance with Lars, who smiled; Drusilla caught the look, and her eyes warmed; she lifted her goblet, and spilled a few drops of the wine.

"To the gods!" she exclaimed. "To all the gods—and may the false become the true!"

"There," said Pelargos, "is a toast I can drink with all my heart!"

POWER! RATHER, the opportunity of striking a blow for freedom, for himself, for them all; a blow such as Rome would remember, a blow for the free people of the world!

His throbbing thoughts stirred Ramnes out of the cottage that night, when the others were asleep, out under the stars. He paced up and down, cloak-wrapped against the night chill, mapping in his brain a thousand things that might be done— if Eryx willed! Within a few hours, he had changed and grown into a different person, as though he had been ripening for this moment.

He was aware of a dark figure, and heard her voice.

"Not sleeping?"

"Planning," said he, falling into step with her. "The world has suddenly become rich and glorious. Ah, if we were in Eryx now!"

"What would you seek to do, if we were?"

"Please you," he said softly. She made no answer for a while, then spoke as she turned away.

"That," she said, "is possible. Goodnight, comrade!"

He slept on the promise of those words.

N O O N O F next day saw Lars Masena off; he had seen the treasure, he knew where to meet them that evening. The winter days were short, the nights long, and he was confident that all would go as planned.

Power! The thought drove unceasingly at Ramnes; not that he cared a snap about power for itself, but for the sake of achievement. It obsessed him that afternoon, as in company with Pelargos he took the horses and heavy armor to the thicket in front of the cave opening, and left them there against the night. The horses tethered, he took seat on a fallen tree and watched Pelargos working with his sling.

"The whole thing seems impossible," he said abruptly. "It's a grand dream to make a song in the heart, but it takes a lot of doing."

"That's life, if you'd live it like a god," said the bald man. "The weakling who's afraid to fight, claims the world owes him a living and tries to sneak it. The strong man goes through defeat and misery, heartbreak, treachery; but goes through. Sometimes."

"Go over to Greece and set up as a philosopher," Ramnes said with asperity. "What do you know of failure and heartbreak, you who last night smoothed out the future with honeyed words? According to your reckoning, we have only to walk ahead to triumph."

"I lied," the other said simply. "This moment, comrade, I'm facing perplexity; I'm at a loss, blocked, baffled! I've been so eager about the other details, that I've missed the keynote of the whole affair. I tried so hard to make you and Drusilla see success, that I left the most important detail to chance—and, confound it, I see no way!"

Ramnes stared at him. "What are you talking about?"

"Remember, I spoke of your contribution? A task, which I didn't envy you?"

"Oh! I remember you mentioned it. Just what is the task?"

"Getting hold of the dagger of Eryx. The one Mancinus has. Croton told you of it. The thing isn't absurd, comrade; it actually works."

Ramnes nodded. "I believe it. Not hard to figure out how it works, either. Why does it matter to us?"

Pelargos surveyed him, lips pursed, eyes troubled.

"Has it occurred to you that Eryx might be slow to accept a new ruler?"

"Why, plague take it, that's what worries me!" burst out Ramnes. "It just doesn't make sense. Priests or not, gods or not, the idea is folly! It sounds good, but lacks in all practical, prosaic value. A handful of gold won't buy the rule of a city; nor will mere superstition conquer reality."

"I know," said the other, and sighed. "Here's the nub of the whole thing, comrade. The ancient prophecy—the real one, not my hocus-pocus—stated that Hercules would come to Eryx bringing back the dagger with him. Remember, it was a gift from Minerva. She and Hercules are the twin divinities of the city. It was the symbol of sovereignty. It was preserved in a temple in Reate until Mancinus seized it."

RAMNES FROWNED. "You're apparently serious—"

"By Hercules, I am serious!" exclaimed Pelargos, fervently. "That dagger's the key to everything! I've racked my brains trying to think up some way of getting it, and I'm stumped. All

The sword of Ramnes slashed... from the man
burst a frightful scream, as his arm fell off.

I can suggest is that you go into Reate tonight with Drusilla,
after we get off, and try your luck. It never leaves Mancinus
night or day, they say; and he lives in the city, not in the camp."

"So you expect me to take such an insane risk, for a dagger?"

"You and she both." Pelargos wore a sulky expression, as
though the problem had so utterly baffled him that he was
ready to snarl at anyone. "Not for a dagger, but for Eryx! I tell
you, it's the key to triumph! The priests there know all about

it, doubtless know the secret of its magic; there's no other in
the world like it."

Ramnes spat out an oath. "If the cursed thing means so much
in Eryx, why doesn't Mancinus plan to make use of it there?"
he demanded.

"He does, he does!" cried Pelargos in exasperation. "He means
to seize Eryx with its help! There's no secret about it; he knows
its value to him. Roman commissioners were here last week.
He's arranged everything with them. Once master of Eryx, he's
to have full prætor's rank. The new consuls, just elected, have

promised him a free hand so long as he sends treasure and slaves and above all, cavalry, to Rome!"

"Then it seems your plans should have begun with this dagger, instead of ending with it. Filled with some subtle poison or some virulent drug, that smears the point on touching a secret spring, eh?"

"Evidently you don't credit the magic of the gods?"

"Bah! No more than you. Well, if I must, I must! Send Drusilla away with Lars. You stay, and lend a hand. We'll get the cursed thing somehow."

"Agreed. Send her out of danger, eh?" The countenance of Pelargos cleared. "Very well. That'll mean delay; we may have to spend most of the night getting at Mancinus."

"She said two Roman senators had been here," Ramnes said gloomily. "She appealed to them and they politely laughed at her. Evidently they were preparing to sell her out all the time, making an agreement with Mancinus; if it's true that the state is taking over all her property, that she's to be a ward—eh? What's wrong?"

"Everything," muttered Pelargos.

He was staring past Ramnes, who turned and came to his feet. Instead of three horses, there were now four. A fourth had come up while they talked, unobserved, and joined the others, and was standing there; something queerly shapeless clung to his saddle, and, as they hastily approached, dripped heavy gouts of blood. A man, horribly gashed by swords, was clinging there senseless.

"Her freedman Caius!" cried Ramnes. "Quick! Something's happened!"

HASTILY PELARGOS helped him get the dying freedman from the saddle. His eyes opened, he looked at them, he spoke faintly.

"Just after—you left. Mancinus. A dozen soldiers. Killed our men—"

His head lolled over, he sighed, and it was his last breath. Ramnes leaped up, but Pelargos caught his arm, looked into his eyes.

"Careful! Quickest to leap, first to stumble, as the saying goes. Three miles to ride." His swift gaze flicked at the trees, the vale, the hills. "I can cut straight across. You ride around; take armor and spear. I'll help you with it."

Ramnes, his brain on fire, turned and hurled himself at the armor.

"Use your head, now," said Pelargos, helping with the stiff ancient fastenings. "You're the shock troops, heavy-armed; go straight in. Trust me to be somewhere. Here's Rome, remember! Meet Rome squarely, comrade. The other fellow always dies first, if you're quick enough; first blow best."

Thought of Drusilla, caught helpless, her men cut down, burned in the brain of Ramnes. Nothing else mattered. The sun was westering, the afternoon well gone. Still silent, grimly silent, he lifted the tremendous weight of the armor into the saddle with his body. Shield gripped on left arm, he took the murderous spear Pelargos handed him, turned the horse, and rode off, without a word.

CHAPTER XI

MANCINUS HAD no lictors now, no marks of office, no toga. Like the others, he was in armor, he had come on a brisk and ruthless business, and here he was at his best; in the role of soldier, he excelled.

His dozen companions were well chosen. Two were Romans, officers of the fifth legion detached on Umbrian duty; dour veterans, impassive and cold men, very efficient in all they did. The remainder were officers from the cavalry training-school, Latins of the southern tribes who hated all Sabines on principle. Four of them stood guard over the assembled slaves and servants, the others were grouped about Mancinus.

Armed with light javelins and swords, the party had wasted no time coming here. The shepherds who attempted to delay them were killed without mercy; to bring home the lesson, a few of the freedmen here, exulting in their new liberty, were cut down before the eyes of Drusilla. The others were cowed and terrified. She, standing before the group, slim and straight and shaken by helpless anger, eyed Mancinus with scorn; the two Romans stood at her elbows, one of them bleeding at the mouth. When they seized her, Drusilla had struck this man with her distaff, which gained her little good.

Mancinus was seated on a stool, arrogantly eying her and the group of slaves; they were in the open, out before the cottage, and a glorious golden light from the approaching sunset flooded the scene. The proprætor was in high good humor. Overlaid by smiling suavity, his lean forceful features were eloquent of character and command. He made no comment, showed no resentment, as Drusilla deliberately lashed the two Roman officers and then the others with chill angered words.

"You, disgrace to the name of Rome, who dare lay hands on me! On me, whose father died with the legions! And you, despicable fawning Latins, who cringe at the beck and call of your conquerors, who flatter this evil man—how dare you stand there even looking at me? If we were in Rome now, the pack of you would be driven to the city gates by lictors. Aye, including you, Mancinus, who shame an honorable name!"

MANCINUS NODDED, smiling, his hot eyes roving up and down her figure.

"For the last time, Drusilla, for the last time, make the most of your tongue," crackled his voice. Beneath its tolerant good-humor burned sarcasm and vindictive resentment, and the flame of desire.

"You're a most intolerable sort of woman," he went on, undershot jaw resting cupped in his hand, gaze devouring her. "Your bitter pride needs chastening. You have beauty, and you don't know how to use it."

"No; a beast doesn't appreciate virtue," she flashed at him. "He hates it and fears it."

"Your old-fashioned qualities," and his sarcasm deepened, "are admirable, but out of place in the world today, Drusilla. You've made yourself objectionable with your insensate pride, your inability to view two sides of a question. Beautiful as you are, you must be brought to hand."

"Scorned and despised by every honest Roman, you now return prating fine words where you were driven out in shame when my father lived," she said.

Mancinus colored, and straightened. He took a scroll from his pouch.

"By this decree of the commissioners appointed by the senate for Umbria," he said, "you are adjudged dangerous to the state, because your authority and position are used to breed discontent and to countenance hostility to the republic. Therefore your estates are taken by the state to be held in trust; you yourself are appointed a ward of the republic, until your marriage to a solid and respectable Roman citizen."

"Meaning perhaps yourself, and the dagger you stole from the Reate temple," she said bitterly, as he finished. "Oh, I know all about your precious plans! And those two senators you bribed. I think you have the most evil heart of any man who ever lived, Mancinus."

His eyes narrowed upon her.

"Too bad I didn't suspect that rascally horse-doctor Croton was waiting to betray me," he rejoined. "So he told you a lot, did he? And all true, Drusilla. All true! You've riddled me with your scorn and contempt, but for the last time. Now the gods have given you into my hands."

"The gods!" she said hotly. "You mean, all the powers of evil!"

He freed the long poniard from its sheath, and turned it over in his hand, as though the sight of it were answer enough.

"The gift of Minerva," he observed, with a thin, cruel smile as he saw the horror leap in her eyes. "A pretty thing, this divine bit of metal!"

A magnificent thing, rather; the blade longer than ordinary, of ancient fluted bronze, not smooth but almost quadrangular in shape, exquisitely chiseled and worked. The hilt, too, was longer and larger than any dagger hilt; an enormous, rough, massy lump of gold in which were set bits of silver as though to help the grip. As a weapon, it was huge and out of all proportion, but as a gift from the gods, it looked the part.

Mancinus thumbed the needle-point, smiling and watching her; but his men eyed the thing askance, with ugly sidelong looks, for it roused their superstition and hatred. It was abnormal, and normal men, whether good or bad, detest all abnormal things and creatures.

RISING SUDDENLY, Mancinus lost his smile; at his gesture, the two Romans seized Drusilla by the arms; she stood erect and unafraid as he approached, her eyes scornful and contemptuous, but her face very pale.

"Aye, Drusilla, this disdainful pride needs a lesson. I'll cure you of it, in the sight of all men," he said, and thrust forth a hand. Catching her gown at the neck, he ripped it open. She did not move, but the blaze in her eyes was dreadful to see. He thrust the dagger at her, so that the point touched her white bosom.

"You'll pay for your taunts and revilings," he said, a snarl in his voice. "I love you and hate you at once! By the power which this weapon of the gods lends me, I'll make you come crawling to my feet, make your proud name a byword for shame, take you to Rome and exhibit you there for what you are—"

The dagger moved slightly. A tiny red scratch appeared on her white skin; a drop of blood gathered and dripped. She said nothing, made no motion, but the look in her eyes seemed to madden him. A harsh peal of laughter escaped him, and he sheathed the weapon.

"Let the gods decide! Loose her, my friends, loose her." He

gestured to the two Romans, who stepped away. She gathered the rent gown together in one hand, then remained unmoving, horror and loathing in her gaze as she watched Mancinus. He surveyed her with exultant malice.

"Mine, do you hear? Mine!" he exclaimed. "Wife, aye; as soon as we get to the city—and slave as well! Here, start your duties aright by carrying this gift of the gods for me."

He slipped off his shoulder the gold-studded leather baldric to which the sheath of the dagger was affixed. Coming to her, laughing, he put it over her head, over one shoulder, so that the dagger hung at her thigh. Her hand went to it convulsively, but he gripped her wrist, caught her knotted hair in the other hand, pressed his lips to hers, and stared into her face with vindictive triumph.

"Mine!" he repeated. She flinched not, moved not; nor, being in his grip, could she. Protesting voices from the servants and slaves made him look up.

"Friends, you might be gathering up these rascals; string them on ropes and we'll march them back with us. The women will come in handy at Rome, now that the strength of every legion is raised to five thousand foot and five hundred horse! Our ancestors stole Sabine women; we'll send Sabine women as slaves to serve the army. Eh, my sweet one?"

He kissed Drusilla again; then, as he looked into her eyes, started slightly.

"It works! The charm works already!" he exclaimed. Stepping back, he struck her across the face, twice, with his open hand, while groans and cries of horror came from the watching slaves and servants. "Take that for your lesson of servility, your first lesson!" broke out his voice, heavy with the hatred in his heart.

At the savage words and action, one of the slaves burst into a cry.

"The gods punish you! May they punish you as you deserve!"

Mancinus swung around. "So? You don't know your master yet, eh? For that, you'll be flogged to death and drawn through

the camp at the tail of a mule, this night! You dogs will learn that when you speak to a Roman—"

A cry checked him, a startled word, an exclamation of amazement.

"Mancinus! Look! Who's this?"

The two Romans, beside him, growled and stared. The group of Latins stared. The slaves stared. Even the dozen horses, clumped at one side, lifted heads and pricked their ears forward. But Drusilla stared not; she looked at Mancinus, her eyes lack-luster and dulled.

IN UPON them Ramnes was riding, slowing his horse, drawing rein as his gaze flitted over them all and touched upon the sprawled corpses, and upon the figure of Drusilla with one hand clutching the gown at her throat. No one knew him, by reason of the wide Etruscan helmet with the bronze nose-bar that came down to his lips.

"Give him a club and lionskin, instead of that spear, and I'd call him Hercules!" said one officer, with a shaky laugh.

"A god! Some god has come!" cried out the slaves with a burst of voices. "Rescue!"

"No such armor as that in the past century and more," said one of the Romans.

Ramnes halted his horse. Carefully he dismounted; the weight of this armor made him topheavy in the saddle, and he needed to be sure of himself. Once on his feet, he lifted the spear and cried out:

"Drusilla! Not hurt?"

A wild shout burst from Mancinus.

"That rascal of a Roman! Here's our man, friends—at him, at him!"

Snatching a javelin, he hurled it, lightning swift. Ramnes, with the deft motion that every schoolboy knew, caught the cast on his shield. A clang, and the javelin slithered off as though it refused to touch that ruddy armor of golden bronze, shimmering in the sunset.

"A god!" cried the slaves. "Ramnes! Lord Ramnes! A god!"

"Mancinus the traitor, rather!" shouted the Roman leader. "At him, everyone!"

"You first, foul cousin," retorted Ramnes, and hurled the great spear.

Mancinus, by a miracle of agility, avoided it; but it went through the Roman next him, through corselet and body and backpiece.

Ramnes instantly regretted his folly in letting the weapon go, but too late. He drew his sword and threw up his shield. They were coming in at him from all directions with javelin and sword. His brain wakened. Upon the flashing moment drove the old maxims of his father: When overpowered, attack! Always attack with everything!

So, as they ringed him in, he suddenly sprang at them, a towering, hurtling figure of ferocity, his face convulsed, a yell on his lips. He crashed bodily into one of the Latins. Carrying all that bronze weight, the breast-to-breast body-blow taught by old Marcus Mancinus was terrific. The Latin gasped and staggered. The sword of Ramnes slashed at his throat. Another

Latin plunged in full tilt, driving with his javelin; it shivered on the bronze corselet, and from the man burst a frightful scream as his arm fell off, lopped near the shoulder, and the blood spurted in air.

Ramnes was aside, swooping, clutching. He got his great beam of a spear, jerked it clear, leaped away.

Swords clanged; javelins drove in. The ancient bronze armor rang like a bell to the impacts, but yielded not. An opening came; Ramnes leaped, drove with that massive spear, put all his force in the thrust. It went through a gay gold-adorned mailcoat like paper, and the Latin in the mailcoat cried out upon death. A desperate leap aside, and Ramnes was clear.

CLEAR, ONLY to find the second Roman upon him, sword hewing. The shield saved him from that deadly stroke, the helmet saved him from another. His spear thrust and went through the Roman's thigh. The man staggered back. Sword ready, Ramnes was upon him, beating his weapon away with the shield, slashing with deadly blade for the throat. The blow went home.

Away again and into them! They shrank not, but met him squarely. Here was Mancinus, sword out; he ducked the mighty spear, but the gold-bossed shaft of it struck him across the eyes and sent him rolling. A javelin flashing for the back—one leap, and Ramnes was away, his open back against a great tree-trunk.

And, suddenly, he was done. Even his giant strength had been sapped and exhausted by those terrific efforts, carrying all the enormous weight of bronze. His lungs burned, his knees were failing. A javelin sang in. He could not lift shield to avoid it, and it struck full on his breastplate, but could not pierce the bronze.

The two Romans were dead, and two of the Latins; the officer with the lopped arm was down, and dying. Mancinus, blood on his face, was ordering the others. They ringed him in; they had him now, and knew it. For the legs, went the word. For the legs! Pin him to the tree with a javelin through the legs, and finish him!

THERE CAME a queer, sickening *plop;* the foremost officer dropped weapons, screamed, and put both hands to his face, whence blood was spurting. Another Latin turned to him in astonishment, only to fling out his arms and pitch forward on his face. The others fell back, all astare. Ramnes, suddenly plucking up hope, strode out and killed the screaming officer with a spear-thrust, and with an angry oath sent the reddened spear hurtling at Mancinus. The latter, with a frantic leap, avoided the cast—so narrowly that it caught in a joint of his armor and ripped it away, and jerked him oft his feet.

A third Latin uttered a terrible cry, with a clang of metal on metal. His eyes rolled, his tongue protruded; he clapped both hands to his breast. Something had struck his corselet and passed on through into his body. He rocked on his heels, and fell.

The shrill, long yell of Pelargos quivered across the sunset. They saw him now, that unearthly tall figure like something inhuman as he stood poised. A wild cry, and the four remaining Latins went plunging for the horses, dragging the reeling Mancinus with them.

As they came to the horses, one of the four pitched over and over, like a rabbit struck by an arrow in mid-leap. The others climbed into the saddle, turned the horses. Once again, the figure of Pelargos uncoiled, and invisible death sang down the air. One of the riders fell over sideways, but his foot held fast and he was dragged for a long way as the horse galloped.

Again Pelargos uncoiled and his arms flew forth. Two men, with Mancinus between them; the Roman swayed in the saddle, bent far forward, then straightened again and kept his seat. The horses pounded on full speed, three men in saddle, one dragging.

Ramnes dropped his shield, put off the heavy helmet, and strode to the group of slaves around Drusilla. Their exultation had died; they opened, in silence and affright, to let him reach her. He stopped dead, and caught his breath.

"Drusilla! Don't you know me?"

She smiled. Her vacant eyes rested on him.

"Of course!" she said. "Of course. You're Ramnes, my dear friend!"

The group of slaves and servants shook with swift relief, then froze again at sight of Ramnes' face. He advanced, caught her arm, peered into her eyes.

"By the gods, what's wrong with you?"

"Nothing, nothing at all, dear Ramnes!" she rejoined. "What was all the noise about? I had a queer dream, but I forget what it was."

He drew back, staring at the enormous sheathed poniard. One of the women came forward, timidly opened the torn robe of Drusilla, who stood docile and unprotesting, and showed the scratch.

"Lord, he did it, and with this weapon that he put on her; he said he was making a slave of her."

A GROAN burst from Ramnes. The dagger of Eryx—there was damnable truth in the legend, as Pelargos had said! He looked at Drusilla, then at the slaves around, with terrible eyes.

"If any of those officers are still alive, kill them," he rasped. The group scattered.

Pelargos came striding up, blithely.

"Ha, comrade! Well fought; I showed up just in time. That rascal Mancinus must have special protection from somewhere; I missed him twice, and got him the third time, but it was too far for full effect. Not that he'll have any joy of the hurt—hello! Hello! What's wrong?"

He checked himself. Ramnes looked up, biting his lip, face livid, and pointed to the weapon. He reached out and took it from Drusilla's shoulder, and thrust it at Pelargos.

"There's your damned dagger. He scratched her with it. Before I got here."

Pelargos looked at him, looked at Drusilla, then turned and went to the servants. His voice rose at them.

"Leave us three horses. Take the rest, take what you like, and scatter. At once! In a few hours there'll be cavalry here to kill every living thing in sight. Scatter! Your mistress goes with us. We'll take her to safety. Clear out, pass the word to any others, and be off!"

He came back to the side of Ramnes and stood looking at Drusilla.

"Lady, do you want to go with us?" he asked.

"Of course," she rejoined. "I'll do whatever you say, dear Pelargos."

Ramnes shivered, stifled a growl of oaths, and turned away from her. The sunset was passing into twilight, the first stars were in the greenish eastern sky.

"Get us horses. Your helmet and spear," said Pelargos in a hoarse voice.

WHEN RAMNES returned, leading the horses, Pelargos was talking with Drusilla. He held out the dagger and baldric.

"Throw away the spear; it's served its use. Take this instead. The damned thing has a queer poise; in the hands of a Hercules like yourself, it'll be a terrible weapon. Well, what are you standing there gawking for? Did you get a taste of the dagger, too?"

With an effort, Ramnes broke the shackles of horror that gripped him.

"I don't know. This—this is too awful for words, Pelargos. To think of her as she was, and as she is now—"

"Well, make the best of it," said Pelargos roughly. "What was I saying to you today? Heartbreak and horror and despair; a man must come through these things, if he's a man. They hit

*"Aye, Drusilla, this
disdainful pride needs
a lesson. I'll cure you
of it, in the sight of all
men," said Mancinus.*

all of us sometime. Come on! Fight through! Maybe this spell
or poison will wear off in a few days."

"You know better," said Ramnes, and Pelargos swore.

"Yes, I know better. Apparently it hasn't worn off those
fellows in Reate. But she's not dead nor hurt, at least. She's not
lost her wits. She's just lost her will-power, it seems. Ah! I'd
give my left hand if that last bullet of mine had just gone twice
as hard! It went straight enough, but it lacked killing force.
Look here, comrade! I'll get some food and wine; she was to
have it ready for us, remember. I'll find it. You take her along
to where the other horses are, where Lars is coming. Maybe
Lars will know something about this deviltry. He may have
some suggestion. We'll get to Eryx—who knows? By that time,
she may be herself again. Fight! The time to fight is when the
hurt's the worst."

Ramnes nodded. He was himself again, but the hurt was
deep.

Deep, and unutterably stunning. For the first time, the wild
and furious exhilaration of battle had seized him, carried him
away. Pitted against picked officers, a dozen to one, he had
tasted the savage wine of victory—his own prowess supreme,

his skill and agility and brute strength flowing in a superhuman stream. All the fighting through the Alps had not been like this, nor left this tremendous realization of supremacy.

But now, now! It had flowed out of him in a minute at the touch of bitter grief. For Drusilla was like a child. She rode with him through the gathering darkness, talked, laughed and seemed herself, yet could make no effort of will, could concentrate on nothing, did precisely as she was told. He even tested her with his sword, and she would have slashed her arm had he not stopped her. To think of her, thus, and in the power of Mancinus who had sworn to shame her before the world, made his brain crawl with horror.

But now she was with him. This thought steadied him; she was a child, and he had her in trust. Rome, Rome! Hatred mounted again in him like a consuming flame. She had been treated as his own father had been treated. Not by Mancinus alone, but by Rome, the devouring wolf. Suddenly, as he rode, he recollected the ivory and gold casket she had taken for herself. He drew rein, turned her around, and they went back and met Pelargos as he was setting forth. He had, it seemed, dug his precious iron bullets from the corpses.

"Get the casket," said Ramnes, "and get a pot of fire from the hearth, to signal Lars."

The three of them rode, at last, to the thicket before the

cavern entrance. There Ramnes lit a torch and plunged into the depths of the grotto once more.

Back in the treasure-room, he looked about, and his eye lit on the small, curious little old casket of bronze; the sacred image of Aeneas, she had said. With a grim smile he plucked it up and went back to rejoin the others. Hatred, indeed! With this, he would take such a vengeance as would make the priests, the true lords of Rome, squirm bitterly!

They kindled a small fire. Drusilla ate, drank, wrapped up against the chill night, compliant with every suggestion, venturing no will of her own; until, of a sudden, a huge monstrous shape upheaved against the stars, came crashing in among the trees, and the voice of Lars Masena reached them in exultant greeting.

CHAPTER XII

AFTER ALL, Asculum proved an impossibility, due to the winding hill roads.

Pushing the horses hard in the wake of the vanished elephant, Ramnes and Pelargos kept on, hour after hour, riding silent and oppressed. In the cold clear grayness of the mountain dawn, a figure appeared on the road ahead. It was Lars, waiting and watching for them, welcoming them with acute relief as they dismounted.

"All well," he said. "The elephant? In a valley a few hundred yards off the road; there's the cart-track to the farm. Safe? Aye. An outpost of the Friends of Hercules; the farmer's one of us. The Lady Drusilla is asleep in the house. We must wait here till tomorrow night."

"Why?" grated Ramnes, who was in a savage mood.

"Because the big bull has not traveled for years; his feet are tender. He's quite tame and handles like a child, but I dare not push him too far. We're only five miles from Asculum. Once past, we're beyond actual Roman territory. I'll get past tomorrow night; there are mountain trails that go around the city. You go on tomorrow, and we'll overtake you in the course of the next morning, and head straight on for Eryx."

"Very well. We'll rest here till noon. Have your friend get someone here to take a message to Rome."

"Rome?" Pelargos blinked at him.

"Yes, Rome! A letter and a box. He'll be highly paid. No danger. Get some sleep first, then I'll write the letter."

The morning was half gone when Ramnes awakened. The farm folk were kindly, hospitable, greatly in awe of the elephant and the guests. Ramnes, with sheepskin and reed pen and fresh bullock's blood, wrote his letter and then read it over to his two companions; his voice was rough with hatred.

"I'll have the messenger leave it, with this bronze casket, on the steps of the temple of Jupiter," said he. "It's addressed to the priests; they'll consider it a miracle, no doubt. They'll know the casket's authentic! Here's the letter:

> *A gift to Rome from the gods; to the oppressor, to the doomed city upon whom falls the wrath of heaven. This relic is one of many things lost by the Senate and the people, through the greed of Lucius Mancinus. If you wish to know more, seek in Eryx. Seek with a sword and you shall find a sword, sharper than your own.*

"Well?" said Pelargos, wrinkling up his face. "Why?"

"I want Rome to know what she's lost!" said Ramnes. "They'll send to Eryx, never fear. The thought of the treasure and, greater, the relics—that'll burn deep! This relic of Aeneas, sent them in contempt and disdain, will prove my words true. They'll send."

"Like a stone from a sling!" Pelargos laughed, and his face cleared. "Right. Mancinus will be at Eryx too, remember. There's your man, here's gold; get it over with, see Drusilla, and let's be gone."

Ramnes arranged with the staring countryman, saw him off with the sheepskin wrapped securely around the casket, and forced himself to meet Drusilla.

It was bitter, yet his heart went out to her with a rush of pity and love; she was sweet and gentle, dazed, bewildered, accepting all with serenity. Ramnes steeled himself to the thought that the effects of the drug might be permanent.

An hour later they were off, with a guide, leaving the armor to be brought on by Lars. Ramnes took the huge dagger, for he was minded to use it as a weapon when the chance came. It fascinated and repelled him, yet in his hands its great weight would prove terrible.

When they were filing off along a narrow hill trail, Pelargos eyed him sharply.

"Comrade, do you realize that you've changed?"

Ramnes nodded. "Yes. No doubt for the worse."

"For the better. You're ten years older than you were yesterday; but the change is deeper than lines in the face. You've found yourself. You've begun to fight the whips of destiny. I can appreciate your feelings."

"Oh!" Ramnes gave him a look. "You think you can, eh?*"

"I felt the same way. When they blinded my wife."

The words came with a shock. "They? Who?"

"The Romans. There was a mistake; she was mixed up with other families of hostages. Some troops had revolted. The hostages were blinded or sold as slaves. They discovered the mistake and freed her, with the two boys. They tried to make amends and let her go. She went to Eryx. This did not help me particularly."

Oddly enough, this disclosure more than anything else helped Ramnes to adjust himself to facts. The simple words were eloquent of tragedy; he perceived what undisclosed deeps of suffering and experience lay beneath the boisterous talk and laughter of Pelargos. He could dimly see why this queer man was so secretive, having been so terribly hurt.

"Apparently," said Ramnes, "I have much to learn."

Pelargos laughed a little. "The best words I've heard you utter for a long time! By the way, I've learned that the priest of

Minerva, in Eryx, is also head of the city council. The priests of Hercules will fatten hugely on our appearance and the fulfill-ment of the prophecies; we'll have to win over the priest of Minerva as well. These two are the chief powers in Eryx. There are other temples, of course, to all the rascally gods of Greece and Rome, to heroes and demigods like Hercules; but these two are the city gods."

Ramnes nodded. He was thinking of that figure sitting beside Lars on the neck of the old elephant, smiling, beautiful with high nobility, stricken.

They hastened on; loaded or not, that elephant would go at twice their speed. All day they traveled hill roads, and with sunset came into a wider and more traveled highway. They were far past Asculum, said the guide, and showed them how the road would turn south toward the eastern sea, and where they would find the ravine and the river that pierced the hills and opened the way to Eryx.

PAYING THE man, they rode on into the evening, without incident, and into the long hours of the night, Ramnes driven by an insatiable desire to be at his journey's end—his brain feverish with a hundred conjectures and plans. In the cold north, the African army was wintering, ere driving at Rome. If this fantastic adventure succeeded, as he began to believe that it must succeed, all the future hope and destiny of Eryx must lie with Hannibal; there lay the death-blow to Rome, waiting!

AT DAWN, the road-fork appeared: A rambling roadside tavern and inn, the road striking off to the left. Ten miles to Eryx. A plunge through hills, out upon the farther marshes to the coast and the city there.

Pelargos pointed to the tavern.

"Wait here, sleep, rest. Tomorrow, go on with Lars and the big bull. Let the news go ahead of us. Remember, it will be only a week or two until Mancinus comes! The loss of the dagger won't worry him; Rome will come, and we must leave no stone unturned to meet Rome with the sword!"

Ramnes frowned. "Eh? You mean my message, my letter and the casket?"

"Oh, that!" Pelargos snapped his fingers. "Comrade, any result from that is a month or two distant. First our noble proprætor will strike. Never mind all that now; eat, sleep, be ready to welcome Drusilla! Our elephant must rest until tomorrow, also. There's a shrine and a grove, beyond the tavern—a good place for them. Be ready to meet them."

Ramnes nodded, drooping with weariness, and they turned in at the tavern. Ten miles! He wondered at the serenity and self-command of Pelargos, with heart's desire so close; he wondered how Lars Masena would look and act, with his own goal at hand.

Noon brought answer to the question: the seamed features of the elephant-trainer alight with eager joy and pride as the great beast padded in before the shrine, where Ramnes and Pelargos waited. The bull threw up his trunk and trumpeted in salute to Ramnes, then sank down. A number of country wagons had halted at the inn, the men holding their affrighted horses and staring slack-jawed.

Drusilla stepped lightly to the beast's shoulder, and Ramnes caught her as she came down, smiling. For a moment his heart leaped, for it seemed that she was herself again; then the hope was gone, as he looked into her eyes. She was weary, but showed only the docile spirit of an obedient child.

The three men fell to work loosing the burden. As Lars pointed out joyously, the bull was in good shape and thoroughly delighted with his change of scene. The African speech and ways, after his sedentary years, had brought back his youth, for an elephant never forgets; and with Lars Masena he was like some monster dog, scarce letting him out of sight. This huge beast from the Atlas, with his curiously segmented trunk

and his understanding of human ways, had a tremendous fascination for Drusilla, who could stand gazing at him or toying with him by the hour.

Lars stayed with the elephant. The others went to the inn, the country carts hastily rattling away at their approach. Drusilla was given a room, and Ramnes composed himself to patient waiting.

He and Pelargos, that afternoon, examined the dagger. To discover its secret was easy. One of the silver knobs in the gold haft sank in with pressure, and from a tiny aperture in the bronze blade, close to the point, oozed a drop of dark oily fluid.

"Some drug," said Pelargos, sniffing it. "Viscous and thick; it's been in the dagger for years, perhaps a century. That would explain the rapidity with which it works. For any proper miracle," and he sneered slightly, "you'd touch a person with this, and tomorrow or next day he'd show the power of the god! But now it works fast. A clever thing! Like some of the wonder-working statues I've seen in temples."

"An utterly damnable thing," growled Ramnes. He fingered the long golden haft, weighed it in his hand, nodded grudging approval. "At need, a cruel weapon in itself!"

"It'll serve, in such hands as yours. What's your first move, once Eryx is ours?"

Ramnes looked up. "To get a list of all Romans in the city."

"Lars can get that in ten minutes, from the Friends of Hercules. And then?"

"Expel them."

"Better to kill them; but you, unfortunately, aren't a god like Hannibal."

"If I were a god, Drusilla would be cured," said Ramnes gloomily. "No; merely a man in the likeness of a god, as you yourself said."

"With that bronze armor, you make a good imitation."

Ramnes cursed under his breath, and Pelargos changed the subject.

THAT EVENING the four of them were sitting at supper in the main room of the tavern, when there came a clatter of hoofs from the inn-yard. Pelargos went swiftly to the window and craned out, and came back, satisfied.

"A man and a woman," he said negligently. "Country folk."

The two came in, talking with the innkeeper. White as death, Lars Masena started up from his stool, then fell back again and hid his face in his hands, trembling violently. Ramnes twisted around. The two arrivals were in Sabine dress, the man a broad countryman, the woman very erect and shapely, holding her head high, a corner of her mantle over her gray hair. At sight of her face, alight and eager and shining with emotion, the truth flashed upon Ramnes, but he could not credit it.

"Is one of you named Lars Masena?" asked the countryman, saluting them.

LARS UNCOVERED his face and came to his feet. The woman looked at him, and he at her. Neither one spoke a word. Their hands went out, they fell into each other's arms with tears of joy, tears that crowded out all other thoughts. Drusilla, with her gentle smile, took them to her own room and left them alone.

"Oh, I had to fetch her!" explained the farmer, grinning widely as he sat and talked over a flagon of wine. He was one Faustus, the brother of Rhea. "She knew he'd be here, and she had to come."

"Indeed? A miracle!" exclaimed Pelargos, with caustic cynicism. "No doubt some god appeared to her with a revelation! Perhaps Phoebus himself, bidding her come!"

Faustus stared. "Eh? Not a bit of it. We heard all about you people yesterday. I belong to the Friends of Hercules, you know; we got word from Reate and Interamna about you. We've been expecting you. Our people in Eryx are expecting you."

Pelargos burst into a wild, shrill laugh.

"Ha! A miracle spoiled by common sense!" he cried, his eyes bright and burning, his face jerking. Suddenly he shoved back from the table so that it nearly overturned and came staggering to his feet, arms outflung. His voice rang hoarsely.

"Comrade, comrade! You've no need of me now. I'll take my horse and ride on, now, at once. There's no miracle for me, there's no work of the gods to aid a blind woman—"

With a rush, he was out of the tavern and gone, but Ramnes saw tears on his cheeks as he went, and sat quiet. Ramnes comprehended perfectly. Something, here at the last, had broken down the man's chill restraint; this meeting between Lars and Rhea, no doubt. Everything, so long pent up, had burst forth in wild impulse. So, in the night, went Pelargos ahead.

THE SUN was still low in the east when the first sight of Eryx broke upon them.

Rhea and her brother rode ahead, on horseback. Lars was perched on the elephant's neck; and behind, on top of the lashed load, Ramnes sat with Drusilla.

They were through the short but rugged hills. Here were the marshes, five miles of them stretching flat and brush-bare, crossed by the causeway and, where the river wended, a long bridge. On ahead, a white marble temple seemed hung in the sky. Drusilla cried out for the sheer beauty of it, and Ramnes nodded to her exclamations. Then it proved that the temple was on a hilltop, and on the other side of the hill, running down into the sea, lay Eryx, as yet invisible to them.

Not, indeed, until they came in between the low hills did the city open up, and all the gray sea beyond; it widened in a sudden vista of enchantment under the morning sunlight, a breath of beauty and life. The high walls and the gate, ahead; the sloping hillside of houses and shops and temples on beyond, running down to the curve of the bay with the warehouses and the wharves, with ships lying there and fishing-boats dotting the glittering waves past the island that formed safe harborage.

And all alive. The roadway, the gates, massed with staring people; the wide street on past the gate, thronged with crowds; voices in roar upon roar of greeting and welcome as the huge Getulian bull padded forward. Even to those who had ere this beheld an elephant, the actual presence of the beast was a marvel; the massive figure in flashing bronze, the smiling, dreamy-eyed woman at his side, were gods come to earth again, Hercules of old and the divine gray-eyed Athene, the Minerva of Etruscans and Romans. The shouts lifted in rolling unison from streets and crowded house-roofs and gateway.

Before the city gates were soldiers, and a group of priests

and old men. Ramnes sighted a figure towering in the background, and smiled with grim comprehension; he could see the hand of Pelargos in this reception.

"Stop before the gates," he said to Lars, as the name of Hercules reverberated in air. "Do you know what you're going to do with this brute of yours?"

Lars flung a grin over his shoulder. "Aye; give him an ocean bath. He's wild for it!"

Fronting the group of priests, the elephant halted, flung up his trunk at the bidding of Lars, and trumpeted mightily. Even the priests recoiled in an access of fear. Then he knelt, and threw back his trunk as Drusilla stepped on his head. It circled her, lifted her, and set her on the ground.

"Athene!" lifted the shouts. "Athene!"

Ramnes followed, the baldric and dagger in his hand. His gaze had already swept the priests. Most of them were priests of the Hercules cult, the old men were city elders; one priest with two attendants was apart from the others. A massive-bearded, dignified old man, with the figure of Athene worked in his robe. The priest, then, of Minerva or Athene, as she was known in Eryx.

"Welcome!" cried the chief priest of Hercules, as flowers pelted all around the two. "Welcome, Athene! Welcome, Hercules! Welcome to your city of Eryx!"

"You are very kind," said Drusilla, smiling.

Ramnes pushed past her angrily.

"We are no gods," he exclaimed. "This lady is named Drusilla. I am named Ramnes. No more of this nonsense about gods! I bring gifts for the priests of Hercules, on the beast yonder. We have come as the friends of Eryx, as the enemies of Rome; if it be the will of this city, I will lead her and secure her against the power of Rome as best I may. But, if the people of Eryx love Rome and welcome her yoke, then we go elsewhere."

FROM THE soldiers and the massed crowds arose wild yells, in an outburst of hatred and tempestuous emotion. "Away with Rome! Down with Rome!" But Ramnes, watching the priests and elders, saw the warmth and eagerness in their faces, and knew there was no question here.

"Where is the priest of Athene?" he demanded, and turned to the stately elder. "Here," said he, extending the baldric and massive dagger, "is something that in past ages the goddess is said to have given to Eryx. Now I give it to you, who represent her."

The priest took the dagger, his face alight, eager, shrewdly suspicious. His expression changed to one of wonder and awe. The crowd had fallen silent, staring curiously, hushed.

"The dagger of Eryx!" exclaimed the priest. He held it out. "Wear it, son of the gods! Wear it for Eryx!"

Applause and shouts welled up from hysteric throats.

UNDER COVER of the tumult, Ramnes spoke impatiently.

"I tell you, I'm no god! Once and for all—"

In the faces of the priests, he read a smile that checked him. The chief priest of Hercules broke in upon him with amused warning.

"Careful, careful! We understand each other; let us have no mistakes. Eryx has need of the gods, friend. Let us each give what the other most desires—eh? If you can give us aid against Rome, we welcome it and you. Get on your great beast again, follow us; there's a dwelling on the temple grounds for you. Agreed?"

In the face of the priest of Athene, Ramnes read confirmation. He broke into a laugh, and threw up his hand at Pelargos, who was grinning happily, holding up a half-grown boy in either arm so they could see over the heads of the crowd, a woman clinging to him. Ramnes took off the heavy bronze helmet, and pushed back his hair.

"Agreed!" he said, and caught one of the roses that came from the eager crowd, and turned to Drusilla. "Tribute, lady! Eryx gives tribute to beauty!"

She took the rose, thrust it in her hair, and smiled. The crowd yelled delirious applause; but Ramnes, glimpsing the face of Athene's priest, saw a flash of comprehension in those deep eyes. His heart sank, but he must see the thing through with good grace, and he handed Drusilla up to her perch again, and followed.

A procession sprang to life, heading through the gates. Priests, city elders, singers and dancers and musicians—no, thought Ramnes, decidedly the Stork had not wasted his time! We understand each other, eh? Those words delighted him, for in their significance lay much that was unuttered.

The temple of Athene was on the height. Below, overlooking the water, lay the more popular shrine of Hercules. For this the procession headed.

Ramnes caught the chuckles of Lars Masena, noted the dreamy smile of Drusilla, saw the tall shape of Pelargos appearing now and again. Eryx had need of the gods; let each give what the other most desires—eh? Shrewd words. Let the people think what they like. There was no deception, no illusion, so far as the rulers of Eryx were concerned; they, too, had bitter need.

He could see it all, as he swayed to the thrust of the beast under him, and stayed Drusilla, holding her hand, against the swing. Now the game was his to play, frankly and with a will, to play hard and all the way, Pelargos backing him, Lars and the Friends of Hercules backing him. Gold and treasure to those who had lack of it, promises here, threats and action there. When that stately priest gave him back the dagger of Eryx, the action was symbolic.

Eryx was his, was in his hand; he, the dictator, the tyrant as the term ran in Greek, the leader of the people—he, the symbol of power! The ragged barbarian from across the Alps had come to rainbow's end, a man in the likeness of a god, hailed as a god, given the power and glory and attributes of a god, leading this city and people against the oppression and greed and injustice of Rome—dream's end!

SUDDENLY HIS gaze met the smiling eyes of Drusilla, and a groan came to his lips; the heart in him turned to water, and the exultation died out of his face. He would have given it all, all, to make this woman herself again; and he could not.

He could not. His shoulders squared at the thought. But, by the gods, he could fight through like a man! And, looking down, glimpsing Pelargos above the heads of the yelling crowd, he waved his hand and caught an answering wave.

Pelargos understood—for was not the woman with him a blind woman?

CHAPTER XIII

FROM THE Friends of Hercules at Reate had come detailed intelligence: A column of cavalry alone, under the proprætor; three thousand of the Latin allies, with Roman officers. A quick, sharp stroke, aimed to catch Eryx by surprise and take the city at one blow. All heavy-armed troops, and mailed horsemen.

Now, from the temple on the hill, Ramnes looked down across the expanse of marshes and the long bridge. Pelargos was with him, and the elders of the city and the priests. As the glittering column pushed out along the wide causeway that led across the five-mile strip of marshlands, his eyes quickened and his pulses pounded. Here came Rome! The trumpets and the standards of Rome, marching to crush him!

For he was Eryx, now. Made *tyrannos* or leader of the city by popular vote, Eryx was his; and he, Ramnes, was Eryx, to stand or fall together. And here rode Rome, to crush him.

From the city to the bridge that crossed the river, midway of the marshes, was two miles in all. Out there was no indication of resistance. The bridge, that should have been defended, was empty. Here, close to the city, were gathered a thousand men, Sabines who had come in to serve against the conqueror they hated; they waited to be led forth, and with them was Lars and the elephant, the old Getulian bull, now clad in armor of leather and mail.

PELARGOS LAUGHED softly. His phenomenal eyesight pierced the glitter of that advancing column.

"A hundred men in advance," said he. "Half a mile in advance; scouts. Heading the column, a hundred Romans, by their standard. Five hundred archers, bowmen; all the rest, heavy-armed cavalry. They march well."

"Mancinus?" rapped out Ramnes.

Pelargos shook his head.

"Can't tell; no doubt, one of the officers with the cavalry, face hidden by his helmet."

"Can you see the boats?"

"I can, yes; but they can't!"

Now, as that long column with its baggage-carts filed down the causeway, where fifty men could march abreast like some glittering snake, Ramnes turned to the others, and in curt sentences showed them the plan of battle.

Along the sluggish stream, as though moored, lay the fishing-boats and other small craft of the city, on both sides of the long bridge. They were crowded with men; but covered over by tarpaulins, would appear empty. Half hidden by brush, they would not be seen readily, and would cause no alarm when the column discovered them.

"A working party attacks the far end of the bridge; the others attack the column, when I meet the Romans," he concluded. Faces brightened; a hum of applause went up.

Pelargos grunted as he eyed the glittering serpent:

"Make up your mind to lose our monster today, comrade."

"That may be," said Ramnes. "But if he serves his purpose, I'm content. Mancinus was a fool to stick to cavalry! One legion of infantry might have smashed us."

"He didn't know the gods were fighting against him," said

*"So you won't talk,
eh? Whenever you
make up your mind
to talk, call a guard
and send for me."*

Pelargos, grinning. "Time's close. Their vanguard is at the bridge. Better get to our places."

The priest of Athene, stately and serene, beckoned Ramnes to one side and surveyed him with gravely steadfast gaze.

"You asked us for help regarding the Lady Drusilla, who was pricked by that dagger you wear," he said. "Have the gods aided you?"

"No," said Ramnes, his face darkening. "There is no help. The wisest doctors have done her no good."

"Perhaps the gods can help, where men fail." The priest smiled slightly. "In the temple archives I've found some information regarding that dagger. I'll sacrifice at once to the gray-eyed Athene, while you fight; if the goddess favors you, bring Drusilla to me tonight."

Ramnes comprehended, and his heart leaped. Face alight, eyes ablaze, he caught the priest by the shoulders.

"I understand. Thanks, thanks a thousandfold! You'll be sure enough of me ere sunset!"

And with a vibrant shout to Pelargos, he was off to the waiting column below.

There they donned armor. All the population of Eryx lined the hills, tense and anxious, awaiting pillage and slaughter and slavery, or the victory that seemed impossible; they were hushed by the sight of the Roman columns, there in the sunlight. Lars stood by the waiting elephant, Rhea with him: Rhea now his wife, a stately splendid woman. Pelargos stooped to kiss his two sons, kissed the blind, smiling mother, and leaped to the shoulder of the kneeling elephant, a shield-bearer at his side, with a long buckler. Ramnes, armed, swung into the saddle and lifted the massive dagger, almost as long as a sword. With a surge and a yell from the waiting men, the elephant started off, and they after it: Footmen, light-armed, light-footed—men used to the treacherous sands and the marshlands. Ramnes headed them, the elephant at slow swing leading the way.

THERE WAS no haste; Pelargos had judged his time admirably. The long bridge was much narrower than the causeway, and the Roman column could cross but slowly. Mancinus had sent no heralds. With arrogant confidence, he had counted upon riding slap into Eryx, cutting down any opposition, and seizing the city at a blow.

At sight of the elephant and the slender force of infantry behind, the Roman column halted, and Ramnes could see Pelargos laughing with impish glee. The vanguard fell back. The glittering serpent took motion once more, flowing forward, constricting to cross the long bridge, and widening out twelve abreast as the horses clattered over. To all appearance the men of Eryx had neglected their best defense, at the bridge, trusting in the elephant and their infantry alone.

Pelargos leaned over to Ramnes.

"Going to talk? Any parley?"

"Talk with your sling," rejoined Ramnes grimly, and Pelargos laughed anew. He stood at full length as the great beast swung along, accustoming himself to the rolling lurch, his ancient Etruscan helmet increasing his height to superhuman proportions.

TWO HERALDS spurred forth from the Roman ranks, waving green branches. Two-thirds of that glittering serpent was across the bridge now, the elephant at slow lurch toward them, Ramnes and his crowding ranks at march behind. Discipline would count for nothing here, and he had deliberately ignored it, that Mancinus might have greater assurance.

Pelargos fitted bullet to sling, and his arm swung. He loosed his cast; a long throw, an impossible throw; but one of the two heralds flung out arms and toppled. A shrill, wild yell arose from the men of Eryx. The Roman trumpets shrilled and the squadron of bowmen spurred forward from the massed column, at charge.

The elephant quickened pace; Ramnes spurred; his men broke into a run. Only a few hundred yards now, narrowing each instant. Pelargos was in swift motion, swinging, loosing, swinging again. Men began falling in the Roman ranks. The archers were pouring forth their shafts, and the twanging hum of bowstrings lifted above the shouts and shuffle of feet.

Then suddenly the elephant lifted trunk in air and trumpeted, as his high bulk merged with the enemy. At this sound, at this incredible shape, the horses reared and fell into mad confusion and panic. He bore on and on, straight into the heart of that glittering serpent, and the result was horrible; the horses, breaking from the causeway, floundered in the marshes. Behind the elephant sped the men of Eryx.

And suddenly, from the rear, welled up terrible voices of dismay and death. The ambuscade was loosed; the men from the boats were attacking, and all that glittering serpent writhed in mortal agony.

Behind the elephant, Ramnes spurred hard, was into the clanging battle before he knew it. Shafts rattled and whistled, but riot for long; quarters were close; horses were plunging; bows were useless. Ramnes battered into the thick of it. The massy dagger was now a sword, now a club. It ran red with blood, crushing steel cap or breastplate with its weight, piercing with the blade. The men of Eryx stabbed horses, cut down the disorganized riders, sent the beasts to flounder in the treacherous mud alongside the road.

The archers were gone. Here were the Romans with their proud standard; then the standard was down, the little band scattered; Pelargos was swinging away, the elephant roaring with fury and pain. Javelins were in him, his trunk gushed blood; dying men stabbed up at his unarmored belly as he crushed them; but he went on.

Ramnes, enormous in that bronze armor, knew not that he was fighting. Few as they were, those Romans died hard. Repeatedly his armor saved him as he crushed his way on. With a wild scream, his horse reared to a javelin thrust. Luckily, men of Eryx were at hand, came rushing, aided Ramnes as his horse went down, and helped him to the saddle of a Roman horse whose rider was dead.

*Mancinus pitched
headlong, and Ramnes
scraped his sandal over
the beard-blurred face,
in open contempt.*

On, now, on among the Latins, the splendid cavalry trained by Mancinus. The elephant had slowed to a halt, but not before his bursts of trumpeting inspired panic among the crowded horses. Despite themselves, the cavalry were forced to break, to scatter from the road, to go floundering into the marsh—and there the light-footed men of Eryx cut them down almost at will.

And all the while, from the bridge where the glittering column was cut, lifted the tumult of death and destruction. The whole column knew now that it was trapped and doomed. The far end of the bridge swayed and was down under the weight of men and horses, with a splintering crash that rose above the clangor of arms and the shouts of men.

RAMNES RAGED like a fury through those ranks, seeking the figure of Mancinus, but finding him nowhere. His second horse was killed; he went forward on foot, crushing and stabbing, searching always for that lean cruel face and not finding it. Desperate, whole ranks of the Latins plunged their horses at the deceptive marshy ground. Others dismounted and made resistance. And in among them, from front and rear, tore the men of Eryx.

The elephant was down, a huge bulk sinking prostrate upon the slain. No weeping now for Lars Masena; a wild and terrible figure, he raged along with Pelargos. Ramnes came up with them, drunk with the battle-madness, smashing down resistance, cleaving the way for the men who stabbed, more drunk even than he with the wine of victory. Victory over Rome! The very thought of it was inconceivable, but here it was.

HERE AT last was the bridge, red with slaughter; the whole column was destroyed, armed men sinking in the marshes, horses screaming, the wagons and baggage captured; there beyond the bridge were a few score riders streaming along in flight. A few score; but among them was Mancinus, as was later proven.

Eryx had emptied itself for slaughter and pillage of those scattered in the mud. Ramnes halted this work with stern hand. Some hundreds of horses were saved; a scant two hundred prisoners were lined up. Ramnes, his bronze helm gashed and battered, blood on his face from a scalp-wound, panted breath into his lungs. Lars Masena was gazing at the dead elephant.

Pelargos limped up,—for his recent thigh-wound had opened afresh—his flitting eyes dancing from one to the other exultantly.

"Here's news for Rome!" said he.

"But the elephant is dead," Ramnes said. "Weeping, Lars?"

"By the gods, not I!" replied Lars. "He died well; who could ask more?"

"Something to that." Pelargos nodded thanks as Ramnes caught a horse for him. "There's always an elephant, of one sort or another, for the right persons. Next time, if there is such, something else will serve. What now, Ramnes?"

Ramnes glanced at the westering sun. "The greatest triumph of all, I hope," he said, and told them what the priest of Athene had said, about Drusilla. "First, a message to Hannibal from Eryx." He halted one of the city officers. "Look up those dead Romans; most of them will be of knightly rank and will wear gold rings. Collect all those gold rings for me."

"Ho!" said Pelargos admiringly. "An idea! Send them to Hannibal, eh?"

"Yes, with the alliance of this city. Rome passes, Rome passes!" The voice of Ramnes rose exultantly. "This is the beginning, and there shall be more ere the end!"

Together they headed for the city.

"Let me take your message to Hannibal," said Lars suddenly.

"If you like. But why?" asked Ramnes.

"I speak the tongue; I know you; I know him. Besides," added Lars, "Rhea wants to see the world; we'll go together."

Eryx was in a delirium of rejoicing. As Ramnes was met by the council of elders, an officer came hurrying, to inquire what disposition should be made of the prisoners; a few of these were Romans; the others were from Latin tribes.

"Scourge the Romans out of our territory," Ramnes said promptly. "Send the Latins home free, with word that our quarrel lies not with them, but with Rome."

So it was done.

A bath, a bandage for his head, a clean toga, and he wearily joined Drusilla. The sun was down; the evening meal was ready; Pelargos and Lars would be along presently. They too had a vivid interest in that evening's work.

Drusilla had heard the news of victory, but it brought no flush to her cheek. She could not be stirred to life; nothing mattered particularly to her. When the four presently walked up the hill to the temple of Athene, the riotous celebration on all sides left her unmoved.

"I understand," Pelargos said to Ramnes, "that they're giving you the old palace of the former kings, as soon as it can be fixed up a bit. Apparently they're satisfied that you're no friend of Rome seeking to betray them."

"You'll move in with me, in that case," Ramnes rejoined. "What I have, I owe to you. Better use some of that treasure, too; send men down the coast to other cities at once. We must raise a force of mercenaries. We need bowmen, slingers, munitions. Lars says we'll have plenty of fighters from the Umbrian tribes, when this news spreads. Also, we want ships."

"Oh!" said Pelargos. "Right. A dozen Roman galleys would bring the city to terms in no time. Plenty to do, eh?"

AT THE temple entrance the stalwart priest met them. He was the titular head of the temple, which had business interests in the city; the temple itself, and the worship of Athene, was entirely in the hands of priestesses. He led them into his own luxurious chambers, and slaves brought in cups and an amphora of excellent Cretan wine.

"Something of a rarity," said the priest, lifting his cup. "A pity to mix it with water.... Well, well, here's congratulations!"

"Did you invite us here for that?" said Ramnes impatiently.

"No, my friend. The sacrifices were auspicious; the magic power which the gods gave to this dagger of yours—"

"Suppose we drop all that talk," Ramnes broke in. "We aren't fools; we know the secret of the dagger. It's not magic power I want, but practical help."

The priest regarded him gravely.

"My friend, the conventions of religion conceal much that is practical; let us, for the moment, accept such conventions, as we do those of society. In the temple archives, I've unearthed an old formula of sacrifice and devotions, which appears to be a cure for the evil of the dagger." He lifted a hand to check a threatened outburst from Ramnes. "Wait! This requires certain herbs, which we have; the treatment and the devotions of the priestesses require a full six days. Leave the Lady Drusilla here with us for this length of time, and let us see what can be done."

Ramnes relaxed. It came to him that behind these words lay many unspoken things; this priest was not revealing all his secrets, by a good deal. He turned to Drusilla.

"Will you remain a week here in the temple, and let these good women try to cure you?"

"Certainly, if you wish it." She laughed softly. "But how can they cure me, when nothing is wrong with me?"

Ramnes did not answer this. He rose, touched his lips to her brow, and pressed the hand of the priest.

"Cure her, bring her to herself, and ask what you will of me."

"I'll send for you when the time comes," replied the grave priest, promising nothing.

HERE BEGAN a week of work into which Ramnes plunged head and ears; now that the Romans were not only crushed but destroyed, and his own power in Eryx was absolute, a host of things that had been pending were in need of action.

Lars and his wife, with an armed escort, departed in style to make search for Hannibal; and along with his message took close to a hundred gold rings worn by Roman knights; some of the bodies had sunk in the marsh, and the rings were lost. Rumors filtered through that the Africans were wintering north of the Apennines. Some of the prisoners said that two new consuls had been elected in Rome, Flaminius and Servilius, and that each of them was to be provided with an army before spring arrived; the republic was making agonies of effort to raise fresh legions.

With Pelargos ever at his elbow, Ramnes went at everything, from the defenses of the city, to the naval possibilities. The best defense on the land side, was the wide marsh; by water, the city was open to any attack. With the bridge repaired temporarily, with an outpost of guards established in the hills beyond, storehouses for grain were prepared and emissaries sent forth to start a flood of food-supplies moving toward Eryx. Envoys were sent to other cities beyond Roman jurisdiction, inviting them to join in a league against aggression. The nucleus of a fleet was prepared.

All of this, and a thousandfold more, could only be started under way in a week's time. Men from the Sabine tribes were flocking in to join the armed force. As the news spread, refugees from Rome began to dribble in from near and far. For many years Eryx had grown fat in peace; both the state and the people were wealthy, and there were vast resources of all kinds upon which to draw.

So, in those days, the work began—work of defense, of construction, of forward-looking to more evil times. Rome defied, Rome repulsed, was not Rome beaten, by a good deal, as all men knew; but in the background was ever the gigantic shape of Hannibal, and Rome must perish, or Hannibal must die. A good gamble, said Eryx, with freedom the stake! On every side Ramnes met with hearty, eager help and coöperation.

Before the end of the week the old palace, a rambling structure built in Cretan style, was turned over to him. Pelargos moved in, with his family; the two boys lent life to the ancient place; the mother was a quiet, kindly, simple soul, over whom Pelargos hovered with an unending care and affection. Slaves abounded and were cheap, but Ramnes was too busy to pay even superficial attention to the running of the palace.

O N T H E sixth day, Ramnes was down at the harbor most
of the afternoon, inspecting two galleys that were outfitting for
naval work. He came back weary and anxious, to find that no
word had come from the temple on the hill.

"They've been hard at it all day, with sacrifices and parties of
women going up there," Pelargos said cynically, forcing him to
relax over a beaker of chilled wine in the garden. "Be patient,
comrade; that old priest is a sly fox, and he'll get somewhere.
They tell me he's been back of many a miracle in his time, and
I don't doubt it. By the way, we've made a grand haul of arms
and weapons, in the spoil from the fight. I'm getting two com-
plete legions, Roman style, whipped into shape."

"Two legions? Why, that's an army!" exclaimed Ramnes. "I
had no idea we had such a force."

"Gold to soldiers, honey to flies," Pelargos said. "We'll need
an army before we get through. We need a few Carthaginians,
too, who understand fighting-ships. Well, we have two months
ahead, before spring arrives. A merchant came in from Ariminium today; he says that all the northern Gauls are solidly
behind Hannibal, and that spring will see a march on Rome.
The only trouble, to my mind, is that Rome will be ready."

"Two armies," said Ramnes. "Good wine! Where'd you get
it?"

"Temple of Hercules; always tap the temples for the choicest wine and women, as they say in the army. Hello! Here's
news."

Ramnes started up. A slave was coming to him, bearing a
scroll left at the entrance by a messenger. He opened it, stared
at it with a puzzled frown. Below one another were written
four Greek letters; at the bottom of the sheet, the words: *"Come
at sunset."*

"What is it?" demanded Pelargos.

Ramnes told him.

"Evidently from our priest. But what those letters mean, I
don't know."

"No hurry; we have half an hour to sunset. What are the letters?"

"*Zeta, Eta, Theta, Iota.*"

Pelargos slapped his long thigh with a burst of laughter, then sobered.

"Now, if that isn't like a priest—to hide behind allusions, avoid saying a thing in downright words…. Hm! I'm not so sure, after all. That man is wise. This may be his way of conveying a still greater idea, which he fears to put into words—"

Pelargos stared at the ground and muttered. Ramnes loosed an impatient oath.

"Well, speak up! Does this message make sense?"

"Oh!" With a quick smile, Pelargos came out of his brown study. "Comrade, if you were a Greek by birth, instead of a Roman with uncommonly good Greek tutors, you'd know. Those are the letters which on a Greek sundial represent the seventh to the tenth hour of the day, the four hours given to amusement and recreation. Put the four letters together, and you have the Greek word '*Live!*' In other terms, during those four hours of the day, live!"

"A H ! A hint that all goes well with her!" The face of Ramnes cleared. Joy, and the apprehension of joy, leaped in his heart. "She's responding to his treatment—he didn't want to raise false hopes—"

"No." Pelargos frowned at him. "Those three words at the bottom relate to her, comrade. "The other is for you. In the devious way of such fellows—liking you, yet unwilling to commit himself, our friend gives you a riddle of advice; a prophecy for the future, he'd probably call it. Live! It may be a greeting, an admonition, or a warning. Four hours of the day—four years of a lifetime—"

Ramnes broke into a laugh, tossed the parchment to the other, and sprang up.

"Hell swallow your croakings! Keep it, if it interests you."

"Thanks; it does." Pelargos caught it up. "Perhaps, after all, it's merely a hint to be yourself, to find other things in life than battle and power, to live more fully, to seek the deeper, simpler life of the soul."

Ramnes regarded the other curiously. "What! Philosophy again? Now that heart's desire is won, aren't you content to enjoy the winning?"

Tucking away the missive, the Stork came to his feet.

"Heart's desire won? It's never won, comrade. Gain one milepost, another looms beyond. Lars is gone, to show his wife the world; he'll come back with some new horizon, depend upon it! Now I have my family again, I think of my two sons. And you? That remains to be seen. There's more to you than the mere makings of a battling and brutal warrior—much more, and this priest knows it."

"Bah! Rome dies; I live!" said Ramnes.

"You've not begun to live yet. Well, forget all this, forget it!" Pelargos, with a laugh, throw off his sober air, caught up his winecup, and emptied it. "Drusilla awaits us—let's go! And here's luck, up above."

They tramped up the hill to the marble fane, faintly golden in the sunset glow; a sound of women's voices chanting a hymn came from the temple. The priest, evidently awaiting them, appeared. He merely smiled at the eager questions of Ramnes, and led them in to the central court, where stood an ivory and gold statue of the goddess. And there beside the statue was Drusilla, grave and starry-eyed—Drusilla once more herself, suddenly radiant at sight of them.

EVEN IN this instant of bursting joy and incredulity, Ramnes could but wonder at the odd depths of his companion, the queerly stifled affections of that devious and scoffing heart. For Pelargos, with a low cry, flung himself forward ahead of Ramnes, dropped to the stones, and caught Drusilla about the knees, in the Greek fashion of a suppliant—caught her and bowed his bald head, with a broken sob.

Above his figure, her hands went out to Ramnes, and her blue eyes greeted him. But he, taking her hands, stood silent and unmoving, his hungry gaze devouring her.

"They've told me everything," she said in her old rich voice, a trace of color rising in her cheeks. "Ah, Ramnes—all the evil dream and the shadows are past—"

His lips trembled; then as Pelargos drew away, Ramnes took her in his arms, and stood silent, her head against his chest, his tears of joy and thanksgiving and heart's desire sparkling on the knotted masses of her hair. Until, presently, her face lifted to him.

CHAPTER XIV

TO RAMNES, life was suddenly rich with new glory; now there was a reason for everything, a pulsing heart in everything. Drusilla was herself again, but herself as he had never seen her, for her grave dignity was all transfigured by the high excitement of their adventure here, and her cool gray eyes were radiant with laughter and eagerness of life and love. For this she did not deny.

"Marriage?" she said to Ramnes. "Yes, my dear, yes; when Rome comes and goes again, it shall be that same day."

"When Rome comes?" he echoed, perplexed. Her eyes danced.

"Yes. Do you think Rome will see her army destroyed here, and do nothing? She may be busy with Hannibal, in desperate straits—but you'll see envoys from the senate here. And don't forget the little bronze casket and the letter, of which you told me."

"Then," said he quickly, "is it a promise? The day Rome goes?"

"If you please me," she rejoined, and went into a peal of laughter at his expression.

Merry she might be, and turning back to girlhood as the days passed; but she supplied the sound practical wisdom that

*Septimus
swallowed hard.
"You could not do
that, Drusilla!"
he said hoarsely.
"You, a Roman!"*

Ramnes most needed now. In no time at all the domestic life
of the palace was organized and running smoothly as the household slaves were fitted into place. Her advice on most problems,
whether of public policy or private, was sound and wholesome;
and when it came to dealing with men, that gray gaze of hers
could unmask a rascal unerringly.

Drusilla never referred to the past but once, when Ramnes
brought her the ivory-and-gold casket containing the books of
the Cumæan Sibyl; then her eyes lit up, and she touched the
casket with reverent fingers.

"I'm glad," she said. "One day we'll have need of this."

Ramnes laughed. "How so? Can you open the box if you
need to look at the prophecies?"

"Better luck to keep the seals unbroken," said she, and put it carefully away.

From other cities came no pledges of help. They were all hanging upon events, afraid to provoke Roman enmity, and the agents of Rome were everywhere. Men came in, and a few ships, and great store of corn and supplies; and ever the men of Eryx stood stoutly behind all that Ramnes did, but it seemed that the whole world was now waiting for the thunderbolt of Africa to strike a death-blow at Rome, or himself to perish by the Roman arms. The Greek colonies and cities along this coast, the hill states, the Latin tribes allied with Rome—all were waiting, breathless. Upon the spring, when the African army would move, trembled the scales of destiny. Capua, the second city in Italy, was rumored to be ready to fling off the yoke and declare for Hannibal, if he were victorious. Meantime, all waited to see whether vengeance would strike Eryx, which had not waited.

RAMNES WAS at the city wharf the morning the galley came in from the north. With him were Drusilla and Pelargos, who had evolved a scheme of harbor defense: From the wharf to the island midway of the harbor was only a few hundred yards. If a causeway could be built and war-engines installed on the island, enemy ships would find Eryx a hard nut to crack. As they were talking, the big trading-galley came sweeping in for anchorage, and was seen to be crowded with armed men.

Boats swarmed about her. The first put in for the city wharf. Pelargos cried out:

"I know that man! Look, Ramnes! It's Giscon, one of Hannibal's engineers—remember the fellow who froze water in the rocks and blasted them apart, there in the Alps? And those are troops in the galley; I see the scarlet of the Spanish infantry, the Berber robes, and the Numidian uniforms…. Ha, here's word from Lars! But Lars isn't in the boat."

The news spread, and all Eryx began tumbling out to see and welcome the Africans. The boat came straight to the city wharf, and Ramnes clasped hands with the dark, bearded Giscon, who wore the purple and gold of Carthaginian nobility.

When he had met and saluted Drusilla, Giscon turned to the others, laughing.

"So this is why you deserted us, Pelargos! Well met, Ramnes. All's well; Hannibal sends you greetings and congratulations. I've letters here from him. Lars Masena is well, and remaining with the army for the present. Here are two hundred men, a mixed contingent, and my humble self at your service. By Moloch! Your city is buzzing!"

PEOPLE MASSED at the waterfront, riotous with delight. Here was token at last of aid and support; the mere presence of a handful of Africans was a tremendous thing, a visible indication of the forces that were tearing Rome asunder.

Ramnes sent off an aide to summon an immediate meeting of the council in the public square.

"An open gesture to all Italy," said Giscon. "I've a nice little speech ready; and for your ears, private words. They'll keep."

His speech, delivered to the council amid the massed thousands, and the drawn-up ranks of African troops, was simple enough—congratulations on being rid of the Roman yoke, full assurances of support and help, and an invitation to formal alliance. Ramnes welcomed him and his men to Eryx, then got his guest away to the palace gardens.

There he and Drusilla and Pelargos glanced over the letter from Hannibal, and Pelargos made the dry comment:

"Two hundred men—ha! Trust a Carthaginian not to spend them unless he gets a thousand in return!"

Giscon broke into laughter. "Precisely; a thousand is what the chief wants, and you with them. In a month, he's breaking winter quarters and smashing directly through the Apennines toward Rome."

"By what route?" Ramnes asked.

"Straight through; one that's never been trodden by man."

"That's an impossibility!"

Giscon smiled. "So the Romans think. Hannibal, his brother Mago, Maharbal and I alone know the plan; there's token of his trust in you! The Romans are exerting every effort, draining every colony and city, to raise men. They're putting two armies in the field, and Hannibal expects to destroy one or both, then march straight on Rome. For these two hundred men, he wants a thousand—and *you*. The Gauls of northern Italy are with us, and your example will start a revolt among the other cities of Italy."

"He must need allies badly," Pelargos observed with a shrewd thrust.

Giscon nodded. "We do. No help has come from Carthage; Roman tactics in Spain have prevented help coming from there. We don't expect much from Carthage, in fact, as political factions there are against us. It's a one-man war, until we smash a way into Rome itself. I must know whether you'll leave, one month from now, and take a thousand men to meet Hannibal; if not, I must send back word."

"Count it done," said Ramnes, and Pelargos nodded assent.

IT WAS three days later that Drusilla caught the spy.

The whole city was possessed by a flaming enthusiasm; for Giscon, taking charge of the defenses, announced that the place could be made impregnable. On the land side, the vast marshes could be made into an impassable bulwark. On the water side, the island in the harbor could be the basis for an engineer's dream, if it were sufficiently provided with military engines. These had to be built, and a causeway had to be built to the island; Giscon was at work from dawn till dark with assistants and plans, while Ramnes got the labor started. Pelargos was occupied with the troops alone.

Ramnes had established headquarters on the long city wharf. He was at work there, late in the morning, making a chart of the harbor depths that Giscon wanted, when Drusilla came hurriedly, accompanied by two of the palace slaves.

"Hello!" Ramnes leaped up from his work, at sight of her white face. "What's wrong?"

"A man," she said, breathless. "I saw him in the market as we were buying provisions. He has a stall there—one of the country folk from the hills."

Ramnes smiled. "Anything wrong about that? The folk come flocking in each market day."

"This is a freedman of Mancinus. He was with Mancinus before—before you came. He used to come to the villa on errands for Mancinus."

Ramnes whistled. He perceived instantly the perilous possibilities in allowing these country people to come flocking into the city. He beckoned two of the guard officers.

"Close the gates, Achillas, and check up on every stranger in the marketplace; no folk from outside are to come in after this except with passes. See to it. You, Criton, come along with six men. Now, Drusilla, show us this fellow."

THE BIG public market was swarming with city folk, fishermen, farmers, soldiers, seamen. Drusilla described the stall in question, one where milk and cheese products were sold by a long, lean fellow in peasant garb. Criton and his men worked quietly around, and with no commotion nabbed their man....

The prison chambers of the old palace were gayly gruesome, artists of old having decorated them in the antique Cretan style with the frescoed monsters, bull-fight figures, and fantastic shapes of the island mythology, but here with a turn for the horrible. One of the cells in particular was given over to monsters of the sea, and here Ramnes chose to receive the prisoner, Drusilla at his side.

Chained, the man was led in. One glance at Drusilla, and a spasm of fear shot through his eyes, and Ramnes saw it.

"Well, Aulus, you see we recognize you. Mancinus sent you?"

Aulus squared his shoulders, and his jaw set stubbornly.

Ramnes smiled.

"So you won't talk, eh? Ready for torture, no doubt. Perhaps you recognize this?" He took the dagger of Eryx from its sheath, and saw a flitting horror come and go in the hard brown face. "You realize, then, that I've only to scratch you with the point, and you'll talk, eh? Well, time enough for that. Now think it all over. Talk, and you'll be set free, with gold in your pocket and protection against Mancinus if you want it. Whenever you make up your mind to talk, call a guard and send for me—that is, unless I decide to give you a touch of the dagger, make you talk, and then send you to Mancinus."

He gestured to Drusilla, and walked out. The guards followed. The door of the cell clanged shut. Out in the gardens, Drusilla turned swiftly to him.

"Why did you do that? What will you do—torture him?"

Ramnes shook his head. "Chances are, it wouldn't break him down; he's ready for it in his own mind. But he's not ready for—nothing. He knows the dagger, and fears it horribly. He knows he'll get rewards and protection if he talks. By tomorrow night, he'll talk."

"Why?" Her gray eyes searched him, and he laughed.

"Hunger and thirst, the pictures on the walls, the uselessness of being stubborn! But chiefly, thirst. A man who knows what to expect, can face it. He doesn't know."

That day a dozen men in the marketplace were clapped under restraint—men who could give no account of themselves. Four of the dozen were guiltless enough, as was proven by the following night, when Aulus talked, broken by thirst.

Eight men and himself, planted here in Eryx. Mancinus was coming with an embassy from Rome, in another three days, coming in disguise, as a slave, bearded and unsuspected. Once in Eryx, he meant to act. How? This, Aulus did not know.

THREE DAYS! Ramnes sat that evening with Drusilla and Pelargos, his brain burning.

"Three days!" he said. "Then I have him trapped. Let him come!"

"Why?" said Drusilla.

"Why? By the gods, you ask why?" exploded Ramnes violently, irritated by the silence and the flitting birdlike looks of Pelargos. "For what he did to you. For what he is. For what he comes here to do—assassination, at least. With nine men who know the ins and outs of the city, he no doubt plans to kill me, perhaps carry you off. What do you expect me to do—forget everything and do nothing?"

There was a little silence, while Drusilla sat frowning at her lap.

Pelargos nodded.

"I understand, comrade. I used to lie awake nights thinking of what I'd do to the executioner who blinded my wife, if I ever caught him. Cost me quite a bit to find out just what man it

was. Then he came up with a detachment to join the army in
Gaul."

Drusilla glanced up quickly. "And—"

"I caught him," said Pelargos. "Got him outside the camp
one night, built a fire, and had a pot-hook at white heat, ready
for his eyes." He shook his head and sighed. "No go; the rascal
whined and blatted like a squealing pig. I decided I wasn't petty
enough to get down to his level; I let him go. All I got out of
it was three days confined to barracks for being absent without
leave."

Ramnes rose and stalked away with a growl of oaths.

DURING TWO days, he fumed and exulted at thought
of Mancinus walking into the trap, and avoided the eyes of
Drusilla when they questioned him. On the third day, he rode
out of the city with the fifty Numidians of Giscon's party, giving
no word to anyone.

They crossed the marsh, wound up the river-gorge beyond,
and so came at last to the outpost of guards and the highway.
A messenger from the Friends of Hercules at Asculum had
arrived with warning that Romans were on the way.

"I know it," said Ramnes. "Take on word to the city, and say
that envoys of Rome are here. Tell the city fathers *to* be assembled in the square, in two hours."

It was nearly noon when the party came riding up to the
defile. An escort of fifty troopers from the Reate camp, two
stern-jawed Romans of senatorial rank with slaves and servants
and baggage-animals, and a long-faced but pleasant man of
fifty with twinkling eyes and an air of keen intelligence, whom
Ramnes recognized instantly from boyhood days. One Septimus, a priest of the Capitoline Jove, a man of family and influence even then, and now no doubt of great importance in Rome.

At sight of the guards and the Numidians, the party halted
in evident dismay. Ramnes, who wore no armor, rode out to
meet them, and the priest hailed him.

"Greeting! You don't remember me?"

"Quite well, Septimus, as I see you remember me," rejoined Ramnes.

"Here are the noble senators Quintus Rufus and Publius Stentor, envoys from Rome to Eryx and its lord."

"They're welcome. I'm the lord of Eryx. Apparently you're in bad company." Ramnes dismounted, and strode forward. "Better keep those troopers of yours very quiet; my Numidians are so used to killing Romans on sight that it would be a pity to provoke them."

The astonished party stared at him. Ignoring the leaders, he boldly broke in among the horses and looked at the slaves. There was the man he sought, new-bearded but unmistakable, hat pulled over eyes. Ramnes came up to him and put out a hand to the horse's bridle.

"Why, here's a queer thing!" said he, mockingly. "A man among your slaves, who used to be a great fellow at Reate! Careful, slave, careful! Put hand to weapon, and I'll tear you apart with my bare hands—and like the job!"

His voice rolled in unuttered fury.

The whole party had fallen into dismayed consternation. The troopers were far outnumbered by the guards and Numidians—those famed African horses, whose very name spelled terror to Rome. Also, the perfect assurance of Ramnes in going straight to the disguised propraetor revealed amazing knowledge.

"What, no answer?" His gaze drove up at Mancinus. "Good cousin, no voice? The Lady Drusilla was speaking of you only yesterday. So were others. In fact, there is some argument as to whether you'd be better impaled before the city gates, or crucified in your slave's garb. Personally, I don't think you worthy of so much trouble—"

MANCINUS' DESPERATE eyes flickered warning, and barely in time. His hand slipped out and a dagger lunged for the throat of Ramnes—who caught the wrist and stepped back sharply.

Mancinus, jerked from the saddle, pitched headlong and lay

quiet, stunned by the fall. So swiftly did it all pass, that before anyone knew what was happening, Ramnes had scraped his sandal across the beard-blurred visage in the dust, with open contempt.

Then he walked out of the group and looked at the two senators.

"Romans, you're welcome; bring your message to the men of Eryx. Send back your escort with that rascal who disgraces the name he bears; no Roman soldiers are allowed on the soil of Eryx, though there's room beneath it for plenty of them."

Rufus, whose reddish hair proclaimed the name, found tongue.

"Are you the son of Marcus Gaius Mancinus, the traitor?"

Ramnes met the cold, hostile eyes with gaze equally cold and hostile.

"Envoys who lend themselves to treachery would do well to choose their words with care. I am Ramnes, the lord of Eryx. Send back your escort; you've nothing to fear except your own dishonest hearts."

The two senators were livid with futile rage, but the priest Septimus was smiling thinly as he listened.

So Ramnes, at the head of half the Numidians, rode back along the causeway. After him came the Romans and their servants, the rest of the Numidians bringing up the rear. To the crowding thousands who massed to watch the entry into the city, and who greeted the cold-eyed envoys with silence or occasional jeers, Rome rode with the bearing of slaves rather than of conquerors.

IT WAS a Roman message, however, that Quintus Rufus delivered in the public square, where the city elders sat in their chairs and the sea of people thronged every foot of space back to the housewalls. Disdaining Ramnes and Drusilla, who sat before the fathers, with Pelargos and Giscon standing beside them, Rufus addressed the council.

"City fathers, you have lifted the sword against Rome. I see that you have also welcomed the enemies of Rome, although the senate knew nothing of this when we started. Mindful of ancient friendship with Eryx, the senate and the Roman people are willing to avert the doom into which the gods seem ready to plunge you. They offer you the choice between peace and alliance with Rome, or utter destruction of your city and its very name. Choose."

"Peace and alliance?" quavered one of the city fathers, in the silence. "Upon what terms?"

"That the traitor to Rome who rules you be sent in chains, together with five hundred of your maidens and five hundred of your young men, to the senate; that you hand over your walls and strong places to a Roman garrison, and pay such tribute as may be imposed upon you."

These words did not at once reach the people, who understood Greek better than Latin, but enough comprehended so that a growl rose ominous and deadly through the crowds. Then Ramnes broke out into sudden laughter, and turned to the African beside him.

"Hear that, Giscon? There's Roman peace and alliance for you! I have a better name for it. Slavery!"

A yell, fierce and savage, pealed up and up from the vast crowd. But the chief of the council rose and held up his arms, and gained quiet again.

"I thank you for the message, Roman," said he. "For this night you are the guests of Eryx, while we deliberate upon our answer. Tomorrow morning, you shall have it."

Rufus assented, which was a bit strange; Rome usually brooked no delay. But, as the visitors were marched away under strong escort, one of their slaves found his way to the side of Ramnes and spoke softly.

"Lord, Septimus the priest desires private word with you."

"I shall send for him tonight," said Ramnes, nodding.

Pelargos chuckled when the slave departed, and winked significantly.

Fleeing folk scattered in terror at
sight of the armed men.

"Here's the result of your little casket sent to Rome, comrade! Now we'll get the real gist of things. It's always the same with these rascals; a big play for publicity and underneath it a secret arrangement with those on the inside!"

Drusilla spoke up quietly. "Ramnes! I want to hear what Septimus has to say tonight. He's actually the greatest influence in all Rome."

Ramnes looked at her, with a quick springing smile.

"You shall not only hear, but have the whole say, my dear! And don't forget your promise—today Rome has come, tomorrow Rome goes!"

She touched his arm gently.

"But today, dear Ramnes, you have the answer. I heard what happened—with Mancinus. And now I'm really proud of you."

Whereupon Ramnes leaned forward and kissed her—in sight of the whole city council and the massed population of Eryx.

And at this, all Eryx fell to cheering madly, for the Greeks loved lovers.

CHAPTER XV

SEPTIMUS THE priest was affable, urbane, polished; in a word, the finer type of Roman whose education and broad culture differentiated him from the harsh, rude, primitive type of hardbitten yokel that had founded Rome.

He could not take his eyes from the table, and Drusilla watched him with a trace of amusement in her face. Ramnes and Pelargos sipped their wine and waited, not quite comprehending the tremendous effect Drusilla had produced on the visitor. For, when she laid on the table the ivory-and-gold casket brought by her from the Sibyl's cave, the effect was instant. No words were needed. Septimus, trained in all priestly mysteries, knew at one glance what this casket was, and what its presence told by implication.

With an effort, he collected himself.

"Someone sent a certain bronze box to Rome," he said. "No need now to ask who sent it."

"You mistake," Ramnes said dryly. "I sent it."

Septimus lifted his head and looked at Ramnes.

"I was sent to ask why," he said gently.

RAMNES UTTERED a harsh laugh; a cynical smile touched the lips of Pelargos; for those words revealed much, as they were meant to do. To the priests and the wise men at Rome, the little bronze casket must have come with staggering import.

For it showed them that the vanished treasures of their ancestors, the sacred things of religion and history gone since the Gauls sacked Rome, whose very loss had been so carefully concealed from the people—that these things were no longer lost. It was no question of treasure alone, but of things more valuable to Rome than any treasure.

And the sight of this ivory-and-gold casket, containing the Sibylline books which were the very essence of Roman veneration and superstition, confirmed the belief.

"Your priests," said Ramnes, "hid away the most sacred things of Rome; and whoever hid them, died. How they became lost, I don't know or care. And what did Rome do? Condemned to infamy and exile one of its truest sons and best soldiers—my father. Why? Because he chose to save Roman lives rather than destroy them in useless combat. One of its best soldiers, Veturis, died from his wounds in Gaul. What happened to his daughter? Rome betrayed her: the senators of Rome tricked her, mocked her, handed her over to the lust and outrage of the vindictive scoundrel who inherited my father's name and place. Rome honors him. This morning I wiped my sandals on his face. And the daughter of Veturis sits here in Eryx, with the secret of all your lost treasures in her heart. I, too, know that secret."

Septimus nodded with an air of regret.

"And I've come to you, begging, as you knew someone would come."

"Precisely," said Ramnes. "You can return and tell Rome—or the colleagues who run the religious affairs of Rome—that the son of Marcus Mancinus has all they lack."

"You were a boy in Rome," said Septimus thoughtfully. "In your heart you must have some veneration for all these things represent."

"To me, they represent Rome," Ramnes answered. "I saw my father's life wrecked, his heart broken, because of Rome's cruelty. I give cruelty for cruelty, hatred for injustice, enmity for tyranny. That's my message to Rome."

"Were your father sitting here tonight," Septimus said softly, "what would he say?"

A shrewd query, and it was his closest bid for success. It did move Ramnes for an instant; then his eyes hardened, as only Roman eyes could do.

"He's not here—which is Rome's fault. I am—which is Rome's misfortune!"

"I believe you," said the priest, and gestured as though to brush aside light talk. "We're practical people, all of us; and practical persons, Lord Ramnes, seldom find it profitable to indulge rancor and animosity. I must admit that I scarcely blame you or the Lady Drusilla for cherishing this resentment; however, what's past is past. There are larger aspects of the whole matter to consider. I should inform you that I have practically unlimited authority to make whatever engagements seem best to me."

HE PAUSED and sipped his wine appreciatively, to let these words sink in.

"Lucius Mancinus, your relative," he went on, "is not a particularly valuable asset to Rome; in fact, he is being ordered to join the armies in the field at once, where he'll command the cavalry. You, on the contrary, might be a highly valuable asset. It should not be difficult, for example, to re-open the old charges against your father; to wipe them out and clear his name, to grant him posthumous honors and to confirm you in those honors. An election to the rank of military tribune, by way of example, would be an excellent way of showing public appreciation."

"For what?" said Ramnes derisively.

"For, shall we say, justice?"

"I am justice. In Eryx."

"Ah, you damned Roman!" Septimus laughed and shook his head. "Have you no price?"

"Hatred," said Ramnes, looking at him fixedly. "To the death."

Septimus turned, with a whimsical gesture. "Can't you persuade him, Drusilla?"

"I agree with him," she said quietly. "Do you think for a minute I'd trust Rome—ever? My future lies here in Eryx."

"So?" And Septimus pursed his lips. "Not, perhaps, such an

indefinite future as you think, Drusilla. After all, there's a good deal of truth in what Rufus said this afternoon; making due allowance for publicity, I'm afraid Rome must move to destroy Eryx."

Drusilla smiled. "Indeed! That's why I brought out this casket. No doubt you're already aware that it contains the Sibylline books. The seals, you see, are intact."

LIGHT DROPS of sweat bedewed the forehead of Septimus.

"I'm glad you venerate the holy relics—"

"Venerate them? Nonsense," broke in Drusilla. "This is a beautiful box, and I love it. I shall take good care of it, and only I myself will know where it's hidden, so there'll be no chance of anyone getting at it. And on the day a Roman army appears, I'll break the seals, Septimus; when the first Roman soldier sets foot in Eryx, I'll destroy the contents of this coffer. Tell that to Rome!"

Septimus swallowed hard. The beads of perspiration increased on his brow.

"You could not do that, Drusilla!" he said hoarsely. "You, a Roman!"

"I'm no Roman," she declared. "Tomorrow, when you're gone, Ramnes and I are to be married. I think Eryx is safe from Rome—for a little while."

Pelargos was grinning with admiration. Ramnes, now seeing what Drusilla must have planned from the first, regarding this casket, chuckled softly. The expression of Septimus was eloquent.

Drusilla went on quietly:

"Out of all the treasure that Rome hid, this was the greatest and holiest thing. There were many other ancient things and symbols of the gods; some we left hidden, some we gave to the priests of Hercules here. There's much of the treasure left untouched."

"Oh!" Septimus gave her one rapid glance. "You gave some away, eh? Then it's no secret that these things exist."

"No secret. Ramnes wears the armor of Porsena of Clusium, for example."

Ramnes, about to speak, checked himself and relaxed. This affair had been resolved, he perceived, into an encounter between Drusilla and the Roman.

"The books of the Cumæan Sibyl!" murmured the priest, his eyes on the casket, the pupils distended, his breath coming fast. He could not dissemble the agitation that gripped him. "The sacred books—the key to Rome's fortunes! Now is when Rome needs them most, now in this hour of crisis!"

"I think she'll need them worse before another year," said Drusilla.

Septimus reached for his wine, sipped it, and mopped his brow.

"The things still untouched," he said in a thick voice. "Tell me—what do you want? I have full authority. I can promise you anything, anything!"

"Dear Septimus, you'll have to trust me to keep this casket and its contents in my own hands," Drusilla said sweetly. "You can trust me, you know. But do you think that anyone on earth would trust you—or the promises of Rome?"

He was slow, in his agitation, to get the finality of her words.

"But I can perform them, carry them out!" he exclaimed. "I tell you, I have full power to act! The College of Augurs, the chief priests in council—"

He checked himself.

DRUSILLA SMILED. "They have given you full powers—precisely! Very well. Go back to Rome and restore Marcus Gaius Mancinus to his name and rank, with posthumous honors."

"At once! At once!" the priest exclaimed. "And then?"

"Then come back; and I'll make a bargain with you for the

balance of the sacred relics. Not this casket, mind. Not the treasure; that goes to Eryx, or elsewhere." Her eyes lifted to Pelargos and to Ramnes. "Do you agree or not?"

"Your game," said Pelargos in delight.

Ramnes assented with a gesture. She looked at Septimus, and his head came up.

"Very well," he said, and sighed. "You drive a hard bargain."

"A harder one, dear Septimus, before you get anything. I want to see the decree of the senate clearing the name of Marcus Mancinus before we even begin to talk terms. That is all."

And it was all.

"He'll be back," declared Pelargos, with his peculiar impish glee. "Oh, he'll be back! Spite of war and battle, politics and earthquake, he'll be back to bargain for even the least of those sacred things! Drusilla, I salute you. It was admirable. Now we can leave you and Eryx in perfect safety. Rome would never risk the destruction of what's in this casket; you've got those superstitious rascals by the neck! But, may I inquire what you propose to gain by bartering anything at all?"

She looked at Ramnes. "You're not angry? I know you swore that Rome should never have anything from that treasure—"

"My dear, it's yours, and whatever you do with it suits me!" broke out Ramnes, laughing. "But I admit I'm curious, too."

"Well, I've practically got your father's name cleared of dishonor," said she. "And you and Giscon were saying yesterday that if you had certain war-engines which only experts could make, and ten really good two-banked war-galleys, we'd be impregnable by sea—"

Ramnes caught his breath. "Girl! By the gods, it'd be magnificent! But they'd never do it. They'd never give up what would be used against them."

"Bah! She's right, comrade," Pelargos exclaimed. "Take a bully like this Roman, or like some of those blasted thickheaded Germans up on the other side of Gaul, and there's only one way to gain his respect; by kicking him. That goes for any uncultured barbarian. The more you kick him, the more he'll do for you. He understands nothing else; he was raised on it at home. Give up their ships? Of course they will. Won't they gain the favor of the gods by doing so?"

IN THE late sunlit morning, all Eryx crowded the public square and the houses and roofs around it. Flowers were everywhere, for these gardens by the warm Adriatic held flowers at all seasons. Word had spread abroad that when Rome left, the shrine of Diana was to witness a ceremony that spelled fiesta for the whole city, and Eryx loved festival.

The city fathers were in their seats. Drusilla and Ramnes, amid roaring plaudits and showering blossoms, took their places, and the two senators of Rome came with grimly solemn tread. The senators saluted the fathers; Rufus asked if the reply to Rome were ready.

"It is ready, noble Rufus," said the chief of the council. "It will be given you by our lord Ramnes."

Rufus, thus forced to acknowledge the master of Eryx, turned to Ramnes, who beckoned an attendant to bring forward a packet wrapped in leather.

"The reply of Eryx," Ramnes said, "to the senate and to the Roman people."

Rufus opened the leather wrapping, while all the ranks around craned to see what this sort of reply might be. Two naked swords were revealed—Roman swords, relics of those Romans who had fallen in the attack on the city. Rufus started back, livid with fury, while laughter and cheers swept through the jammed sea of people, in a roar of voices.

So Rome came, and went again....

That evening in the sunset Pelargos stood on the sandy beach of the harbor, with his blind wife and the two boys, who were stripping for their evening swim. He gazed seaward, and presently, as the swell of hymeneal chants came from the temple of Diana above, he fell to staring at the horizon. The two boys questioned eagerly what he saw there, and he smiled.

"What do I see there? Why, my sons, that's a hard thing to answer. It looks to be a man, in the likeness of a god, who has gained all of heart's desire—only to find that instead of the road coming to an end, it is barely beginning."

CHAPTER XVI

THE THOUSAND were filing out of Eryx—some city men, but mostly Sabines, eager to be in at the death of Rome—a thousand cavalry, splendidly equipped and mounted. And, with them, certain others who were to return ere long.

These last weeks had seen feverish activity in the city. Now the mole out to the harbor island was nearing completion; in the workshops men were laboring on various parts for war-engines; and other squads were completing Giscon's plans for the marsh defenses.

"We can well leave Eryx," said Pelargos, as he and Ramnes waved farewell to the white figure of Drusilla, and set their horses to the road. "She's safe. The city loves her, Giscon has a shrewd head, and that ivory casket of hers will prevent any Roman raid for the present. Trust her!"

"Aye, even at the worst," assented Ramnes. "Even if Hannibal is now destroyed, even if the weight of Rome crushes him and us."

Pelargos chuckled. "Gloomy heart at leaving wife? Think of fame ahead! Fame and glory and the plunder of Rome—not to mention the remainder of that treasure we'll send back."

"Fame and glory be damned," said Ramnes. "I've had my fill. But Rome? Aye!"

To empty that cavern of treasure and send it back, to ride with a thousand men through the heart of Umbria, was by no means so mad as might appear. Of late, news had come in from all quarters, and a very carefully phrased letter had arrived from Lars Masena.

NOW, THIS spring, was the death-grapple; Rome knew it, Hannibal knew it, all Italy knew it. Africa must be destroyed on the Tuscan plains, or Rome must go down to ruin. To put armies in the field, refusing to call back her legions from Spain, Rome had stripped her Latin allies and the hill states of every available man. The huge training-camp at Reate was empty, every city and town was empty. The suspense everywhere had become intolerable; all business, commerce, political activity, hung upon the issue with bated breath.

The letter from Lars, so couched as to do no damage if the courier fell into Roman hands, gave explicit instructions. Ramnes was to bring his thousand back to Reate, then on to the Cassian Way and north to Clusium, below Lake Trasimene; there, Lars would meet him. Hard riding would do it handily,

Suddenly, the ambuscade was loosed; the men from the boats were attacking, and all that glittering serpent writhed in mortal agony.

and the hill cities would have no warning, no time to levy men to stop him.

Also, hinted Lars Masena, any gold that could be spared would be welcomed by the chief.

"So the armor of Porsena returns to Clusium, where it originated!" Pelargos laughed thinly. His own heavy armor, and that of Ramnes, was packed on one of the few baggage animals. "That's fate for you, comrade."

They poured through the hills to Asculum, unhindered. The squadron in advance was equipped with Roman armor, giving out word that those following were riding to join the armies of Rome; they clattered on day and night, each man supplied with a week's emergency rations.

Asculum was past now, and the first task lay ahead. The

advance squadron posted on to Reate, gathered carts and horses, and came back to the Villa Veturis, now all desolate and empty. There outside the grotto of Lamnia the force made night camp, and was off at sunrise; the escorting squadron and the carts back to Eryx with treasure and relics, Ramnes and his thousand, each man loaded with gold for Hannibal, off toward the Via Cassia, with Pelargos heading the advance squadron.

It was a hard, swift push through the hills, day and night in the saddle, horses pressed to the limit. Half the towns in Umbria and Etruria might have been captured in such a raid, but somewhere on ahead lay what dwarfed all else. Rome or Africa, and the scales of destiny at balance—there was the driving, compelling force that bound Ramnes and his men; they passed by every town, unheeding.

THEY WERE on the wide-paved Cassian Way at last, pounding northward. All Roman country here, rich and thickly settled. But a trickle upon the wide road became a stream and then a flood—refugees, by horse and cart and on foot, with wild tales of the Punic terror driving down at Rome. Not too late, then!

Clusium in sight at last, refugees in torrents, the smoke of burning farms on the horizon; and, in the afternoon sunlight, a squadron of Numidian horse meeting Pelargos and pealing exultant shouts to the blue sky. Pelargos came back on the gallop and drew rein, his eyes glittering.

"On! Lars is here, in the town! Come along, let the men follow with the Numidians!"

Ramnes gave the squadron leaders orders to follow and halt in Clusium to rest men and horses, then was off at a gallop with Pelargos and the Numidian captain. They pounded into the old Etruscan capital, and amid wild Berber yells from African throats, slid from the saddle and stiffly flung themselves upon Lars Masena.

IT WAS a new Lars who took them into the crumbling palace of King Porsena, and ordered wine and food in haste. A

Lars breathless with excitement, glittering with gold and gems, great with authority—a man like a sword, at keen high tension.

"Just in time, just in time!" he exclaimed fiercely. "I was afraid you'd not get here. We've not an hour to lose. Hannibal and the army stop at Cortona tonight, come on past Lake Trasimene tomorrow. The consul Flaminius is hard after him, and Hannibal means to trap him and destroy him. I don't know just how or where—it may be happening now. We'll ride back and meet the army."

"Where's Rhea?" demanded Pelargos.

"With the baggage and the other women. By the gods, she's seen a few things, let me tell you! It was terrible. Worse than the Alps, far worse."

"What was?" demanded Ramnes, gulping at his wine.

"The push across the Apennines. Marshes swollen by the winter rains. We were six days and nights in water up to our waists—can you realize what that means, you two? Men died like flies in the first frost."

Pelargos laughed harshly. "What does that matter, to a god?"

Lars snarled at him. "No mockery! I tell you, Hannibal's no less than a god himself! He's been laid out with fever. He's lost an eye—infected. He's worn to skin and bone, but he's never faltered! The last of the elephants died—all except one; it carried Hannibal when he was at his worst, and I drove the beast. Death? We've left a trail of the dead through those mountains! But we got through, and we're here."

"How many left?" queried Pelargos with skeptic air.

"Somewhere over thirty thousand. Flaminius has between thirty and forty thousand. Our drive at Rome was too fast for them. The other consul's somewhere up in the northeast and out of it. If we destroy Flaminius, Rome's open—open to us!"

Lars choked on his own excitement, then demanded the news from Eryx. He could scarcely hear it, however, or put his mind upon it; he was in a perfect flame, and not he alone. Everyone was the same. Ramnes caught the infection. Today, tomorrow at this time—Rome or Africa, and the fate of the world!

"To be frank about it, the army isn't in too good condition," admitted Lars. "You know what shape it was in when we got out of the Alps; now it's worse. And we're clean out of supplies. The country's pretty bare at this time of year."

"Ha! There's ice for the sherbet!" exclaimed Pelargos with caustic asperity. "In plain words, the army's on its last legs; Hannibal has fever and one eye gone—and you talk of sacking Rome! The truth is, you're all on the dead run with Flaminius chasing you!"

LARS LOOKED up, a fervid glow in his eyes.

"And Flaminius," he admitted slowly, "knows it. Some of our men have deserted to him with the news. He knows it. He knows we're driving straight on Rome, plundering and burning the Roman countryside as we go. He's determined to stop us."

Pelargos blinked. "Ah!" he said in a different voice. "So that's how the wind blows! A good thing for Rome that Hannibal hasn't lost both eyes; then he'd be master of the Seven Hills in a fortnight! No use sitting here swilling wine. Let's be going!"

For the Stork had kindled to the infectious fever of it all. Now he flung his cynic caution to the winds and went flaming forth with them, and the three rode north with the squadrons of Eryx somewhere behind, and ruddy sunset gilding all Etruria....

Pelargos was in a fury of wild exhilaration. All the way, into the night, they breasted a continuous flood of fugitives and fleeing folk, who scattered in panicked terror at the sight of armed men. Country people, peasants and nobles alike, laden with burdens of family wealth, pushing barrows, old men and women hitched to carts, girls and children flushing away like frightened quail.

Some were out of their heads with fear. One stalwart gray-beard maniac, a veteran of the first Punic war, strode along shouting that the world was at an end, that the gods had turned against Rome, that fire and blood would consume all things. Groups of priests scurried, laden with sacred temple gear. Women carried babes; peddlers and merchants from the city, wounded soldiers in flight—all of them with hysteric voices of pillage and death and slavery. A sudden roar of laughter escaped Pelargos, as he waved an arm at the fleeing multitudes.

"Make way, make way for the gods! There are your fine Roman folk, comrade, Etruscans of the ancient stock, fleeing like leaves before the tempest! When the gods ride forth, the people of earth are broken and cast adrift on the whirlwind. Husbands like you, fathers like me, wives and children like ours—loosed upon a sea of blood and rapine and pillage, dying, their corpses strewing the fields and the roads!"

"Are you mad?" cried Ramnes at him. Pelargos laughed again, shrilly.

"Aye, mad, drunk with glory of the gods! And tomorrow night we may be like these, scattered afar in wild flight with death at our shoulder. Here's war, comrade, brute passion unleashed, mankind chased down and speared like running deer in the forest—blood, blood, blood! And all the doings of the immortals, of the gods, of men in the likeness of gods! Rome perishes, and we put the sword to her throat. Well done!"

For a bit Ramnes thought this was rank insanity, though he was too weary to think much about anything; but presently Pelargos fell silent, and afterward made no mention of his wild words. They were, all of them, a little short of madness, what with the bursting tension and the hard riding, and the world won or lost on the morrow.

ABOUT MIDNIGHT, it was, they came upon the one man who seemed oblivious to the mounting storm of human fury, and untouched, unmoved by the tremendous strain of tension all around. A man whose giant frame was haggard and worn, thinned by fever and suffering, wasted to a mockery of what it had been, with a bandage around his head, closing one eye. And with him the boy who was now aged into manhood: Hannibal and his brother Mago.

Without rising from the campfire, he stretched out his hands to them, greeted Lars and Pelargos warmly, made Ramnes come and sit beside him. All their words fell away suddenly, before his tranquillity, his unhurried, commanding presence, his quiet voice. He beckoned two of his staff officers, and ordered Lars and Pelargos away with them.

"The Balearic slingers are awaiting you, Pelargos; go and command them, and learn the dispositions as you go…. Your wife, Lars," he said, smiling, "is with the baggage; go to her. A remarkable woman, that; give her, I pray you, my warmest regards."

Their figures faded away. This was in the valley of Trasimene, and from the lake a heavy night-mist had arisen that blotted out the stars. Wine was brought, and Ramnes was thankful for it.

HANNIBAL TURNED to him.

"Well, my friend, I know your story from Lars. You served me well, there in the Alps; the gods have served you well. Or, indeed, did you serve me at all?"

"I think my hatred of Rome was the thing I served," said Ramnes slowly. "I've brought you gold, and a thousand horse, the squadrons of Eryx; they're close behind."

"Ah, good, good!" Hannibal beckoned another aide. "When they come, bring them past us here, and feed up the fire a bit, then take them to camp beyond my bodyguard. Ramnes leads them tomorrow, with me."

"Whither?" asked Ramnes. Hannibal drew his purple cloak about his shoulders against the mist, and leaning forward, traced with his finger in the dust.

"Here's the highway that comes down beside the lake, yonder—the water on one side, the steep hills on the other. At the north end is Maharbal; here at the south end am I, with the heavy-armed troops; along the hills are the slingers and light-armed men—all hidden. I am not hidden. I have men posted on the hill up above, who'll be seen above the mist. Flaminius will march for me—the trap will close on him. It is all very simple."

No exultation, no fiery words; the man seemed unutterably weary.

"Then he must surrender—but a consul of Rome does not surrender," exclaimed Ramnes.

"I fear not, my friend. In that case, not one man of his whole army escapes. Now tell me about your city. Is it an offshoot of Eryx in Sicily—a Greek colony? Tell me."

Ramnes obeyed, seeing that the other wanted mental diversion. Hannibal listened carefully, questioning now and then.

"The alliance of your city means everything to me," he said at length. "Not for itself, but for what it will mean; Eryx starts what the rest of Italy will follow. The yoke of Rome is ended. Well, well, I envy you Pelargos! I see clearly that he's for you, not for me; a remarkable man. Have you armor?"

"Coming, with my men. I must thank you for sending Giscon to Eryx; he's being of immense help to us."

"We must do what we can," said the other musingly. "A good motto, that; we must do what we can—for ourselves, for others, for the world! Chiefly, I fear, for ourselves."

He glanced up as an officer rode up, dismounted, saluted, and spoke swiftly.

"Ah! Your squadrons." Hannibal rose. An aide brought him helmet and sword; the bandage was concealed. He stood beside Ramnes, in the firelight, as the shadowy shapes of weary men and horses appeared.

At an order from Ramnes, the squadron leaders fell out; the files of men wended past, and in passing, each man flung down before Hannibal the package of treasure he had brought. The pile grew and grew. From the staff, from the African officers crowding about, came cries of amazement.

The worn and haggard man had vanished. In his place stood

a Hannibal aglow with the old eager vitality, the astonishing personal charm which made him unique in his age. He stood beside Ramnes, a somber and gigantic figure radiating strength and power.

THE LAST squadron filed past. Hannibal turned to the squadron leaders, greeting them with a grip of the hand here, a few words there. From all sides officers and men came running, to stare at the immense loose heap of golden coins as they crowded about, and to welcome the officers of Eryx. More than one greeted Ramnes with eager recollection, and the warmth of friendship banished the chill misty night.

"I thank you, Ramnes, and you his officers," Hannibal said. "We welcome you, we're proud of you and of Eryx. Eh?" He turned, as one of the Numidian captains spoke a few words. A laugh broke from him, and he flung out his hand at the pile of gold.

"Oh, that! Leave it where it is; a guard, of course. Leave it there. Either we shall have great use for it by this time tomorrow—or we shall not. To rest, friends, to rest, and remember that he who sleeps soundest, is surest to have the gods on his side tomorrow."

Which, reflected Ramnes, sounded uncommonly like an echo of Pelargos.

CHAPTER XVII

JUST BEFORE the dawn came a rapid drumming of hooves. A courier flung himself from the saddle and panted out swift tidings. Ramnes, awakened, gathered that it was word from Maharbal, at the upper end of the lake.

"Very well," said Hannibal, rubbing his one eye. "So the consul and two Roman legions and the pick of their cavalry, are in the van! Excellent. Send me Pelargos; I want him with me, and half the slingers as well. No other change. Serve out

Sword to sword, shield to shield, eye to eye, the two men struggled— until the blade of Ramnes crashed down on helm and skull—and life.

food and wine at once, what there's left of it. The staff with me. Ramnes!"

"Here," said Ramnes.

"Come along. We're going part way up the hill. They're in the trap."

Under the mist, which continued thick and heavy, was a stir of movement as the ranks of heavy-armed Spanish and Carthaginians, which closed this end of the trap, wakened and fed. The horses were brought up. Hannibal spoke rapidly, as he ate and armed.

"I've posted your squadrons under the hill to the left, Ramnes;

when I give the word, take them into the Roman horse. Until then, with me."

They mounted and rode blindly through the fog, for Ramnes; but for the others, who knew the ground perfectly, it was only a little way to a shoulder of the high hill. Here they dismounted again and waited, resting, relaxed. The first grayness was lifting through the world; soon the spears of dawn would strike up across the sky.

Silence, and the heaviness of mist, cloaked everything. Impossible to realize that men by the thousand waited. Impossible to realize that through this dark and fog were coming thirty thousand and more Romans, stretched out in column, doubtless, for a couple of miles. Here with the hilltop above barely visible,—since it was above the mist,—all was stillness and waiting.

Then, upon this heaviness of suspense, lifted a single voice in Greek. Perhaps one of the men from Eryx, perhaps not; no telling. It quavered up in a song, a snatch of plaintive simple words, perchance caught from some Greek poet. One of the staff officers moved quickly as though to have the voice checked, but Hannibal lifted a hand in restraint; he was listening, his face thoughtful, to those oddly incongruous, careless words.

Am I not with thee in the time of trouble,
Dread specter of thy youth, companion of thine age?
I am neither evil destiny nor guardian angel,
Although I am so named by men.

Where thou art, shall I be alway
As a brother inseparable,
Even unto the end of thy days
When I shall be seated on thy gravestone!

In sadness, seek my solace freely,
But in joyous days avoid me warily.
Ever must I follow thy path
Yet never may I touch thy hand—
For I am Solitude.

The voice died away abruptly, as though checked by some officer. The staff and aides looked one at another, most of the Africans speaking Greek fluently. Then a new voice, lusty, bold, energetic, broke from the mist.

"Ha, comrades! You heard that fellow singing? There's an omen for you, Chief!"

Hannibal looked up, smiling, as Pelargos loomed above them.

"I thought you had no use for omens, worthy Stork?"

"Oh, I never avoid any good thing," Pelargos said cheerfully, with a wave of the hand to Ramnes. "Of course an omen can be read any way you want to read it; I read this to mean luck! You sent for me?"

"I want your eyes," said Hannibal, "when the mist rises. Your slingers?"

"Half of them at hand, as ordered."

"Good. I understand the consul is in the van, with two legions and the cavalry—that will be ten to fifteen thousand men. You'll have first honor here, as at the Trebia. I want the officers picked off; if the cavalry charge you, retreat to cover of my ranks."

DAWN SHOWED—A rosy streak growing from the eastern sky. The ranks on the hill, above the mist, broke into motion; they had seen the Roman approach coming, through the swirls and eddies of fog below. A silence fell, dread and ominous with tension.

The mist began to thin. Out below, closing off the way southward, Ramnes began to see the ranks of heavy-armed Spanish and Carthaginians, with Hannibal's bodyguard. Slowly, slowly came a measured cadence, at first almost imperceptible, then growing in force; the marching tread of unseen feet in unison, thousands of them.

"Ah! It's time Mago attacked!" muttered Hannibal, frowning anxiously. His brother was in charge of the light-armed troops stationed along the hills in hiding, on the Roman flank.

A trumpet rang out, unseen but startling in its nearness. As though this were a signal, the mist eddied and thinned, the sun was lifting. The golden rays struck down through the vapor and there was a dull glinting like the glint of water: the spears and mail of the Roman column. The mist became clearer; another trumpet blew with sudden urgent voice.

Rome had seen her prey awaiting her.

For a moment, nothing moved. The serried Roman ranks were halted; then horsemen began to work forward.

Pelargos said, peering at the masses of men:

"The consul, Hannibal! I see him, there in the group of cavalry! He's staring at our lines, at the hill, at us. Those are the Latin horse raised by Mancinus. There's Mancinus himself, comrade! Ah—what's that?"

From the invisible north, where the lake and valley were still clad in mist, came a rending tumult, a clangor of arms mingled with voices.

"That's Mago!" exclaimed Hannibal, his face lighting up. "To your slingers, Pelargos! The officers, remember!"

Thinner grew the mist. More and more of the Roman column became visible. Flaminius knew that he was attacked from the high hills in flank; he did not know that Maharbal and the Numidians had closed in behind him and were slaughtering his rearguard. This, in fact, was something he would never know—for, in the rising tumult and confusion, came the shrill voice of Pelargos:

"For you, Hannibal! Flaminius down—for you!"

The slingers were almost invisible. Ramnes could scarcely see those figures stealing over the ground, afoot; but a hail of death was striking the ranks of Rome. The mist now was blowing away.

Hannibal turned.

"Ramnes! Those horse will be charging in a moment. To your squadrons! Cut up those cavalry yonder, then strike in on the left flank of the legions."

Ramnes swung into the saddle and was gone. His gigantic

figure, clad now in the bronze armor of Porsena, seemed unnatural and superhuman. To his voice, the squadrons of Eryx seemed to spring out of the ground, as the Latin horse began to move. The first squadron, the second, the third, swept past, struck into a gallop, and went rushing like the wind for those gleaming ranks. Heading the last two squadrons, Ramnes followed; he carried no dagger of Eryx today, but sword and javelin.

A C R A S H; the first squadron was swallowed up. The second followed and was lost in the Roman ranks. The third plunged on headlong. Now all those ranks were in wild confusion. The serried legions were moving forward, and Ramnes with his last two squadrons hammered home the blow that broke the Latin cavalry.

Broke it, scattered it, sent it in wild flight, then wheeled and struck at the flank of the legions. Here was Rome itself; here were the citizens of Rome, the old blood and stock of Rome, facing about as though on parade, taking the shock, dissipating it. The charge was scattered, but had served its purpose. Momentarily halted, the Roman ranks were now met by the storming infantry of Spain and Africa....

And here the world stopped, for them and for Ramnes as well. He, plunging through the wildest of the fight, saw the face of Mancinus rising before him; sword to sword, shield to shield, eye to eye, the two men struggled, until the blade of Ramnes crashed down on helm and skull—and life. The dead figure pitched out of the saddle, and Ramnes, suddenly conscious of the stoppage of everything, drew out of the struggle to rally his squadrons.

There was the queer thing, as the mist bore away and the long valley was disclosed—everything had stopped. From the north, the Roman rear had rolled up, what was left of it, until the ranks of legions now ran along in one solid line. The cavalry had completely vanished. Hannibal and his bodyguard still occupied the lower slope of the hill; all the other Punic forces had moved in upon the Roman mass, on three sides. The lake itself formed the fourth side. And movement had ceased.

Yet the clangor of iron upon iron dinned up from front and rear. Only in the mass had motion halted; the ranks were fighting, breast to breast, stubbornly and terribly. Ramnes was awed by the scene as its meaning stood revealed. Here was no trickery of surprise or advantage. It was man to man, Rome against Africa, and those who slew best and quickest, would win. But killing—that was the business of the legions! They were trained to it!

Ramnes gathered the squadrons of Eryx, dismounted them, and hurled them into the stubborn battle, led them against those ghastly pale set faces. The Romans gave no ground, but rank succeeded rank as they died and fought on and died. They were overmatched, man for man, ferocity for ferocity.

Suddenly Ramnes felt himself shaken from his feet; he reeled, recovered, saw the men around him staggering as they fought. In the air, from the ground, reverberated a dull and grinding roar, and the earth shook and trembled.

No one heeded; javelins flashed, swords drove down, the serried ranks struggled on in a blind and mad ferocity. And presently Ramnes was amazed to realize that the Africans, not the Romans, were doing the slaughtering. On to the northward along the lake, that mighty column was breaking asunder, splitting into smaller divisions; thirty thousand men were dying. Here and there, parties of the Latin allies were flinging down their arms, but not the Romans. The legions fought on—and slowly, slowly perished.

The world was lost, and won.

RAMNES SHEATHED his sword. Excitement held him; furious exultation seized him and shook him, as he made his way toward the general and the staff. Couriers had foamed in from the north. Hannibal's features were blazing, as he put out a hand to Ramnes.

"Not a man of them, not a man of them!" he exclaimed.

"Some cut a way out; Maharbal has them surrounded. Not a man will escape! The whole army, do you understand! From the consul down—the whole army! Do you know what it means?"

Ramnes gripped his hand, swung him around, pointed southward.

"That's what it means, Hannibal! Look—through the dust, above those trees, over the horizon—see them? Do you see those seven gleaming hills? The road's open to them, the road to Rome! The end of tyranny and injustice and treachery is there; now to take freedom to those seven hills. To Rome! On to Rome!"

The staff officers echoed his words fiercely: "On to Rome, Hannibal!"

There was a laugh. Ramnes turned, Hannibal turned.

A long, incredibly tall figure, bald pate shining in the sunlight, blood spattering armor and arms; it was Pelargos, striding toward them, juggling a Roman sword, flinging it high in air and catching it again, and singing.

"Ha!" he cried out, and saluted. "A sword for you, Hannibal! The sword of the consul, Flaminius—a gift for you! Plunge it into the throat of Rome!"

HANNIBAL TOOK the sword, and held it up. His gaze lifted to the horizon, and widened, as though the vision of those seven hills came to him, also.

"The end of the road—right!" he exclaimed. "Right, Ramnes! Right, my friends! This day, Rome has perished!"

Pelargos came to Ramnes and gripped his hand.

"All that I promised you in Gaul has come true, comrade. Content?"

Ramnes nodded, voiceless, as the thunderous rolling cheers of victory swept down the bloody ranks. His heart swelled to it, his breath came quickly, his eyes glinted with exultation; here was triumph such as few men had ever known, or would know again—Rome, gasping out her life under the bright Etruscan sunlight!

"It's finished," he said slowly, as the last reeling clumps of legionaries went down. "Finished."

Pelargos rubbed his long nose. His lips moved, as though to say that nothing was ever finished—but the clamorous acclaim of voices drowned his words; and with a slight shrug, he turned away.

ABOUT THE AUTHOR

H. BEDFORD-JONES is a Canadian by birth, but not by profession, having removed to the United States at the age of one year. For over twenty years he has been more or less profitably engaged in writing and traveling. As he has seldom resided in one place longer than a year or so and is a person of retiring habits, he is somewhat a man of mystery; more than once he has suffered from unscrupulous gentlemen who impersonated him—one of whom murdered a wife and was subsequently shot by the police, luckily after losing his alias.

The real Bedford-Jones is an elderly man, whose gray hair and precise attire give him rather the appearance of a retired foreign diplomat. His hobby is stamp collecting, and his collection of Japan is said to be one of the finest in existence. At present writing he is en route to Morocco, and when this appears in print he will probably be somewhere on the Mojave Desert in company with Erle Stanley Gardner.

Questioned as to the main facts in his life, he declared there was only one main fact, but it was not for publication; that his life had been uneventful except for numerous financial losses, and that his only adventures lay in evading adventurers. In his younger years he was something of an athlete, but the encroachments of age preclude any active pursuits except that of motoring. He is usually to be found poring over his stamps, working at his typewriter, or laboring in his California rose garden, which is one of the sights of Cathedral Cañon, near Palm Springs.

www.ingramcontent.com/pod-product-compliance
Lightning Source LLC
Chambersburg PA
CBHW061521020726
47502CB00006B/2178